Contrary Angel

Books by Mike Barnes

Calm Jazz Sea (1996)

Aquarium (1999)

The Syllabus (2002)

MIKE BARNES

CONTRARY ANGEL

The Porcupine's Quill

National Library of Canada Cataloguing in Publication

Barnes, Mike, 1955–

I. Title.

P S 8553.A 7633 C 65 2004   C 813'.54   C 2004-901532-X

1   2   3   4   ·   06   05   04

Published by The Porcupine's Quill,
68 Main Street, Erin, Ontario N O B 1 T O.
www.sentex.net/~pql

Readied for the press by John Metcalf; copy edited by Doris Cowan.

Represented in Canada by the Literary Press Group.
Trade orders are available from University of Toronto Press.

We acknowledge the support of the Ontario Arts Council
and the Canada Council for the Arts for our publishing program.
The financial support of the Government of Canada
through the Book Publishing Industry Development Program
is also gratefully acknowledged. Thanks, also, to the Government of
Ontario through the Ontario Media Development Corporation's
Ontario Book Initiative.

 Canada Council **Conseil des Arts**
for the Arts **du Canada**

ONTARIO ARTS COUNCIL
CONSEIL DES ARTS DE L'ONTARIO

FOR HEATHER

Contents

*

Don and Ron

Over in potwash, Don was yelling at Ron. Across the hospital kitchen, Lewis stopped loading dishes in the Hobart for a moment; he stood on the rubber mat that raised him slightly off the wet floor, listening. Fragments of the altercation made it through the din of clanking, rumbling machines, the knock of crockery, and dozens of separate, murmured conversations. Strings of shrill accusation: *Why the fuck did you ... How the fuck'm I s'posed to ...* Interspersed with bits of whiny self-defence, excuses that could mimic the volume, but not the scathing spirit, of attack. *For chrissakes, I was only ... Aw shit....*

In places around the huge, low-ceilinged room, others had paused to listen too. White-hatted chefs, mist-shrouded priestly figures with carving knives or gleaming ladles or plasticized recipe cards; clear-plastic-gloved sandwich makers, buttering and spreading and slicing at the long low prep tables; porters pulling squeaky-wheeled carts to the hose-down station. Some of these carried on with their jobs, oblivious or indifferent to the ruckus. But here and there, Lewis saw a head tilted to one side, a pair of gloved hands held poised for a moment.

It was an old song. Don was a hothead, with a crippled foot and a drinking problem. Heaps of dirty pots surrounded him. Lewis had filled in twice for the sickly Ron and had experienced first-hand Don's sweating and screaming, his spittle-flying tirades. Add in Ron's resemblance to an easy target – round, simple, and slow-moving – and the duet was scored. The supervisors had long since given up trying to silence it. Potwash was a hellish slot to fill, and Don and Ron had been cursing and bumbling their way through it for a decade together.

A supervisor moved now through the centre of the kitchen, shaking her head as she consulted her clipboard. Those who had been listening got busy again, their faint knowing smiles dissolving under the constant pressure of time. 460 beds, 3 meals a day, 365 days a year. Down at the other end of the Hobart, Lewis's partner was standing an eloquent step back from the machine, eyeing the black rubber belt moving emptily past him. Stacks of plates, cutlery bins and green wash racks surrounded him like mute allies.

Lewis began feeding the dishwasher again. In his brief pause, the round table between him and the clearing line had filled up. Hurriedly loading plates and bowls, he glanced over at Krista. She was on scrape-down today, third in the line of four women who received cafeteria trays through a little window and stripped them for washing. She could glance up and see him without turning, but Lewis didn't expect her to. Not today. It was partly her embarrassment at the way she looked in her hairnet and beige smock, 'the most sexless outfit imaginable', she claimed. But it was mostly last night.

They'd been to see a movie at the Broadway. *The Tenant*, by Roman Polanski. Krista had never been to a rep cinema before. This surprised Lewis, since talking about movies on their coffee breaks, sharing enthusiasm if not tastes, had emboldened him to ask her out on this first date. But then, he reflected, most people did prefer the new releases. It was being at McMaster for three years that had made his tastes more exotic. A glance around the Broadway lobby – funky with berets and leather jackets and goatees – seemed to confirm this. Another good reason to be at the hospital, he thought. Get back in touch. Hanging back by the *Eraserhead* poster while he bought popcorn, Krista hadn't looked particularly ill at ease, but Lewis thought she'd be good at hiding that. What she had looked was out of place. In some vague, gnawing way that he couldn't pinpoint. Was it her clothes: new-looking, sensible? Jeans and a brown turtleneck sweater. A tan, belted overcoat that was both too long and too short to be cool. When they'd taken their seats, he leaned close to say, 'I like the smell here. It smells like old movies.' A thought he'd shared before. 'It's must,' said Krista, fishing in her purse.

Another slightly awkward moment occurred during the screening. Twice, actually. Lewis was just beginning to chuckle at an on-screen grotesquerie, one of Polanski's bizarre images that leapt past horror into camp, when he felt Krista stiffen beside him. The first time, she seemed to shrink, her body sliding down deeper into her seat while her chin dipped into her turtleneck collar. The second time, she actually jumped and clutched his sleeve, letting go of it immediately. Lewis glanced around the darkened theatre to see if anyone had noticed, but a wave of laughter like his own was still rippling through it. People were having fun.

So was Krista, he realized later. They were at the Black Forest Inn, waiting in the crowded bar area for a table to open. A line of customers trailed through the double doors out into the May evening. Krista and Lewis sipped their beers. Someone at a nearby table exclaimed over the 99-cent price of draft, management's gift to its legions of PATIENT & VALUED GUESTS said a wooden plaque below a cuckoo clock.

'Hamilton heaven,' Lewis remarked. And Krista giggled, sliding up a hand to cover her mouth. It was a reflexive gesture, another thing besides her trim figure that made her seem girlish at times. He hadn't had to feign surprise when she'd told him she was thirty-six. She hadn't asked his age, but he'd told her anyway. 'Twenty-one!' another kitchen lady had cried. 'Spring chicken!'

'Younger than this chicken anyway,' Krista frowned, sawing at the lunch special.

That was another thing he liked about her: her sense of humour. Quiet and irregular, but also dark and sharp.

'Did you like the movie?' he asked over their jägerschnitzel. She'd said so as they left the theatre, but now that they were eating together, he wanted to hear her answer again.

She nodded seriously. 'Very scary.'

'Did you think so? Really?' He was surprised again, as he had been in the theatre dark. Also curious: Krista had been working in the kitchen fifteen years, scraping other people's slop, one-eyed cooks groping her in the freezer (*He almost lost the other one*), Don and Ron's bitching crescendo in the background. What could scare her?

'A woman in a full body cast, screaming after her suicide attempt?'

'Yeah, exactly, but that's what takes it over the top.' He leaned forward in their booth, excited to be explaining it to her. 'That close-up of her screaming mouth, like a cave the camera falls into. It's black comedy. A horror spoof.'

'Hardy har.'

'No, it's still scary. That's why it's *black* comedy.'

'Like the young guy dressing up in drag.'

'That was Polanski.'

'That was kind of funny. Creepy. But funny.'

'He was becoming the girl. The former tenant.'

'Yeah, I got that.'

'Or how about the tooth in the wall? Him pulling out the cotton and finding it, root and all, in the plaster chink. That's gotta be –'

But he stopped when he saw Krista shudder. Her hand came up to her mouth, her typical gesture, but not to cover a laugh this time. More self-protectively, in sympathy with the madwoman in the movie. The gesture with her hand was becoming decipherable to him; at least, he had an inkling about it. Her teeth were good, white and even. It seemed more an unwillingness to show feeling. To be *caught* feeling? Fifteen years scraping plates, he thought again. She was sipping her coffee, smiling at him, eager to get past the moment. But her back was stiff against the back of the booth, as if something had truly frightened her.

A nice spring evening, they'd walked along King Street, past Gore Park and Jackson Square and the Sheraton, toward Krista's house on Market Street. 'Your own house. Congratulations,' he'd said, curious at how she'd managed it on kitchen wages. 'I'll pass that on to the bank,' she replied. Lewis wanted to hold her hand, but he couldn't for some reason, even though he sensed she wanted him to. They strolled through the mild sweetish air in a silence that felt calm at first, then awkward and strained again.

'Don was in fine form today,' he said, to break it.

'Don's an asshole,' she said. He glanced at her. No sympathy for Don's foot? he wondered. Don had his locker in a corner of the change room, but Lewis had come in early one day and had caught a glimpse of something impossibly thin and white, like a parsnip, disappearing into Don's heavy, built-up orthopedic black boot, the one he swung wide and clomped off quickly to make himself walk.

'Ron seemed to think so.' Today's counter-attack particularly feeble, high-pitched bleats and moans that made him think somehow of a great cornered vole.

'Ronnie's pathetic,' Krista said, a bit more gently. The diminutive *Ronnie* seemed to capture a truth, while also softening it. No *misplaced* sympathy, Lewis decided.

Market Street was a row of small working-class bungalows tucked in behind King Street off the west end of Jackson Square. It looked vaguely out of place, like a neighbourhood from an older, harder time, slated to be demo'd and reno'd when the economy picked up. Which, in Hamilton, might give it a long shelf life just as it was. Lewis had grown up on a similar, though no doubt sootier street in the east end, in the shadow of the steel company where his father worked. Market Street violated his belief, unchallenged till now, that Hamilton became steadily more affluent, greener, as you moved westward. There were exceptions, it seemed.

'Here we are,' Krista said. Behind her stood a low, shingle-fronted house with two small windows set high on either side of the door, like eyes above a long nose. A walkway planted on either side with what looked like marigolds, glimmering a dull polleny gold in the pale streetlights. No lights on inside, like the other houses they'd passed. Bedtime by ten for a six-o'clock shift: that too was familiar.

'I had a good time. It was interesting,' she murmured. Which parts? Lewis wondered.

'So did I,' he said.

'I'd invite you in for a coffee, but I live with my mom. She'll be sleeping,' Krista said, with a glance at the dark house behind her.

He nodded. No mention of her dad. Had he died already?

By the way she lingered in front of him, her hands worrying the belt of her coat, he thought it would be all right if he kissed her. Desire surged up in him, hot and surprising. He wanted to bundle Krista up in her baggy coat like a blanket, lift her off her feet, squash her to him. Krista, who might be small, but was definitely not weak. Not helpless.

She gave her head a shake, as if ending an inner struggle, and raised her chin decisively. 'You're beautiful,' she said, her hand going up to his cheek. And he was shocked for a moment, not so much by what she had said, as by the concentration in her voice, how she was saying just the one thing only. *You're beautiful*: nothing more. Nor less; though that wasn't what struck him then.

She turned and strode to her door. Fiddled with her key, and the door closed behind her. No light came on, though Lewis stood on the sidewalk waiting for it. He saw an image torn from romantic movies, Krista standing with her back pressed against the door, dying to invite him in. He began walking back toward King Street, where a bus would take him to the room he still kept near the university. As he walked he tried out the image again, Krista waiting in the dark, breathless. Deciding it could fit, he walked faster.

After two days of general training, trailing around behind surly porters, doing fifth-wheel stints with various cooks and cleaners, Lewis had been dumped in potwash when Ron called in sick. His trial by fire, it was darkly hinted to him. By the same people who'd first pointed out Don and Ron, Laurel and Hardy gesticulating and bellowing in a cloud of steam. His first impression of Don, close up: tall and skinny, his face greasy-grey. Heart-trouble or drinker or bad-food-in-a-basement grey. Or all three, since they went together. He and Lewis worked side by side at the huge double sinks, orange water and pulped food and sauce and gravy splattering their white uniforms, four hands flying to keep pace with the piles of pots. They had to scrape down enough layers of cooked-on sludge to load them into the revolving steam cleaner. Don silent, except for ritual growled curses at the cooks when they brought another armful. *Motherfucker. Cuntface. Blow me, asshole.* Lewis chuckled at these comments. Don seemed more harried comedian than the cruel, intimidating force of his kitchen rep.

It wasn't until two hours in, when they got clear of the scrambled egg and porridge pots, that he got his first inkling of the source of Don's power.

'Fuck it. Break time.' Don swung his bad leg back in an arc, clomped onto the other one. Screened by the potwash machine, where the steam was thickest, and by Lewis standing in front of him, he lit up a smoke from the pack in his shirt pocket. A violation of kitchen rules, of course, but supervisors were not much more likely to visit potwash than anyone else.

'So where'd they find a beauty like you?' Don asked, exhaling. Something in the drawled question telling Lewis he already knew. The two hours until now amounting maybe to bided time, the sizing-up period cultivated by a boy with a bum leg in many schoolyards, seeking the chink in the armour of stronger bodies, finding it in weaker minds. The paper kitchen hat atop the long face comical, the same sharp folded crease and rolled-up sweat-catcher Lewis wore, like a kid's paper boat capsized on the skull. The eyes beneath it gimlet-sharp.

'I just finished university,' Lewis answered.

Don cackled weirdly, the sound spilling around the cigarette in his mouth. 'Finished, not graduated, eh?' He butted his smoke straight down in a lasagna pan, conceivably to retrieve later. Swinging back to work, he muttered, 'Well, we can always use another lifer.'

Which left Lewis stunned, amazed at Don's summary read of him. And wondering why he *had* said *finished*. He still had another year. *Lifers* and *students* were the two species of people making up the kitchen staff. They could usually be identified at a glance. Lifers: going nowhere, wearing that knowledge; students: at a way station, feeling chipper or sullen about that. Even the work paces were distinctive. Lifers: slow and steady, paced for the duration. Students: frisky-fast at first, then zoned. Lewis had been hired at the end of April with a batch of other students, summer replacements for the holidays. But he couldn't feel like one of them. He'd had a bad scare, something none of them looked like they'd endured. Only a month before he'd been caught submitting an essay he'd bought from a graduate student. Not the first essay he'd bought or plagiarized, as the prof, after a Don-like silent appraisal, had surmised. 'Count yourself lucky it's a zero on the course and not a faculty expulsion,' he'd said, the words clipped, white-collar anger bitten back. He even looked like Don: lean, grey, stooped amid heaps of papers in a book-cramped cubbyhole. Alike, but oh, so different. Dr Newark's cheap tweed suit seeming resplendent beside Don's gravy-ketchup-egg-carrot blazoned whites (though again, the colour schemes were similar). For a few days Lewis had stayed in his basement room. Feeling depressed, oppressed, sorry for himself. And, mainly, surprised. A sudden, stinging sense, a coming-to, like being slapped in the face. Various forms of fudging were so common that most students, he included, didn't consider them *real* cheating. It'd been years since he'd mentally revised his A average a grade down, or told it to anyone feeling anything but pride. Now his sense of himself, as well as his future plans, of graduate school or law school, seemed to collapse. Only rent, his student loan run out, had pushed him out the door to look for summer work. When he'd got the job in the hospital dietary department, he'd gone over to his parents' house for dinner. His father wore his usual wan smile at the news, the all-purpose crease that had helped push Lewis out of home at age seventeen. But seeing it now, he wondered why he'd ever found such mockery in it. It was clearly just a tired smile. He was a lifer

15

in the cold mill, and tending ton after shining ton of cold rolled steel seemed to have convinced him that nothing made much difference. 'Buy some rubber gloves,' his mother called from the kitchen. Though Lewis couldn't recall her ever wearing any.

He counted it as a small victory that he worked well enough to keep clear of a major Don rampage. Not that a rampage needed to be justified, but Don preferred some kind of hook to hang his rage on. Lewis never gave him one. He worked at furious speed, his hands often doing entirely separate tasks, while his eyes spotted new ones and his mind sequenced them. It came to him in a pause that this was all he'd needed to do at university. Work. Why hadn't he? *Not smart enough.* The fear had lurked. Dictating procedures to avoid confronting it.

Don had to content himself with tirades about the weather, the Leafs, the supervisors. Each topic was broached via a bland, innocent-sounding question: *Didja hear… Whaddya think…* Lewis's answer, no matter how mild and uncommitted, would trigger the volcanic spew. *Course it's gonna rain! Y'ever listen to the fuckin radio? … 'A bit better,' he says! Have you watched a game lately? Are you fuckin blind? … Wait'll they short-pay you and then tell me the cunts are all right….*

Lewis had the impression of a Dr Frankenstein, building a makeshift Ron out of available parts. The likeness could only be broad. Not slow, not stupid (not *as* stupid); but deaf, blind, green.

The next day he found himself pencilled in to potwash again. With Ron this time; the partners' illnesses geared together, like their personalities. Or else Don paying Ron back, a day for a day. Again Lewis sensed himself being fitted for the role of the absent man. Ron's tactics more transparent, comically so. A round pale face, with rubbery lips and watered grey eyes, turned up into his: *Case you're wondrin about them cake pans, I'll get to them.* Childish eyes looking up at him, trusting in correction. When Lewis said he hadn't been wondering, Ron's jaw sagged. He worked even slower, seeking abuse in the usual places. Lewis picked up the slack. *I ain't workin faster! I can't!* Lewis didn't answer the whine. When he came back from break, Ron was slouched at the sinks, one hand scratching his ass while the other picked at a flabby white belly behind the missing buttons of his shirt. The same pot from fifteen minutes ago doing slow spirals on top of scummy water, world's ugliest ship on its filthiest ocean.

Bug-eyed terror at Lewis's approach. *Don't look at me! You never saw what they brought in!* Lewis glanced about: nothing new. Muttering and stomping about the little space: *That's right! Go to break at peak time! Then come back and start yelling!* 'I'm not yelling,' Lewis said. But, finally, he was beginning to.

Shortly after, he graduated to a steady shift on the dish machine, inheriting it when a student quit without notice. In last position on the clearing line that day, across the big round table from him, was a fairly young woman. A lifer, not a student, but not bad-looking by kitchen standards. Her cheeks were pebbly, perhaps from old acne scars, but her face was open and pleasing, with shiny-bright brown eyes.

'You survived potwash,' she said, her smile faint and wry.

'Barely,' he replied.

'Barely is outstanding, around here.'

A taut mind, Lewis thought. To go with the taut body he'd already noticed. *Taut. Taught.* Her darkish skin brought to mind the Mediterranean sea on his desk map.

He extended a hand over the table. The fingers dripped milk and oatmeal flecks. 'Lewis.'

Her hand went up over a chuckle for the first time. 'Krista.' The hand came down as she turned away. 'You need some gloves.'

Gloves. All of the students wore them. So did some of the lifers. Krista did; she recommended putting cream inside the fingers. Don never wore gloves, but Ron did, sometimes. When he remembered. When a serving woman was away, Ron filled in on the lunch and supper lines, taking his place as a solitary man among the dozen or so women who stood beside movable steam tables on either side of a long conveyor belt, dishing out their portions of the meal according to the menu boxes checked on the trays moving past. The supervisor, who stood at the end of the belt monitoring the trays as the porter loaded them onto the carts, always strode up to Ron's niche and inspected that his gloves were on and intact and clean, before returning to her place and pushing the start button. Ron's occasional place on the serving line was, to Lewis, one of the more unfathomable kitchen policies. Not just from the standpoint of efficiency – though they usually gave Ron the rice/potatoes niche, a yes/no proposition – but mainly from the standpoint of hygiene. There were cartoon posters around the kitchen showing gleaming hands and giant suicidal germs, beetle or amoeba-shaped, in lurid Smarties colours, who begged the staff to WASH UP! KILL US DEAD! But Ron's hands, when they weren't in dishwater, were busy at the back or front of his pants, and Lewis had been in the change room when Ron barged in for one of his sudden washroom breaks: a few minutes of fussing and bumping sounds in the stall, followed by a hasty belt-buckling exit, no water much less soap required. But when he asked Krista about it, she just said, 'Would you rather have Don screaming when the line backs up? Maybe throwing trays?' An answer which, when he probed beyond its superficial logic, left Lewis with a buzzy, swirly feeling in his head; as if the kitchen was not a set-up that could be tinkered with according to logic and necessity, not at all, but rather a place that ran on deep and unassailable truths; dark, choice-less matters that only an outsider would question or find absurd.

When his shifts allowed, he still went home for Sunday dinner. His mother had developed a ritual of checking his hands. By now these were red and chafed, the cracked skin peeling in places; his mother held them in her own, similar-looking hands, and clucked disapprovingly. 'Gloves, I told you. Get some latex gloves. Use moisturizer at night, or put some inside.' Krista's advice. 'Do you want your hands to look like his?' And his father, as if they'd rehearsed this, obligingly held up his hands in his living-room chair, without turning round or taking his eyes from the TV. The hands were battered, deeply creased paws, a middle nail blackened, the rest yellow and horny-thick, having gone black and fallen off and regrown many times after heavy things had fallen on them. The fingers, Lewis also noticed, curled naturally, as if his father were supporting a globe above his head.

'It's only a summer job. In three months all I'll be turning is pages,' he said.

Now his father turned round, swivelling his armchair. The curved paws cupped his kneecaps. He smiled, and for an instant Lewis saw Don leering at him. It was a hallucination: his father, squat and amiable, looked nothing like Don, but for a moment Lewis had the same sense of a superior, malign intelligence, something that knows your real future and takes pleasure in hinting at it. He blinked hard to clear the vision. It was abetted by the fuggy kitchen smells of baking chicken and simmering peas and steaming rice. And also, no doubt, by his late night with Krista, only three hours between the time they finished up behind her house on Market Street and the time he had to turn on the lights and various machines and start the oatmeal water boiling for the first cook. *Early Man*, his Sunday designation on the job sheet.

If you stood behind the hospital, as he sometimes did after his shift, you got a good general view of Hamilton. The brown hospital buildings were on Concession Street on 'the mountain', as residents called the Niagara escarpment, which cupped the older part of the city like a huge limestone palm. Beyond the staff parking lots, at a chain link fence between a narrow strip of grass and a three-hundred-foot drop, Lewis could look out and down and see everything spread out before him. To his right, east, were the two steel companies and the other heavy industries, chaotic conglomerations belching smoke and flame twenty-four hours a day. To his left, a little farther away, lay the university and its leafy lawns. Between them was central Hamilton: low office buildings and concrete malls, shining high-rise apartments and dilapidated ones, their rusted balconies hung with laundry and plastic toys; civic renewal projects next to scummy, run-down zones; vacant lots, some chained off and with a booth for issuing parking stubs. Lake Ontario sticking a tapering blue arm along the northern edge. The water did look blue from this height, though Lewis knew it was brown and sludgy and smelled bad. Far out ahead, visible on a clear day or when a stiff enough west wind drove the smog back, Toronto's mirage-like spires, gleaming Bauhaus slabs and the postmodernist hypodermic needle which was the 'world's tallest freestanding structure', if not quite a building ... shimmering in the sun like an Emerald City to all the Steel-City Dorothys drooping in the poppy-fields of work.

From this height it all looked plain as a diagram. A diagram with a simple caption, the unchanged continental message: *Go west, young man!* In this case, *Go left!* He was hovering at the apex of a huge lopsided triangle, with the simplified choices height gave. He could fly a short way east to one corner of the triangle, where his father would hand him a hard hat and a time card. Or he could flap his wings hard the other way, soaring in a high arc down to the gentler tip where girls in tight jeans and cableknit sweaters listened to a tweedy guy talk about Thomas

Hobbes and his *Leviathan*. There, for the price of coughing up a few essays and exams a year – a price, strangely enough, he had found too high – you were free to attend discount films, swill cheap draft and dance to roaring bands, sleep late and wake up with a cappuccino series, flash copies of Chomsky and Foucault at people who might actually be impressed by them.

It was a very simple choice, really. No choice at all. But he had fucked it up.

Fucked it up, he stressed internally, branding himself with the message as he wheeled from the fence and went to his bus on Concession Street. Riding along in a stew of self-accusation, he was as oblivious to his fellow passengers as to the streets that went clicking past. The vast residential plateau on top of the mountain was not part of his diagram. That was only where you lived, in a mansion on the brow or in a bungalow on east or west-something street, after you had made your lifelong choice. It was a final tally. Nor did the city centre, the confused assortment he was snaking down through the Jolley Cut to enter, really count. Though that, he realized dimly, was where a good many people still lived. Not east, not west, not above. Just there, somewhere in the muddled middle. Lots of people. Including Krista, whom sometimes in this mood he was on his way to meeting.

They saw each other on Saturday night. Krista worked seven to three, Monday to Friday, *days* her sole reward for her fifteen years of service. Lewis was summer relief, on call; he worked anywhere, anytime. He often worked the early shift Sunday, and might be off on a weekday, but Krista was firm about Saturday being their only night out. 'I need my sleep,' she said, 'and Friday night I'm too baked.' It was one time she sounded old to Lewis. At university he'd developed a capacity, even a taste, for all-nighters. He liked the stretched-out, buzzy feeling, running on adrenaline. *Le dérèglement de tous les sens*. Rimbaud, courtesy of his first-year French prof.

In some ways it was like having a secret affair. Since they'd started 'going out' – Krista's phrase, another time she seemed old-fashioned – Krista didn't like to have their lunches together, or at least no more often than chance would justify. She also insisted on meeting downtown. 'You have no idea how women talk,' she said. He wondered if she meant her mother and if she needed him to be more inexperienced than he was. *My sweet young thing.*

'Come,' she would murmur, sometime around midnight Saturday, and she would lead him by the hand down a thrillingly thin strip of lawn between the brick side of her house and some dense, face-grazing bushes, through a latched wooden gate, into her backyard. This would be after they'd seen a movie and had dinner, then taken a walk through the warm soup of a Hamilton spring evening, up and down random streets, or through Victoria Park, or to a Tim Horton's for another coffee and dessert. But all of these activities felt preliminary, preparatory to the moment when they entered Krista's small, dark, bush-shrouded backyard. Lewis certainly felt so; he thought Krista did too. They couldn't go directly to her yard, not early, in the light; but that was where every other moment, every milked and savoured pleasure, led to.

The yard was small, very dark. Market Street was asleep. No light, and hardly any sound, pierced the screen of friendly hulking bushes. The first time Krista led him back there, lifting the gate latch with a soft click that sent a complementary throb through his balls, she put a finger to her lips. 'Shh, my mom,' she whispered, a moist wind in his ears. Which seemed also to explain why they couldn't go inside. That first night, on their second date, they sat in two lawn chairs pushed together, kissing awkwardly over the plastic armrests. 'Come,' she said, and they lay on the damp cool lawn, stretched out by a bed of petunias that showed shy colours in the dark. She didn't seem fond of kissing, and he didn't really like the way she did it, with quick, darting movements, her tongue flicking at his then pulling back. She wasn't teasing; the kisses were more like pecks. What she did do that he liked, and soon craved, was the all-over body cuddle. Though *cuddle* hardly captured it. Squashed tight against each other from head to toe – face to neck and hair, breasts to chest, hips locked, groins twisting, thighs sealed, feet scaling calves, toes (shoes off) clenching. Pressing and caressing and clenching and rubbing and grinding. Friction in all its crazy-humid glories. He thought someone seeing them would have been confused at first, as he was once when he saw two snakes mating, a coiling wrangle of flesh that only on close inspection could be separated into distinct forms.

The first two weeks, she broke off abruptly, with a panted, 'No, hon,' when he fumbled at her belt. 'No, hon, no.' Short minutes later – it felt like seconds – he found himself walking down Market Street, still breathing hard, sparks shooting up from the bulge in his jeans up through the top of his head, dazzling his eyes. Krista he imagined panting behind the door again, or else sprawled across her bed, her hand speeding between her legs. As his would be as soon as he had endured the bus ride with its taunting bumps and jolts.

Krista's body was lithe and firm, alive with hot energy. The third Saturday, she let him unbutton her white cotton blouse and two hot black nipples popped into his mouth, one after the other, as the small firm mounds they sat on were thrashed back and forth. He brought his knee up between her legs and she gripped it. Both of them were moaning, whimpering with urgency. He would be on top, then she, grappling like wrestlers. Then he was on his back and she lifted herself a little away; through the open blouse he saw her nipples shining glossily where he'd sucked them. She began to ride him with a steady rhythm, sliding back and forth over his crotch. When he fumbled to undo her belt, she let him. He pulled her zipper down, felt wiry hair, hot flesh. She moaned and arched backward, face to the hazy night. He tried to push his hand down far enough, but their groins would not unseal. He pulled her down again, her face in his neck. With her jeans unbuttoned, he could slide his hand down the back of her pants, over round hard haunches thrusting with a rhythm that made him think of pistons; he could feel her buttock muscles bunch and lengthen, the piston head driving up and down, up and down. At the very end of his reach, his middle finger found wetness with a firm ridge at the bottom, the ridge that just flicked his finger at the uppermost height of each piston stroke. The motion quickened into frenzy, agonizingly pleasurable. Agonizingly teasing, too: the clenching and unclenching of her ass, his thrusting hips, the whip-flick piston-stroke that brought ridge and fingertip into momentary conjunction. They gasped, faster and faster. He shuddered and came.

A moment later, Krista stopped too. She held herself very still, poised in mid-air, then lay down on top of him. He didn't know if she had come. He'd known before, with other girlfriends. He thought he had. But he couldn't tell now if her stillness was the stillness of completion or of a simple halt, an abandoned project. No movement in her betrayed a lingering desire. But he wasn't sure. There was something almost too still about her. For some reason he thought of her gesture, the hand up over her mouth to hide, or stop, a laugh. Pleasure – observed pleasure? – caught and stifled. He wanted to ask, but he was too embarrassed. Embarrassed and a little afraid. Afraid of what? Even in his satisfied stillness, the questions multiplied.

Not smart enough. Even here, even now.

'C'mon, babe,' she said, half moaning it, when he began nuzzling her neck again. That meant no: he was sure this time. But did that mean she *had* come? Or that she didn't expect to, so why start up? She rolled off him and they lay on their backs, staring up at the sky. There were rustlings in the huddled bushes, and a cricket chirping, sounding close by although you never knew. It was funny; walking back to the gate, he had heard only a deep silence, a pounding nothing in his ears. He took her hand, which felt limp, unresponsive. Indifferent? He pointed up at the stars, a handful of the brightest glimmering through the haze. He breathed deeply through his nose. 'It smells like rotten eggs, doesn't it? Even in springtime.'

'Always has, always will,' she said. He turned his head apprehensively, but she was smiling at him.

Questions nagged him as he rode the bus home. He felt more desire for Krista than for any woman he'd known. The sight of her bucking above him had been like a lash coming down, something that made him writhe and whimper, almost twist away just thinking of it. He was sure she felt the same way, but there was the curious way she'd stopped, so controlled and automatic. Like the Hobart belt when he pushed the black button. And there was also her lack of curiosity to explore under his clothes, though she'd felt him all over *through* them. Shyness? He didn't think so. What he sensed was cooler than that, a decision taken calmly and obeyed. *Don't get too involved.* Was that it? Leave a layer of cotton between herself and her pleasure, the hand between the laugh and the person causing it? Don't flatter yourself, warned an inner voice. She didn't mind your hand in her shirt, down her pants. Yes. He always felt he was getting closer to the truth of things when his ego took a beating. In the murmured endearments she had begun to use with him, he sensed words unspoken, left off the end. He supplied them now in his mind. *Come* here, *come* along. *No, hon,* stop that. *C'mon, babe* ... be reasonable. It was the language, the advising shorthand, you used with a loved child. Reminding, admonishing, encouraging, correcting; acquainting him with the facts of the world and with the requirements of the moment. A soft and patient Don, if Don could even be imagined that way.

But when they'd gone round to the front of the house, she'd stopped him in the brick-bush alley and hugged him tight; her lips *had* found the gap between his shirt buttons and left a moist kiss there. 'You're beautiful,' she'd murmured again. A bare whisper.

So: back to square one. Not indifferent, not aloof. Not controlled; not completely, anyway. Afraid of losing control. Of getting too involved. Wanting to keep the limits of something clearly in view. He believed her scattered comments about her mother – crotchety, infirm, prudish – but he also believed they made for a good excuse. When a relationship went indoors, went home, it went deeper. Went deeper or stopped. He hadn't invited Krista for Sunday dinner at his parents', and she hadn't seemed surprised or hurt that he hadn't. It wasn't just the fifteen-year age difference, though he knew that would bring his father's *Gotcha* smile floating into view and amplify his mother's cooking sounds in the kitchen. It wasn't *just* that, though what else it was he couldn't quite say. She hadn't even been to his place, accepting his description of its squalor with a muttered 'Bachelors'. One of the reasons he'd rented the grubby room on Broadway Avenue, besides getting away from his parents, was to have a place to take girls to. He'd done that a few times. But he was reluctant to bring Krista there, not that he thought she wanted to. If he was honest, he supposed he didn't want to drag any of the points of his aerial triangle over onto another. Let the influences, if they mixed, mingle in the middle. *Summer romance*, he summarized to himself, a concise term that sounded breezy but evoked poignant depths, making him feel crass but also clever. Older and wiser.

The bus was speeding through Westdale now. Only a couple of other passengers, gaunt, dishevelled men who'd seen last call, slumped against windows. Lawns and maple trees and Tudor homes blurred past the smeary glass. Out where Lewis rented the city petered out and got grotty again, but Westdale was prime real estate. Professors and professionals and retirees, cutting the grass and sweeping the walk. It was pleasant to picture himself living here some day.

* * *

'L sat?'

Krista said it that way, like a moron's best guess or the climax of a Beckett play.

'L S A T,' Lewis corrected, erasing the wry little pause she had inserted between the L and S A T parts.

'L sat,' she repeated, making the question a statement but not otherwise changing it.

They were in the Tim Horton's at the corner of King and Caroline, a few blocks from Krista's house. Lewis had brought along the L S A T information book that had arrived in the mail a week ago, plus his notes from his first few practice sessions at home. He thought he was doing well, getting maybe three-quarters of the questions without too much trouble, but he had to see his success reflected in someone else's eyes to make it real. Krista's eyes. 'Will there be an exam afterwards?' she asked when he met her at the theatre. He'd chuckled, liking the way she levelled one demolishing stare at his zippered briefcase but did not inquire about its contents.

'Law School Admission Test,' he said.

'You said you had one more year. If you go back. Four years, Polly Sigh.'

He turned the booklet around so she could see the front of it, but she kept her eyes on him. 'I do. I don't know yet,' he muttered. At the back of his brain it had started. *Not smart enough.* An aggrieved chant, still soft yet. 'You take the test to apply. I have to be ready in *case* I go back.'

'What about graduate school?'

'I don't *know*. Now *you're* sounding like a lawyer.'

'Not me, boss. Me plate-scraper.' She held up her hands, her proof. But actually her hands were silky soft, the nails clear and rounded; she was fastidious about her gloves and cream regimen. The fingers did look strong, though. Capable. His looked ravaged but effete.

'Look, I just thought we could look at a few problems together. Some of them are actually kind of interesting.'

'You want me to help you study for law school?' She glanced at the book's cover. 'The test's on Tuesday.'

Despite himself he felt a lurch of panic. He turned the book around. Sure enough, the first test date was June 17. 'I'm aiming for the October one,' he said, calmly enough.

Whatever effect he'd been aiming at was shot, but he felt stubborn about finishing what he'd started. He wasn't going to let the plan, embryonic as it was, get squashed. It had come to him on one of his upper-deck observations of the Hamilton triangle. *Test yourself,* a voice had said to him. *Prove yourself.* Climb back into respectability. The cheater reformed. Short of morals once – *mea maxima culpa* – but not short of brains or bounce-back pluck. It had a ring he could live with.

He got refills for their coffees and another cruller for himself. When he came back, Krista was leafing through the book. She didn't seem very interested, but not affectedly bored either. To her credit, Lewis thought. He showed her the questions on reading comprehension and logical reasoning. 'Jesus,' she said, scanning a passage. Which pleased him enough that he didn't need to show her his answers, which were mostly right. He saved the analytical reasoning section for the last, a little embarrassed by the artificiality of the questions, parlour games concocted by smart people to fool other, maybe not-so-smart people, unconnected to anything that made the world really work. Surprisingly, though, Krista saw more sense in them than he did. Or as much sense in them as in the others.

From a group of seven people – D, E, F, G, H, I, and K – exactly four will be selected to attend a special dinner. Selection conforms to the following conditions:

    Either D or E must be selected, but D and E cannot both be selected.

    Either H or I must be selected, but H and I cannot both be selected.

    H cannot be selected unless F is selected.

    K cannot be selected unless E is selected.

Followed by questions about the lucky diners.

'These things are very silly,' said Lewis.

'Not if you're the one missing din-din,' Krista said.

Or making it, he thought. Or serving, or washing up after. 'They're hard,' he said. An understatement. He was only averaging about fifty percent on them, and taking far too long.

'Well, let's see,' she said gamely. He took out his paper and pencil and showed her the fill-in-the-boxes format that was recommended for this kind of question. She watched while he ran through what they knew and didn't know, what could be eliminated and what might still be possible. She reminded him of a couple of the parameters when he overlooked them. After a few minutes they agreed on an answer for the first question.

He looked up the answer in the back of the book. Wrong. *'This is considered a difficult question; only 37% of test takers answered it correctly,'* he read out.

'Well, pardon us for trying,' she said. Her smile of solidarity did not hearten him, though he tried to return it. He knew what Krista didn't: for someone with a B+ average – his best, he figured, without illegal help, which he was determined to shun – the top 37% wasn't a finish line. It was the starting gate. *Not smart enough* started chanting again, a little louder. *Lifer* chimed in, a harsh medley.

'Where's J?' said Krista.

'What?' He sagged inwardly. Back to kiddie talk.

'We've got D, E, F, G, H, I, and then K. They've left out J. Is that some kind of lawyer code, or are they just being cute?'

'Trying to be cute,' he said. 'Maybe to fool us.'

'It worked.'

They walked to Market Street in a sombre silence that Lewis couldn't find the will to break. They didn't hold hands. It felt like their first date, minus the hope. 'You should finish school,' Krista said at last. He nodded bleakly. His mind was casting ahead to the awkwardness of parting at the dark front door as they had that first night, with no trip around back. It seemed inevitable. The desire that would normally be building in him at this point, an itching pressure below his belt, was absent, left behind with the three saps who missed dinner. What a joke. Which didn't change a thing. What he banked on was Krista finding a way to do it naturally, with the least pain to both of them. Experience counted.

But, no. Fifteen minutes later, to his surprised relief, he came with a wheeze and the double bucking stopped. Krista was still, the dark yard was still. No one had to be selected for dinner. Even the cricket started up again.

It wasn't until he was waiting for the bus that the inner trial resumed. *My question goes to motive, Your Honour. Proceed then, Counsellor, but tread warily. Yes, Your Honour, thank you. I repeat: Did you dry-hump the defendant before he returned to school because you feared his rates would rise? Milking the cow a last drop, if the Bench will forgive a coarse metaphor. Or did you, with no malice aforethought, simply lust after the defendant, regardless of his status then or, forgive me again, to come?*

The witness is instructed to answer.

I will put the question another way. Is it door A: a last quickie? Or door B: a quickie?

Perhaps counsel could rephrase the question.

By the dim light of the bus, he read another passage at random. *If Pergoy and Mosley earn the same salary, what is the minimum number of partners that must have lower salaries than Arnsback?* Before he'd left, Krista had murmured close to his ear, 'Sometimes I'm glad you don't wear gloves.' Woozily he thought of her wet satin ridge, driving up to get flicked by the raspy callused pad of his middle finger. He closed the book, let it lie across his, after all, happy groin. Closed his eyes then, too.

Don was raging. Raging out of control and over the top, even by Don standards. Apparently this happened often on pay days, though Lewis had not noticed the synchronicity before. It made sense, though; by the fourteenth day, Don would have been dry a day or two, his money gone, and now had to endure several more hours of potwash before he could get to a glass. Lewis snuck glances at Krista's beige smock stretched over her rounded bottom. Lascivious thoughts came often to him in the kitchen now, an indulgence abetted by the sluicing water, spongy substances, basic smells. Mentally he tore open the uniform again, though this time he left her hairnet on; a weird, new little thrill. All the while loading the Hobart, his partner unloading glumly ten metres away. Don screaming at Ron. *Step it up a fuckin notch, we're falling behind. I'm workin, I'm workin … Yeah like a goddam old woman. Rinse those pricks so we can run em through the goddam machine. I was scrapin off … Jerking off, you mean.* Ron burbling weakly, never joining the fray even in his partial way. Another payday rite, maybe, both men polarized, their split selves grappling in some primal clarity. Lewis noticed that, this time, no one paused to listen. You didn't need to listen in order to hear, for one thing. But also, he thought, loading the Hobart steadily himself, you didn't want to add even the iota of psychic energy an audience would contribute. You didn't want to be involved. Glancing over, he saw Don leaning against one of the sinks, skinny as a bent nail, his head swivelling to rail at Ron as he bumbled about beside and behind him. The picture blurred by steam, severed by passing bodies, seemed dream-like. Or like a memory flashback in an old movie, misty veils disclosing piercing bits.

Finally the senior supervisor stalked over to potwash – her grim face, pumping clipboard and flapping coat hems telling less of determination than of a need to find determination. There was a short hush in the kitchen while she said her piece – some heads cocked now, hands poised – and then Don's bellow split the air: *Me and Ronnie're busting our fucking balls!* Me and Ronnie, when it counted. The supervisor fled to the office, her leathery old face glowing with rage. She'd find a desk facing a nice blank wall, an hour or two of paperwork to sop up her unused adrenaline.

Lewis looked to Krista, forgetting that she was on paper toss today, pitching milk cartons and serviettes and muffin cups into the trash, her back to him. Over in potwash, Don and Ron could be seen muttering together, a temporary truce of shared resentment. Lewis thought of a whip-thin crazy mother and her fat simple son, the mother screeching accusations one moment, then soothy-chummy the next. Don didn't look like any woman Lewis would want to meet; that's what made him think he was remembering a movie. Flashes of dry prairie dust around a clapboard house, the widow with the cracked mind and the feckless son. The pictures were spotty, but clear. He must have seen it somewhere. But he couldn't remember the name.

After picking up his pay stub, he stood for a long time at his observation post behind the hospital, at the edge of the brow. Tomorrow was the solstice, the official start of summer, though already halfway through his four-month break from school. *A break?* Hamilton was undergoing one of its 'inversions', a term no one understood except that it meant the air, hot and hazy and smelly to begin with, perfected these qualities under a grey lid, acquiring an extra density and richness. A simmering stew of pollution, gases and sweat and just raw heat. The smoke from the factories curdled into the haze in gooey spirals. He thought of the grease hood over the giant griddle, how the drippings from its curved surface seemed to fall in slow motion, buoyed up by dense acrid fumes. Just standing here, he could feel sweat prickling his arms, legs, back, all over his body. The sun cooked his neck like a study lamp at close range.

His old admonitory triangle – east, west, me – was as blurred as everything else by the heat. Maybe it was that – helped by the Don and Ron show today – that decided him to take his practice test tonight. Since trying the question with Krista a week ago, he'd been practising hard, reading the L S A T questions in his room, recording his answers. He was getting better; day by day, he could see it. It was time to step up. Middle of summer break, see where he stood. See whether he was going forward (which, he reflected for a moment, meant going back, back to school) … or – no, he didn't want to know about directions other than forward.

His room was cool, at least. Basements had that going for them. There was a dank musty smell, and the German landlords argued late every night and then stomped about the rooms, hate walks that were hammer bangs on Lewis's ceiling. Something nasty seeped through the curling tiles in his shower stall, something white and gluey … and when he'd gone upstairs to complain, about this and about the nighttime racket, he'd been met by two bland moons: *Huh, seepage? Noises?* He'd backed away and the door had closed, ever so softly. But it was cool.

He sat at the desk, one of three articles – along with a chair and a single bed – that allowed the room to rent as *furnished*. The desk was small and low, child-sized, with a map of the world on its plasticized surface, a grinning sperm whale with a sailor's hat spouting a plume of water near Hawaii. He had to sit with knees akimbo, like a limbo dancer, or else side-saddle in the chair, turning to see the page. He chose the first option now, the pressure on his knees a good spur to alertness. He laid his pages out on the continents, checked his time. He was following the rules: four sections, thirty-five minutes each. No going back, no borrowing time from one section for another. He had his paper, pencils. Coffee his one indulgence. For the second test, he'd cut that out too. He'd read in the introduction that you had to supply a thumbprint along with pieces of ID when you took the real test. *A regrettable necessity, but stand-ins have been used by testees in the past, and L S A T results must be absolutely reliable.* He tried to fight down a sense of personal slight, also a sense of entrapment. Super-smarties, who'd seen him coming.…

No. Stop that. Clear mind, now. Clear. Mind. Second hand ticking ...
30 ... 25 ... 20 ... 15 ... 10 ... 5, 3, 2, 1. Go!

Go, man, go!

Exactly two hours and twenty minutes later, he laid down his pencil. Not even finishing the last question, playing it straight up the middle. After a quick bathroom run, the coffee and nerves doing a number on his bladder, he started checking his answers. God, it was a temptation to change the wrong ones. One flick of the eraser, new box filled in. Even here in his room. He didn't, but the thought kept hammering away.

A few minutes later he had his totals. Sixty-one percent correct. The analytical reasoning better than before, but still dragging him down. 'A pass!' Krista might have said if she'd been there. He was glad she wasn't. You didn't *pass* the LSAT. You creamed it, you did very well, or you flunked. Three simple grades. He'd flunked.

He arranged his papers into a neat pile, tapping them on the desk until they looked like one thick sheet, placing the booklet over them at one corner of the surface. He stared at the coloured world. His eye went straight to a place it had gone before. A dot that at times, times like this, could loom larger than Asia. It was the Mariana Trench in the West Pacific, the deepest water in the world. He leaned close to read the fine print, though he knew it by heart. *Greatest known ocean depth (36,200 ft. at the Challenger Deep).* This time his mind snagged, not on the stupendous numbers, seven miles of black water straight down, but on the sly little word *known.* One thing the LSAT hammered into you was the importance of little words. Known. Greatest *known* depth.

A few inches away, only a couple of thousand nautical miles, the whale grinned moronically. Moby Dick on a caffeine jag. Or his idiot brother, Dopey Dick. Little Dick?

Oh, stop it! Stop it, now!

Don was absent as expected the next day. 'Pie-eyed', 'blotto', 'totalled', 'wasted' – people seemed to enjoy finding their own term for his assumed condition. Lewis was on the dish machine to start the shift, but after about an hour he heard the student who was in potwash complaining to the super that he couldn't handle it. 'Man, that guy....' He imagined a pained look, a grimace summarizing Ron's fecklessness; craning his neck, he could see the bottoms of four white-trousered legs below a counter, the rest of the bodies hidden by intervening kettles and the swing-down mixing bowls. 'We're falling behind,' the voice whined. When the supervisor came to ask Lewis to swap, she spoke dismissively of the student, a new one. 'We've got a weak link,' she said, and Lewis saw the image, the kitchen a clanking chain, an endless belt of forged links. He put some of the same scorn into the look he levelled at the blond guy walking toward him, pulling on gloves, tossing his bangs. Dumb enough to expect to keep a job while rejecting its tasks; or was it smart enough? He was the one in potwash.

His mood already sour from the LSAT debacle, he felt the day getting worse. Ron was behind a teetering wall of dirty pots, scratching himself. The sight of Lewis started up a defensive blather. 'I was hustlin. He wasn't doin nothin. Cooks were –'

'Shut up,' Lewis said. Ron did.

As he watched his hands flying over the work of pots, a sequence of actions without pause – *grab, scrape, rinse, scrub, rinse, soak or load* – that allowed him to make minute gains against the inflow, he found himself thinking about that *Shut up*. It had come out naturally, clipped and smooth. The language of efficiency. What was required. He could think these thoughts like a robot, its brain and hands controlled by different programs. It occurred to him that it was hope that made the students so slow and unreliable. Daydreams, sparkly plans, that blew their attention away like dandelion puffs and made their basking bodies go soft and idle. The wall of pots shrank by a layer or two.

Meanwhile Ron was rearranging pots, draining his sink and refilling it with water, staring at greasy tiled walls, scratching himself, squeezing flabbily behind Lewis and back again ... he was doing lots of things. What he wasn't doing was washing pots. Not one. Lewis thought he understood. Ron, big baby Ron, had heard there was a parent on duty. *Shut up.* Now there was only a maniac worker, a blur of hands and sweat. He was trying to make the parent come back. His understanding grew apace with his anger, both of them encased in a hard clarity like amber, neither of them affecting the other. He wasn't going to play.

Finally, though, Ron took off his apron – a fussy, two-minute job in itself – and mumbled, 'Washroom break. Be right back.' Disappeared. To discipline his anger, Lewis told himself to expect him back in fifteen, no, make it twenty minutes. Don't watch the clock, he warned. Work.

The trouble was, he could watch the clock *and* work. He could do any-thing and work, now.

Fifty-four minutes later, Ron appeared. In that fifty-four minutes, the cooks had brought the bread pudding pans, the quiche trays, and the roasting pans from yesterday. *Sorry, must've forgotten these,* yelled the cook from New Zealand, the one who climbed rocks. Lewis had ratcheted his attack up yet another impossible notch, kept that pace up for several minutes, then, quite suddenly, had stopped. Exhausted. He was standing by the double sinks with a metal spatula, poking at chunks of black stuff, when a block of white appeared hazily in his peripheral vision, fussing with its belt. He laid the spatula down. Turned.

He took one giant step to where Ron stood and clutched him by the shoulders. His fingers sank in softness.

'Eek!' Ron squealed, like a massive mouse seized by an owl.

'Now look, you! Your ass stays here! Not out for a crap, not jerking off! Here! Your hands start working! Ass here, hands working. Got it?' Despite his rage, the power that filled his chest then roared out his throat, he could still hear himself from a little measuring distance. It was Don's voice, but with a difference. Less scattered, more focused. More controlled. Meaner, maybe. Rage had to aim itself to be cruel. The way Don's had with him, Lewis. Ron blinked watery eyes up at him. Almost colourless, almost empty eyes. Grey, blond-lashed pools lit slightly by fear, by fitful focus, maybe – it was possible to read this in them – by gratitude.

He looked across the kitchen – a few faces turned, interested – and saw the student up on the rubber mat behind the Hobart, smirking. Krista ... no, it was Saturday.

A while later, the leathery-faced supervisor came by potwash. Ron was working fairly steadily; Lewis had taken to poking him in the side when he fell into reverie, something that produced a sound, a Pillsbury Doughboy squeak, but also a few minutes of activity.

The supervisor pretended to consult her clipboard. 'Do you have a date of termination?' When Lewis didn't answer immediately, she added, 'I know it's not even July yet, but we do like to get a sense of how long students will be with us. For scheduling purposes.'

He doubted this. Students lasted for a period of days or weeks, the best dropping off near Labour Day. They were mayflies or butterflies, summer phenomena.

'I may not be terminating,' he said. It just came out. Like *shut up.*

'Oh?' She pretended to be surprised. 'Well, you're always welcome to submit an application. In the meantime, thanks for helping out today.' She jerked a friendly scowl toward the figure bent over the sink, scrubbing the corner of a pan Lewis had already cleaned.

That night he met Krista outside the Broadway. On his way past the Odeon, he saw there was a new James Bond playing, and thought that something bland and frothy might have been a better choice. He was dead tired. But Krista had been interested in the Hitchcock double, *Vertigo* followed by *Psycho.* She remembered seeing *The Birds* as a little girl, the crows pecking the shrieking schoolchildren.

'I kind of lost it with Ron today,' he said when they were seated.

'Oh?' Her expression neutral.

He shook his head. 'The pots were piling up and he was doing nothing. Nothing.'

She shrugged. 'You do what you gotta do.' She bit her brownie and snuggled close, taking his hand. 'Ready to get scared?'

Afterwards they went to the Black Forest, which had become their spot. They ordered the special, Hungarian goulash with spätzle. Sipping his beer, Lewis found the smells in the restaurant a little too primal and pungent – meat and spuds, spuds and meat, fried in oil with onions – to let him escape the kitchen. When the heaped plates went past, he saw the pots that each had produced. Somebody was back behind the swinging doors, behind the painting of a Heidi-girl in braids and a dirndl. Back there, sweating and cursing....

The beer helped, as always. The 99-cent glasses that came and went, replenished by the grinning platinum blonde with too much pancake on her face and breasts that heaved yeastily out of her embroidered 'peasant' top. The Hitchcock had helped too. It wasn't as campy as the Polanski, perhaps because you never lost the sense of a controlling intelligence, a malicious and entertaining guide who would never quite succumb to his own fantasies. It struck him as light entertainment, like the Bond, but far more witty and engaging. Stylish.

But it was Krista, more than he, who wanted to talk tonight. The Hitchcock had stirred her up. She was mainly interested in the sudden shocks and falls both movies had. 'Like the policeman at the beginning. The one you saw his face screaming, all the way down.'

'*Vertigo*.' He sipped his beer.

'Or the detective on the stairs.'

'In *Psycho*, you mean?'

'Yeah. It was funny, when he was climbing the stairs you knew he was going to get it. But it was still a complete shock when the old lady jumped out.'

'Which was Norman Bates.'

'Oh, *really?*' Her eyebrows twitched. It was authority figures she liked to see brought low, he thought.

'Seeing her pop out with that knife.' She shuddered.

'It was everything,' he suggested. 'The slow climb. The way we only saw her from the back. The knife raised, held for a moment, poised. Then that chopping arm, like a piston. Him tumbling down the stairs.'

She was looking at him in a discouraging way. She liked celebration of moments, replaying scenes and dialogue, not analysis. But he went on anyway. It was habit, partly. 'If you think about it, both movies were about double identities. Trading places.'

She sipped a new glass of beer and made a face. 'This is sour.' He hailed their waitress, who came with Germanic haste. '*Al-so*. I take it away and bring the lady another.'

He continued, musing. 'Jimmy Stewart trying to turn a woman into someone else, Anthony Perkins trying to turn himself into his mother … but they were both … I don't know. Twisted. Wrong-headed.' His mind reeled around thematic depths in Hitchcock he was glimpsing for the first time, slivers and layers he couldn't articulate, though he could see them, flitting. Krista was watching him.

Their food arrived. 'Mmm, smell that?' she said encouragingly.

He did. He did that. He inhaled the hearty fug from his bowl of meat and gravy, the sideshow of fried noodles like oily commas. It *was* good. He told himself to relax, stop trying to comment on the obvious and the unsayable. It *was* a habit. One he wanted to lose. One he needed to.

After coffee, they walked their full bellies slowly up King Street. In the protracted light of the solstice, people seemed to be moving in slow motion, stunned by the day's length and heat. 'First day of summer,' he heard Krista say at his side. He nodded. *First day,* yet for a week now the weather had been unchanged, an enveloping fluid of hot rotten smells, an organic soup gone off, like a decaying womb.

'Hey, I'm kidding.' He felt a poke in his side, and looked down to see her dusky heart-shaped, pleasantly pock-marked face. A face I'd trust, he thought, surprising himself.

Up ahead, in front of the Holiday Inn, a crowd was gathered. Curious onlookers, a jumble of them spilling from the sidewalk onto the road. A policeman was directing traffic away from the curbside lane. 'Accident,' Krista murmured. The crowd huddled round in a ragged semi-circle, straining forward; ahead of them another policeman had his arms stretched out, limiting their advance.

They paused at the outer rim of the crowd. By a touch on Krista's arm, he told her to stay, while he pushed forward slowly, ignoring the hisses and clucks as he squeezed through. Taller than the others, he could see the scene over their heads. Two cars, a big blue Ford and a Yellow taxi cab, were sitting skewed in the lane, a little ways apart, like boxers who'd done battle and been ordered by the referee to neutral corners. The Ford had a punched-in front fender and the cab had taken a sock in the middle, a body blow, leaving a crumpled circle in the rear passenger door. It didn't seem that serious. The two drivers were standing, each beside his car. But as he scanned the scene for more details, a few curious facts met his eyes. The taxi driver was staring at the ground, arms folded. The other driver was also looking at the pavement, staring intensely down; Lewis saw him swipe his forearm quickly across his eyes. They weren't arguing; they weren't even looking at each other. Another thing he noticed was that one of the taxi's windows had been shattered. Cracks spidered the window above the impact site, but looking through these, he could see a clear square bordered by a few tiny icicles of glass. Just as he shouldered his way right to the front, sweaty arms rubbing along his own, he heard a man say, 'How could a guy go through that little window?' His companion said, 'From the smell of him, he was mostly liquid.' He was still trying to absorb this image when he got close enough to see the space the policeman with the raised arms was protecting, a patch of pavement between himself and the cars. On it lay a long lump, a body obviously, covered by a grey plastic sheet. The sheet struck Lewis forcefully; grey and shiny, it didn't look like anything a normal person would have handy; he wondered if police cars carried

it, standard issue for times like these. Then he saw, just off the corner of
the sheeted lump, the black boot. Even lying on its side it looked huge.
Broad sole and wide square heel, the top built up several inches; the
whole thick-looking, solid even when empty; and all black. A giant's
boot. In his mind he saw the tiny white foot yanked out of it like a
parsnip out of the damp earth.

He pushed his way back to Krista. 'Jesus,' he said. 'It's Don.'

Her face went blank with bewilderment, just for a moment, and then
seemed to fill with recognition. She bit her bottom lip. 'Poor Ronnie,'
she said.

'No. Don,' he told her.

She stared at him, the blankness seeping back into her face. Belatedly
they heard the ambulance siren. Faces looked about, seeking the flashing
lights. The police must have said the call was non-urgent. No one living
and hurt, here.

They began walking away. They walked for a long time, saying no
more than a dozen words in all. They walked north on John Street, all
the way down to the docks. Stood for a few moments looking at the flat
grey-brown water, sailboats putt-putting or becalmed. At the other end
of the funnel-shaped bay, the freighters were moored off the steel
company's artificial shores, piles of coal dust and iron ore and something white, like mounds of pepper and cinnamon and salt ... he kept
peering into a giant's world, for some reason.

Hand in hand, still silent, they walked along the shore to the Yacht
Club, people in shorts and T-shirts having drinks amid the fetor, then
up to Barton Street and along it to Dundurn Park. Krista's hand felt
sweaty in his; it was a good feeling, a clammy warmth, the liquids from
their bodies mingling. In Dundurn Park they walked among the cooler
shade of the trees, down the lawns, pausing by the cannons pointed out
toward the lake. 'Defending Hammer's shores,' he'd joked on another
night. They walked a little way along the edge of the bluff, the railway
tracks below, the bay beyond. Finally they crossed York Boulevard and
turned to begin the walk back. His legs felt leaden, and Krista was limp-
ing a bit; she said the fifteen years of standing had ruined her feet. 'You
wouldn't want to see them,' she'd said, in a way that made him think he
never would. Her limp, the cemetery groves beyond the wall next to
them, traffic whizzing past on the other side – conjunctions brought him

repeatedly back to Don, his anomalous flight through a small window, head first he assumed, no one else hurt. *Mostly liquid,* the onlooker had said. It wasn't an image that would have occurred to Lewis to describe Don, but now he couldn't shake it out of his head. The boy with the faulty body, dissolving its imperfect solidity in alcohol, shot by ounce by bottle. Except that alcohol didn't dissolve, it preserved. It turned things into rubbery, pickled artifacts in glass bottles. Bottles that could drop. Drop and shatter.

At Krista's house, they hugged tightly by the walkway. They embraced clammily, their groins glommed together, then drew delicately apart, still hugging from the waist up. 'Poor Ronnie,' Krista whispered again. In answer he pressed her tight. She pressed a kiss into his neck and turned up the walk. He watched her. After a few steps she paused, turned and came back to him. She took his hands in hers, her face serious and determined, as it had been that first night. 'I *do* think you're beautiful,' she said. And then, déjà vu again, she was gone, slipped away into the black house.

No light switched on.

He walked slowly, contemplatively, away. For once he thought he understood their goodbye. There was no more hurry now. It was a working rhythm. Which didn't mean that it would last, just that it had found its pace. It was a link in a moving chain, a sequence of causes and understandings, a round of scheduled tasks and breaks, even a pause for sudden deaths. He couldn't find much in himself to object to it.

The new student, the blond one with bangs, met him at the door to the change room the next morning. He looked excited. 'Didja hear, man? Didja hear what happened?'

'I heard,' Lewis said. He opened his locker and began to change.

'No, man, listen. Last night. What's-his-name, that tall guy in pot-wash –'

Lewis turned on the bench to face him. 'I know all about it,' he said.

The boy made a face and went away. A minute later another one came into the room and Lewis heard the story babbled. It sounded strange in someone's mouth, not just in his, Lewis's, head. Both more and less real. Don on a twenty-four-hour tear with his payday money. On the way home, his cab in a minor collision. No one hurt, but Don,

like a contrary angel, finds a small window and hurtles head first
through it. Broken neck. He wondered if the student was making some
of it up. After all, the news was only a few hours old.

He checked the schedule and found that his name had been
scratched off the dish machine and pencilled in for portering. Portering
was a cushy, coveted job, one that he had not had since his training and
had not expected to get except by a fluke. Today, of all days, he had
expected to land in potwash. But then he remembered his conversation
with the supervisor yesterday, his fuzziness about leaving: was that his
fluke? A hesitation that should be rewarded, this slacker, cleaner job the
only tidbit available in the kitchen? It made sense. Looking at the schedule with its boxes and codes, names crossed out and rewritten in various
pens and pencils, he thought of the LSAT problem he and Krista had
worked on in Tim Horton's. ... *four people selected for a special dinner ...*
She was right: you did have to figure these things out.

The strange thing about the porter's job was that it kept him out of
the kitchen almost entirely. He walked about the hospital, among
doctors and nurses and blue-suited maintenance men, riding elevators
to different wards to deliver the breakfast carts. Then he reported to an
alcove in a corridor past the change room, where a supervisor was waiting with a clipboard and pencil, a hooded parka and gloves. When he'd
donned the outerwear, she opened the big door to the main freezer.
White air puffed out, a frost giant's breath. Clutching the clipboard in
his gloves, he took a step into the ice cave. 'Remember, just ten minutes
at a time,' he heard from behind him as the door closed. Inventory was
weird. Weird and kind of fun. You walked about the stacks of frozen
meals, rubbing the front of foil pans to read the magic marker label,
then counting the pans to the ceiling. Food was stacked on shelves
around the four walls, and on shelves on an island in the middle; you
squeezed between them delicately, avoiding the searing metal. The
minus-forty-degree chill found the legs, the face, the hands when the
gloves came off to write; it found everything but it found these first,
making the skin go numb and rubbery in a loss that was like pleasure.
Ten minutes is nothing, he had thought, less than ten minutes ago, but
long before the thump came on the door, he was sure the supervisor had
forgotten. When he emerged into the corridor again, his legs wobbled
embarrassingly. Water welled up out of his eyes and dropped hotly onto

his cheeks. He shook off his gloves and pressed his hands to his face, feeling half-frozen flesh shift sluggishly. 'Here.' The super – young, with dirty blond hair, not unattractive – had a coffee for him.

At break time he sat with the tray-strippers, glad that Krista was off so he could join them. He listened to the kitchen gossip like an outsider, like the bored ward clerks who sometimes came over to get the latest Don and Ron story. But the stories had diverged, at last. Don had sailed, quite literally, out of his place and into a new legend, a bizarre and violent dream. His story dominated, as he had dominated. But Ron came up for mention too, still a counterpoint, if only in terms of how he was coping. He had apparently taken the news calmly, perhaps uncomprehendingly, and was working almost steadily. People were keeping an eye on him. 'Blondie do okay,' said the huge scraper, the lascivious kidder. She tossed her oily bangs in parody, and Lewis found himself roaring with the others.

Ron took his place with the potato scoop at lunch time. Lewis was at the end of the belt, beside the old supervisor, who was now openly cultivating him. Her normal demeanour was grim and tense, but today her lined face cracked in a smile, like a dried-apple face splitting, and she tossed him some crusts of encouragement. 'No sweat, you'll see. You'll do fine.'

And he did. The belt started moving. As trays came down he scooped them off the end, checked their designation, and slid them into a slot on the proper ward cart. Every so often the super would push the black button to stop the belt and query something: salt on a no-salt tray, a cookie package on a diabetic menu; regular utensils, not plastic, for the psych ward. The server who had made the mistake would scurry down and correct it. Ron made his usual share of mistakes, missing checks or seeing checks where there weren't any, but was otherwise working normally. Lewis could feel the relief along both sides of the belt.

Then, when his carts were about half filled, the illusion snapped. He was crouched down, inserting a tray in a lower slot, when a wrinkled hand reached down and pressed the Stop button by his head. He heard a low-voiced disturbance, a flurry of murmurs and whispers. It was strange to be able to hear it amid the cooks' clatter; he thought it was because it was a different sound. Or maybe because he, all of them, had been waiting for it.

Sure enough, when he stood up again, he saw everybody looking at Ron. It was the reactions he noticed first: one server leaning back from her niche, hand beside her mouth, to say something to her neighbour; a woman darting meek glances at the supervisor while she pointed at Ron; up and down the line, expressions of surprise, dismay, annoyance. At the end of all of the eye-lines, hand-lines, Ron was standing with his shoulders slumped, very still. Staring down at his steam table, as he often stared into the sinks in potwash. Checking the belt, Lewis saw that none of the last half dozen trays had mashed potatoes on them. 'Ach, Gott,' he heard from beside him, the supervisor lapsing out of English in disgust. He looked back at Ron. There was a stain, brown and spreading, in the seat of his baggy white trousers. A few hands were pointing now, unnecessarily; no one was speaking. Everyone was staring with one pair of eyes at the confession of Ron's body. For a moment the kitchen seemed to stop, hung in a balance: the poise of someone's indignity balanced by the onlookers' shame.

Only for a moment; and then, in a flurry, the world started again. The super snapped her fingers at the woman just behind Ron. She had been gaping; now she turned and watched as the super jabbed a finger at Ron and then jabbed her thumb at the door. In other circumstances the repeated mime might have been funny. Finally the woman understood; she stuck a forefinger in the air – *Ah yes, good idea* – and came out from her niche to lead Ron away. She touched his arm and Ron plodded after her. All eyes followed as they walked slowly toward the doors leading to the change room, the stain in Ron's pants still visibly spreading.

When they disappeared there was a moment of confusion, a pause when no one seemed to know how to proceed, as if the script for one scene had ended and the next page had been misplaced. The supervisor strode toward a phone on the wall, to call whom Lewis couldn't imagine. Security? Psychiatry? When she was almost there, she turned and strode back to the belt. 'All right, let's go,' she bellowed. She handed him a pair of plastic gloves and pointed to Ron's vacant niche. 'I'll load,' she said. On his way up the line, he passed the woman who had led Ron out, returning with a grimace, her teeth bared and her jaw vibrating, like someone in a centrifuge: the universal expression for revulsion.

He took his place and checked his double metal bins. Mashed, mashed-no-salt. It was hard to make a mistake. 'Gloves on?' called a voice from the end of the line. A cheery voice; time to jolly the troops back to normal. 'Yup,' he answered.

As he scooped, he marvelled at how two men had been erased from the kitchen in the space of one day. There was a buzz of activity, normal talk and clatter that amounted to cathedral hush. He'd tasted it before on the days when both of them were off. Though it couldn't have been that fast, he told himself; things have to happen over time. Not knowing if the thought was naïve or cynical or just realistic. Wishing he could ask Krista. He kept looking at the server a few places ahead of him, on the other side of the line. She was the one who'd murmured from behind her hand, but it wasn't just the similarity of gesture; she had Krista's firm, tidy body; a neat body, dipped in clothes like a second skin. Grace under efficiency: Hemingway's courage definition, adapted to the kitchen. But when she turned, catching his eye with a fleeting smile, he saw that she was fifteen years younger. Fifteen years *too young*.

The job's mine if I want it, he thought. Not knowing where the thought came from, even surprised by it. Had it grown over time too, then hatched suddenly; like Don bursting into death, Ron dribbling after him? Like a lifer, he thought, scooping.

'Tired of the faculty life?' his father said around his fork at dinner. Lewis had never heard his father use the word *faculty* before; was surprised he knew it, actually.

'Well, we've all got to eat,' he said.

'That's one thing they've taught you.'

The atmosphere around his announcement was light-hearted; he had wanted it to be. 'I'm taking a year off to work,' he'd said, which cued his father to say, 'A year off. Well, I guess I've been off twenty years. A nice holiday.' With that smile that Lewis read now as a kind of lawyer's smile; smug, clever; satisfied to milk a word for all its treacherous and absurd implications. Where had that word savvy come from? From all the break and lunchroom banter, the word wiles to survive it? His father looked to his wife to share the joke, but her face was blank. Alone in her kitchen, she worked to deeper, wordless rhythms. Any decision worried her.

When he was helping her with the dishes, she said, 'If you're seeing someone, you should bring her over for dinner. Let us meet her.' She said it offhandedly, while scrubbing the potato pot; that meant it was a serious comment, the product of long deliberation. Lewis thought his mother, whom he loved, was unknown to him. That also made him take her seriously. 'I will, Mom,' he said, patting her back. She nodded at the water rocking in the sink.

Back home, he found himself in a jittery mood. Instead of flopping on his bed, he paced the small room restlessly. He felt uneasy. He wondered why. It had been a deeply strange, eventful weekend, especially the last twenty-four hours, but he knew it was more than that. It must be because tomorrow was his day off, since his mind kept returning to that. What to do with it? There were no LSAT preps to do. But even more – since those sessions had never amounted to more than a few hours anyway – there were no future plans, the goals that backed the LSAT questions and made them solid. Time off was just time off. What to do with it?

He tidied the room, throwing out pizza boxes and arranging his laundry in piles to take to the laundromat. He felt like someone preparing a clean surface to work on … but what was the job? What would he build or fix?

He opened a garbage bag and gathered up the newspapers and magazines scattered around the room; then, after a moment's thought, he dropped in his school notes too. He opened his three-ring binders and shook the pages free. He was just about to close the bag when, suddenly, he swept into it the LSAT papers and booklet from the little desk. It wasn't that he thought he was through with school and the LSAT; he didn't know that yet. In fact, what made him anxious to be rid of them was the sequence of tactics whispered by the trash in the bag. *Buy better essays, maybe from the internet. Get some A-pluses if possible, at least straight As. Keep practising the LSAT. Look into the thumbprint situation. Someone must have thought of it.…*

The thoughts had to be bagged, they had to be twist-tied, they had to be removed.

The plop the bag made when he tossed it beside his landlords' trash was a judgement. A judgement he'd have to live with. *Not smart enough.* He didn't know how to live with it yet, but not fighting it any more was a first step. Already he felt a bit calmer.

* * *

Later, it was almost midnight, he found himself walking toward Krista's house. He wanted to walk, though it was a long way; the tiredness in his legs helped him think better. It was only a day since he and Krista had taken their exhausted walk, but it felt like a week had passed. Events were receding rapidly behind him, or he was accelerating away from them. The decision to visit Krista had come on him suddenly, a sweeping urge like the discarding of his papers and plans. Sitting in his room he'd felt his loneliness. It was nothing abstract, not a hollow feeling; rather, a buzzing itch that started in his crotch and spread down into his legs and up, through his chest and down his arms, up into his head. Desire. Desire for Krista. He had to see her. Excitedly, he glimpsed a new way they could be together. It was their old way – he wasn't getting rid of anything – but with strong new elements added. Part of the new life he was glimpsing for himself – with fear, yes, but also with growing anticipation – involved the necessity of bold action. A grey background of work, but lit by flashes of impulse, pleasures snatched from drabness. Unannounced visits. Visits to her house. Visits to his. Meeting each other's parents. The end of a summer romance, and the start of … something else. Not knowing was part of the thrill.

Come, babe. It was his turn to say it. To need it and want it. To demand it.

Resolve carried him quickly to Market Street. But then, as he turned the corner, his steps slowed. There was a light on in Krista's house. It was what he had hoped for, why he had walked quickly, but it slowed him with its stark promise of a meeting. *I need my sleep.* Well, you couldn't always have your sleep. No one could.

He hesitated at the foot of the narrow walkway. On either side, the marigolds glimmered palely atop their neat black mounds. Nipples on breasts, he thought; except that the colours were reversed: they should be dark on tan. He stepped softly, his eye on the glow behind the curtains. He reached the door and knocked.

A sharp-faced old woman peered out from behind the chain lock. Her chin jutted out beyond a toothless mouth, making her face seem to be collapsing on itself; but with her shower or night cap on, there was still a strong resemblance to Krista. Words jumbled in his mind: *I'm sorry to call so late, Mrs –* For a moment he could not remember Krista's last name. *Would your daughter be up still?* It was only when her hand flew up protectively to her mouth that he had a sudden, piercing sense of how careless he'd been.

Urchipelago

St. George Station

The southbound subway train came to a stop. The doors didn't open. Looks of surprise on the faces outside on the platform, and on those waiting inside.

Then the lights went out.

Tension. A shiver in the air like an electric ghost. Earphones came off heads, books got closed. The station lights were still on, so the car was not completely dark. It was more like deep dusk.

'Jumper,' said a voice opposite me.

A black man's face came into focus – wide and heavy, with coal-black eyes and short, grizzled hair. Though very dark, his face emerged from the shadows more clearly than the white faces, which remained smudge-like. That surprised me.

Another surprise was that he seemed to see me better than I could see him. For one thing, he wasn't peering or squinting. And he spoke right to me, not casting about.

'Maybe,' I said, not wanting to think about it.

'For sure,' he said. Which irritated me.

'Please,' said a woman to my right. I looked over. She was sitting with a child on the seat perpendicular to mine. Though closer than the black man's, their faces were blurrier, like out-of-focus snapshots. But I could make out a woman who was at least sixty, and a boy, perhaps four, who held a shopping bag. They looked like grandmother and grandson out for a Saturday afternoon shopping trip. The boy had his face cocked to one side, perhaps so he could see all three of us at once.

The intercom popped on. 'Please take your seats,' said a man's voice. Some people did. 'Service will resume shortly.'

That was all. But the line, hissing faintly, stayed open. A few moments later, another voice continued, in a crackly lower register, like someone mumbling over a bad telephone connection, '… someone at track level … the interruption.'

47

At track level. The black man's eyes gleamed at me, as if to say, *See.* And I tried to project back a decent scepticism. Yet neither of us knew anything.

The boy and his grandmother had a whispered exchange.

'What's Saint George?' the boy said out loud.

The woman answered in a brisk public voice. 'Saint George is the patron saint of England. He was a knight who killed a dragon.' She struck me as a liberal sort of person, someone who would never not answer a question but who might skim over the details.

'What dragon?' the boy wanted to know.

'A big one, I should think,' his grandmother replied. To avoid the black man, who was still staring meaningfully at me, I had shifted my gaze toward the pair, the woman peering about as if absentmindedly, and the boy taking us all in.

Now the intercom popped again, and the crackly voice, which might be meant to be public or private, said, 'Crews … from both ends of the tunnel.'

I looked straight back at the black man. To me, *both ends of the tunnel* implied a straggler, someone on foot. Confused perhaps, maybe crazy, but not squashed under the wheels. He glowered defiantly at me. I could see the boy's face out of the corner of my eye, a pale moon hovering, as the black man and I carried on our silent disagreement about the dragon in the dark.

C'mon, I wanted to tell those knowing eyes, *Don't just assume. Let's give him a chance.* Feeling angry and determined and not at all ridiculous yet, though we were strangers and neither of us knew anything.

Just then, the lights flickered on and 'Service resumed' with a fiery sigh.

You're Up

You're up because you spent the night arguing with your lover. Your right hand bloated, the bones throbbing, from when you punched the wall to make your point. *What point? Can't remember.* Ice in a plastic bag your boxing glove, clinging to pink knuckles as it melts.

Or there is no lover. She's, he's, gone. You're between lovers, and you're up because there is no other body to pin against the fact of night.

You go pinwheeling down a spiral galaxy of stars and dark matter. Nebulae of memories. Supernovas.

Black holes.

You're sick. You've caught a bug. You ate too much, or the wrong thing. The fact is, you haven't eaten in days. Your bowels twist on air.

Anyway – every way – you're up.

You're up.

And staring at garbage.

The garbage you put out at midnight, half a century ago, looms in the sluggish dawn. Glad bags and the neighbours' can and two plants somebody got tired of. Wisps of dispersing darkness curdle around the mounds like Spielberg ghouls.

A car coasts up and stops. An old grey sedan, stately and rusted-through. A tall man in a windbreaker gets out and walks to the curb. No furtive glance, but he moves efficiently. Carries one spider plant in its plastic pot back to the car, an Impala you see now in the streaky light. Pops the trunk, sets it inside. Casts a look back, and you hear him decide not to push his luck. *Float like a butterfly, sting if you can.*

The car rolls down half a block and stops again. He eases something large and spindly from a pile. *A chair?* You can't see.

Stand in the flare of pumpkin over rooftops, coffee bubbling black, and imagine the room a person might construct before daybreak, piece by piece, week by week. From things bought or stolen, given or discarded. Found.

A chair. A plant. A table and some food. Clothes for the coming season.

Walls, ceiling, floor.

A window facing north?

Courier

The things you saw, driving for a living. Not just the normal dumb show of mouths and fingers, everyday snarls that meld you to the machine. The siren floating behind the spinning lights. The slow motion flames.

But even more, the small mysteries, puzzling seeds that find an untrampled patch of mind and put down slender roots.

Things that connect you back to the idea that someone else is behind each wheel. Things that stay.

Like the clothes – pink, blue, yellow, white – scattered along the Allen Expressway at dawn. A long ragged line, as if they had been fed out gradually. So conjecture starts: Spring cleaning? An eviction notice? Red underpants – past too fast – catching the crescent sun.

Or coming up behind a man who keeps turning to speak to his companion. His hand reaches over too, to prod or caress. Mouthing and touching, with just quick glances back ahead of him, at 120 kilometres an hour. But no one is visible in the seat. When you pull out to pass, glancing over you see the cassette tapes spilling out of a shoe box. It's them he's talking to, singing along with.

Sometimes a head can be so still it looks carved. No movement at all, even to ease muscle cramp. Though the eyes, you think, might be darting inside that ball. Just then the tail lights flare, you slam the brakes to keep from rear-ending him. Witty as a Gershwin moon, up pops another head, tight blond curls above a slender neck.

Drive on with new rules, new exceptions. The rootlets budding into stems and flowers, curious hybrids.

Smiling to yourself as you see the next mouth working, the hand pushing down at the tapes. The lips wide, yelling. Heavy metal? Then, unprepared for it, the little pale arm, like a peeled stick, floating up by the passenger window, fingers stretched to touch the cool glass.

Steel

'Push mama?' the Italian charge-car drivers would say if they caught you smiling in the lunchroom. Or, more often, 'No push mama?' when you were frowning or just glum. It was a simple binary explanation of mood. Push mama, no push mama. With helpful finger-through-hole gestures for the rookies.

And the lunches *their* mamas packed. Soft powdery buns stuffed with prosciutto, provolone, roasted red peppers. Plums, pears, oranges on the side. Slabs of cake and butter tarts. Thermoses of *latte*.

They were veterans of five, ten years tops. No transfers out of the coke ovens. We said they couldn't last past fifty, lungs carbonized. But who knows?

Our lunches were peanut butter sandwiches and machine coffee. But then on nights we had tabs of Sunshine or Windowpane, the flames and green-purple plumes a gorgeous Boschean dance.

Some guys up from the labour gang only lasted an hour. Or two and twenty minutes, if they wanted to keep their steeltoes. The trick was to hang over the sides of the battery, suck up what air you could. Then rush in with your pry bar to do your lids while holding your breath.

In theory. Trouble was, if one lid stuck – and it always did – you ran out halfway through and sucked in cancer green right down to the base of your lungs.

Canetti said his first sight of me I was mid-air, leaping backwards with my gloves over my crotch. Someone hadn't bled the gas from the gooseneck – a common shortcut, especially if stoned – and the flame roared out between my legs and twenty feet beyond. We became partners.

'Lifer?' he'd wink when I was reading on my twenty minutes down. It made him cackle to watch the drops of sweat roll down my nose and splotch onto the page. I was actually reading *One Day in the Life of Ivan Denisovich*, the margins black from my turning.

Pictures were crude, the lines cartoony. 'Thass honky work,' a black guy said, departing without his boots. One guy was crushed to jam between an oven and the pusher-car. Fractures and sprains common from the charge-car, which loomed huge in the smoke, a tiny clanging bell.

Canetti quit first. When I left, at a year, I was second senior lidsman. Five years later I ran into Canetti outside a Tim Horton's at 3 a.m. I was writing ten poems a day and wouldn't have cracked *The Gulag Archipelago* for blood. Canetti looked sullen, his eyes downshifted.

'No push mama?' I said. He looked at me like I was a talking parrot. Then asked if I knew where he could buy a gun.

Do Not Stand
Outside the Grande Restaurant

The crude and prominent sign made it our natural meeting place. Seven words in slashing black capitals, on a square of cardboard taped inside the window. No 'Please' because there didn't need to be. Mrs Soon, the owner, came out regularly to chase us away. 'For customers. Not crazy people,' she would hiss. 'Go haunt some place else.' *Haunt* or *on*: her accent made it hard to tell. Sometimes she even waved a broom, like a Grimm's witch.

⚘

Enough of us drifted by sometimes to make it like a mini-Ward. Like the loose knot we used to form outside OT in the morning. Or outside the dining room, the kitchen porter glancing nervously at us as he braked his cart.

There was Jaz. Karl Jazurewlski. A few years older, so in and out longer than the rest of us. Who one day got the bright idea of kicking in a window (not Mrs Soon's) when the weather turned cold. 'The food's shit and so's the company. But hey,' he grinned, 'what's new?' The hardest part, he said, was standing there listening to the alarm bell clanging until the cops arrived.

With his rippling red hair and beard, huge paunch, and wild, bewildered eyes, Jaz looked like a Santa Claus some kids had set on fire. He always brought Mrs Soon out soonest.

⚘

Billy. A porcelain depressive, whom you always saw coming a long way off. Stumble-floating between his canes like a puppet. 'I can't go by fast,' he used to say. Which was a different, and maybe worse, outcome than any he'd envisioned from his perch atop the Skyway.

Clover. With her rancid breath and quasi-occult mutterings. Unlike Billy, she always appeared suddenly, without warning, like a ghost.

53

Beside your bed in the middle of the night, muttering strange prayers or prophecies. Reporting. 'Satan raped me,' she'd say, with that foul breath, a crypt kiss. 'Go back to your room,' I'd instruct her, patting her little body through her nightgown. And off she'd float.

'Clover' had come from a movie, she said. It wasn't until years later, on the late show, that I saw *Inside Daisy Clover*. A Hollywood yawner about Natalie Wood becoming famous but keeping her head. I think Clover had it confused with *Splendor in the Grass*. Natalie Wood going mad but staying beautiful. It must have been the height of Clover's fantasy.

⁂

Old Sparky. The Thorazine Kid. Largactil. Mellaril. Electro-Lite. Electrode. Gurney. Pharma-Shock.

Thinking up names for myself was as much writing as I could manage then. It filled the hours it had to. The medical words fascinated me, and were the ones I mostly remembered.

⁂

Standing in a row in front of Mrs Soon's establishment, we'd recite our diagnoses to startled passersby, like a line of soldiers sounding off their ranks and serial numbers.

'Bipolar,' Jaz boomed.

'Depressive,' Billy admitted.

'Schizophrenic,' Clover whispered, the syllables like smoke wisps.

'The gamut,' I declared. Jaz scowled; Billy watched him. 'The spectrum.' Which wasn't quite true: no one had called me a depressive without a hyphen. But I was trying to remember the words.

This would be after we had pooled coins for a round of coffees – never quite enough – and before Mrs Soon emerged.

⁂

There really couldn't have been that many meetings. Not with all of us. But they're strung together in my memory.

Psycho pearls.

For one thing, even though we all lived in the same neighbourhood, all of us were getting discharged and readmitted at different times.

To halfway houses or to 'independent living'. To pissy, roach-ridden rooms in either case, though the one had less supervision.

There was one time, though, when we all assembled together. A bright and spangly April day. It's a trustworthy memory because Jaz marked it by saying, apropos our simultaneous discharges, 'Spring cleaning.'

Even Clover laughed. The sun was steely-white, spiked with rays. It scoured the surfaces of things until they shone.

෨

They tell me it happened several dozen times. Several *series*, they called them. 'An unusually intractable episode,' mumbled one resident, clearly embarrassed by the numbers.

෨

Open my eyes. Beige, tilting. So dizzy.

Close.

Open. (Later.)

Buzzy headache. Not bad, like sandpaper scraping. *Where'm I?*

Wha'ppened?

Going to throw up. Wish I. Filthy, oozy feeling. The beige. And the dirty brown-orange. Tilty, angles. Close eyes. Better. Deep breaths. Deep and slow. A musty farty smell, something scratching my cheek. Move feet, slowly. Lying on something. *Whatsa call'?*

Sleepy coming again.

When the lady comes, you don't know at first she's a nurse. No white uniform. You're sitting on the shit-brown couch, taking slow breaths, trying not to stare at the wobbling beige walls or orange carpet.

She is smiling.

'Hello, sleepyhead.'

You put your hands up to your temples. Something scaly there, flakes of something. Some flakes off, milky scales like dried glue. Like someone came on your head.

'It's ten o'clock,' she says. 'Come on.'

She has a wrinkled face with fuzzy brown-orange hair. But she's smiling.

'Come on.'

As you walk slowly up the hall, her arm crooked in yours, she fills you in.
You had E C T at 8 this morning. Electro-Convulsive-Therapy. You know
there's always some transient memory loss.
How would I know?
She stops at a door. A black sign says Treatment Room.
'Anything?'
You shake your head. Then: flashes. Rolling on a stretcher. Cool sheets,
ceiling tiles. Faces, clustering. Old man says: 'Little prick now.' Taps the
back of your hand. 'You'll go to sleep now.' Sick sweet smell up throat, in
nose –
How many?
This is your sixth treatment. In this series.
Series? World series. Cereal.

Later she opens a drawer. You're sitting on a bed in another room, dying
to sleep. 'See. You used to write poems. Many poems. See these books.'
You see them.
'I've got an idea. Why don't you write down what I've told you before
your next treatment. Write down what you want to know afterwards.
Like a letter to yourself.'
Dear Sir:
'Then you won't need me to tell you everything.'
Exactly.
'You can read it all by yourself.'
Exactly!
'It might even help your memory.'
Exactly!!

'What's your name?'
'Kay.'
O-kay. Oh, Kay. K-Mart. K.

❧

After a couple of years everybody moved on. You just did. Forces tugged
you away. Not necessarily to anything better. But different.
Ten years flutter like an eyelid. One day I meet my old doctor in the
liquor store.

'How're things?'

'Up and down,' I say. At the moment I have a part-time job, an apartment. A sort of girlfriend.

He nods. 'You know, it's funny. I was just thinking of you the other day. Reviewing some old files. That's what shrinks do for nostalgia.' He had a suave, ironic manner that had picked me up when I'd let it. It made me feel with-it too. 'And it hit me – it was obvious right away – that your diagnosis was wrong all along.'

'Which one?'

'Good point. All of them. It should have been bipolar from the start. It was the violence of that first episode that threw everyone. Threw me, I'll admit.'

We were in a corner of the liquor store on a Monday. Nobody but glass and spirits around us, but I still looked over my shoulder.

'I see we're on the same scrip,' was all I said, indicating the Smirnoff forty-ouncer in each of our baskets.

He smiled. He always smiled easily, though I never heard him laugh.

'Give me a call sometime,' he said.

And I did. And eventually, after a few disastrous trials, found a drug that seemed to work better than the rest. It was milder, with fewer side effects. Mainly it let me sleep better. Six hours on a regular basis the best therapy yet.

❧

The first time I was actually *in* the Grande Restaurant – and I was only ever in it twice – I was dressed in a suit. I was in Independent Living, and my case worker (though by this time they'd switched the name to Advisor) had me on a job search. We bought the suit at the Sally Ann, charcoal grey, and she took in the waist herself. She was just starting. I had a routine crush on her.

I went into the Grande as a kind of lark. Expecting Mrs Soon to throw me out, but feeling hazardous and feisty about it. I was probably swinging up, because everything, even my useless résumés, had a fizz and pop and sparkle. Life was a science experiment, the kind where you mix two colourless liquids together and watch them flame or smoke or turn colours. Or explode.

Inside, the Grande didn't look too different than it had through the

57

dusty window. Not quite as dusty, but the wood around the booths was still nicked and scarred, stuffing bulging out of torn vinyl seat covers. Cigarette pall. Calendar pictures of Switzerland, framed in black.

Mrs Soon approached me with her coffee pot. 'Never-Empty Cup' was the other, smaller sign in the window.

I looked up calmly, but my stomach flipped. You can't get shooed away so often without its leaving some mark.

But she said, 'Would you like a refill, sir?'

Sir.

That's exactly what she said.

To confirm I wasn't hallucinating, she even repeated it. 'Would you like a coffee, sir?'

৶৶

I got another lesson in a suit's magic, years later, when I stopped a businessman for the time. With his bird-like features, he looked less bovine than the rest. I was in a down phase, looking pretty ratty, and I was sick of getting brushed off at the 'Do you –' mark.

'Sir?' I said. Then: 'Billy?'

What made it doubly eerie, like seeing a ghost, was that a few days before I'd seen one of those terrible jumper diagrams in the paper. The kind with a dotted line from the overpass to the highway below (as if you couldn't imagine the route gravity would take from A to B). *Billy*, I'd thought, when I saw the dots. And I kept thinking *Billy* even after I'd read the other name.

Even now it was like seeing a ghost.

What made it creepier still, though, was when our eyes locked for a moment, and by the way Billy said my name, I was certain he'd seen the same picture and thought the same thing. Only about me.

We compared notes. Billy didn't seem embarrassed to be talking to me, but it was part of his illness never to be impolite. Jaz had disappeared long ago. No sightings of him in years.

'Maybe he kicked the wrong window,' Billy said.

'Or too many of the right ones,' I said.

Billy's smile still looked sad.

Clover you didn't ask about. If she was still alive, it had to be somewhere nasty.

I watched Billy walk away. His two-sided limp made for a kind of sailor roll, but at least he'd got rid of the canes. Someone looking at him now, skinny in a Tip Top suit, would probably assume he'd twisted his knee jogging. Or skiing.

He said his company had a good health plan.

❦

For my thirty-eighth birthday I bought myself a spiral notebook. Giant Scribbler, it was called.

Great name, I thought.

I started writing again. About fifteen years after Kay had suggested it. *Better late than never* may be a terrible phrase, but sometimes it's all you've got.

Kay was right, too, about it being like a memory prompt. Instructions to a lesser self that you know is coming.

'Memo to Tomorrow' got published in *The Fiddler*. I got a free copy and a cheque for $25.

The news was good. But coming just before another birthday, my fortieth, it had to be a little mixed. Not exactly *I greet you at the beginning of a grand career.*

But nice.

❦

Often it was just lists of words in the Giant Scribbler.

Redaction.

Gallimaufry.

I'd forget them. Study. Forget, study.

❦

'Don't get lost in the past,' a friend said.

Which made no sense to me. What else could you do in the past?

'Learn new habits,' she also said. A very brutal person, which accounted for most of her charm.

Even if she's right, she's wrong, was my take.

❦

'This' – she was looking through the window – 'it looks like a dump.'

'It is. It's a real mess,' I said happily.

She crossed her arms and gave me a strange look. She must have seen how happy I felt. I felt I could scale walls.

'Then what are we doing here?'

'Nothing. Let's move on.'

We started walking away. After we'd been walking for a while, she said, 'You're not a very open person. You keep stuff locked away.'

I started to deny it, but who was I kidding?

We walked some more. Not saying a word.

'Let's find some place and go inside,' I said finally. 'Let's get something. Okay?'

But we couldn't. Not together anyway.

⁂

One day I'm walking past the Grande and I see Clover through the window. She's sitting inside, with an older woman. Her mother, it turns out. Naturally, I'm surprised. But not too surprised. It's another time when the tumblers are starting to click.

I go up to their booth. Clover returns my greeting and introduces me to her mom. Then she invites me to join them. It was always spooky how Clover could do certain routines normally. She phased in and out.

Mrs Soon brings another coffee and menu with only the harassed look that is her resting expression. It's been a couple of years since we were steady loiterers, but presumably she's got our faces in a deep file. Neither of us looks too grungy, though, is what's throwing her. Clover's in Independent Living, it looks like, and I'm on my own, working again.

'I knew Clover on the Ward,' I have to admit to her mother, who's been skipping these politely nervous glances at me.

'Oh,' she smiles, obviously relieved. Which throws me for a minute. Then I realize: she thinks I'm staff. I've shaved, I'm using the laundromat, getting six hours most nights. Sometimes that's all it takes.

Clover looks good too. Too good. Her mom's got her dressed up like a little doll, in a red jumper, with nylons and black pumps that I can hear tapping under the table. She has white powder on her face, and careful red lipstick. She looks like her mother. Clover must be around twenty-five, like me, but she looks like a matron out for tea with an old pal.

'Put the ponies inside,' Clover says, shredding the illusion. There's an element of madness that's sheer stubbornness. Fighting the bit even as your teeth bleed.

'Now, honey.' Her mother flashes an exasperated look at me. But Clover's watching me calmly, waiting for my next move.

'We'll put *all* the animals inside,' I say.

'Ha!' Clover puffs. A rank breath still. I notice a roll of Clorets by her mother's purse. But though her mother gives Clover's arm a little slap, at the same time pleading, 'Honey, c'mon, be nice,' I know we're safe for a moment. 'Ha!' means your answer's crossed a threshold. It's bullshit, clearly, but it will do. No need for screaming or howling just yet.

We drink our coffees and eat our toast in relative peace. Mother and I making small talk.

'We will go through a door,' Clover announces.

Her mother's mouth tightens slightly. Her eyes, I've been noticing, are shiny but glazed. Set in deep, lined sockets, they look like marbles in leather pouches. The way we used to keep them, loosening the drawstring for trades or challenges.

'Will you excuse me while I go to the ladies' room?' she says to me. She trusts me.

☙

Clover is looking slyly at me, twirling her spoon in her untouched coffee. Within her madness she's a bit of a flirt. Or it could be another default routine.

'Clover, I had a dream.'

She perks up even more. Dreams always interested her. Maybe she felt they put her on more of an even footing with people.

'My dad grew clover,' she tells me.

'Did he?' I say, momentarily distracted by the sheen of something. Clover has a great way of opening doors a crack, showing you slivers of light. But I press on. The thing is, I really am starting to feel a bit steadier. And in this bout of health I've been reading books – on illness, on vitamins, on drugs – recording my dreams. *Studying* health. Seeing if I can learn it like a subject, pass. And Clover in her oracular phase just might provide another clue.

'It was up north, in this place where my dad and I used to go fishing. This lake with swamp and weeds all around it. "Paradise for frogs and

61

fish," my dad used to say. "Just don't try to get out to take a piss."

'I was going fishing again. Only this time it wasn't with my dad. It was another older man, someone I didn't know, but he looked a bit like my high school chemistry teacher. Kind of goofy-looking, with thick glasses. But nice.'

Clover is still listening. Looking at me anyway.

'He tells me that we have to find the perfect frog, for bait. It's bright green, he says, like wet grass. I tell him there's nothing like that here. Just the usual frogs, leopard frogs and bullfrogs. That's when he gets impatient – something he never was at school – and tells me again to find it. "*Look*," he says in this stern voice.

'So I get out of the boat and start mucking around in the weeds. Walking along the shoreline in my rubber boots. Frogs scatter all around me. Then I see something green up ahead, just sitting on top of this oily black mud. It looks like a piece of broken glass, like a ginger ale bottle, it's so green. The frog, I realize. I sneak up on it as quiet as I can, but it doesn't even move until my fingers close around it. Then it wriggles a bit, but not much. It seems sleepy in the sun.

'Behind me, my teacher is shouting. "Bring it here, bring it here! You got it!"

'When I hand it to him is the first time I realize I'm a little kid. His arm is big and hairy, but mine's like a little peeled stick, white and skinny.

'The next thing I know, we're back out on the lake, fishing. I'm still wondering what we're going to do with the special frog, when suddenly I notice it's on my hook. Just hanging there, like a limp green jewel. Not even kicking.

'Anyway. To cut it short, I cast the frog into the weeds and catch a huge pike. You know what that is?'

Clover nods.

'I'm so excited that I forget all about the green frog. Before, as I was casting, it made me feel sick to think of him getting chewed on and swallowed.

'The teacher hauls up the anchor and starts the motor. It scares me the way everything about him is in a hurry. He roars us into shore and jumps out with my pike and a knife in his hand. I'm crying, but he doesn't pay any attention. "You'll see. You'll see," he's muttering.

'Then he does a terrible thing. Instead of cleaning the pike in the usual way, he just pokes the knife in its belly and slits it open. The pike is still breathing, its gills opening and closing. I'm bawling my eyes out by this time.

'He roots around in the pike's insides and finds the stomach. Squeezes it so the lining stretches tight, and pops it open with his knife. As soon as the sharp blade touches it, it splits open.

'The green frog falls into the grass. Some of the skin's torn off its back and legs, it looks woozy, but after a moment it takes a little hop. Then again. It hops toward some long grass. "You see?" the teacher says. "But you have to move fast."

'Excited, I start to go after it. This is a frog I want to keep. But the teacher grabs my arm. "Give him another day to recover," he winks. "We'll come back tomorrow."

'That's when I notice it's starting to rain. Big, splashy drops that pock the mud.'

࿐

Plock. Pock. Pock pock. Plock.

I can still hear the sound of the rain on the mud. In my dream. It's hard to come back from the dream, it was so vivid. I shake my head to clear it. I'm still in the dream, I haven't woken up. Or else the dream has followed me back here. I don't know which is worse.

Clover is looking at me. Through the eyeholes in her mother's mask of powder and lipstick, combed-flat hair. *Inside Daisy Clover.*

Her shoes, I think, remembering the tapping sound. But when I duck my head to glance under the table, her black patent leather shoes are lying flat on the floor.

Between them, a slow stream dribbles from the orange leatherette to land – *plip plip* – in a little spreading golden puddle.

It's a different dream.

࿐

No flicker in Clover's eyes when I straighten back up.

She's gone.

࿐

63

'Go to the washroom, Clover,' I say.

Maybe she just hears *go. Beat it.* Because she gets up, rising with that drugged rigidity that can approximate dignity, and walks over to a corner of the restaurant.

There, where the two walls meet, she hikes up her mom's red jumper, squats down lightly, and pisses.

Pisses hard. It hisses and spatters on the linoleum.

The faces in the other booths turning, the hornet blur of their voices, are no more than crazy spinning shapes in a midway. Right at the back of the trench of eyes, against the canvas of the freak tent, only Clover is in focus. All menstrual red and fossil white, squatting in a hiss like silence.

Ward basics kick in.

The next thing I know, I'm standing just in front of her, my back offering a narrow wall of privacy, my face to the freaks. Their faces are still just smears, I can't bring them into focus.

Clover's mother comes out of the washroom. She takes in the scene without much reaction. Her shoulders slump a bit, and her face.

She comes over and goes behind me. I hear her whispering, rather gently actually. Then, out of the corner of my eye, I see her standing beside me. You can't move someone *while* they're pissing.

❧

Of course, someone's been missing from this scene, and she arrives now. Mrs Soon comes late, but she makes up for that with ferocity. She storms out of the kitchen swing door with her broom held outward like a lance. Fire in her pasty face.

When she is halfway down the aisle, I scream at the top of my lungs: 'Fuck *off* you *monstrous bitch!*'

So loud it hurts my throat, scrapes it raw.

Whatever articulate monster bellows this is able to weight the key words exactly.

Mrs Soon freezes, broom rampant. Everybody does. There's a few moments where it feels like my scream has carried off not only all sound, but movement too. Leaving a bunch of statues frozen in an airless storeroom.

❧

The first movement I'm aware of is Clover's mother. Who backs into my vision with an accusing stare.

I'm not staff.

No. Nor was, nor ever shall be.

The next thing I know I'm far away. Hustling down street after clutching street, it's a long time before I can suspect that that particular dream is over.

Though it's only another dream that replaces it. And another.

They slide over each other like maggots.

～

One day you go back. No particular reason. You've thought of it many times, almost every day it seems, and then one day you just do it. You can't be a sad spook forever. It helps to have your lover with you.

But there's a problem. You can't find the Grande anywhere. Maybe you have the wrong street. No – there's the dry-cleaning place, just the same. And the florist's shop. The Grande was right between them. But now there's nothing between them.

It wasn't that long ago, just a few years, that someone told you that Mrs Soon no longer runs the restaurant. Her son operates it now. The kid who used to wash dishes, bent over when the door swung open, scrubbing.

There's a man in front of the florist's, though. Kind of a scaled-down Jaz. Bushily bearded, but small, with dull eyes behind thick glasses. Wearing dirty pink sweat pants and a brown ski jacket.

'Speyadahgehambah?' he says loudly when you come near.

It comes out as a garble, but you're only a few seconds translating it. Spare a dollar so I can get a hamburger? It's no harder than a musician transposing keys. Moving from C major to one with a few more sharps and flats.

He scares the one you're with.

'He's not dangerous,' you tell her.

'How do you know?'

But that's hard to explain. You haven't told her everything yet. He can't afford to be dangerous, just as some others can't afford not to be. Economics of power. It's in the eyes.

'Do you want to talk about it?' she asks. And that's when you realize you've been walking a long way in silence. The neighbourhood of the Grande is far behind.

'Sure. But let's find a place to go inside,' you say. Because it's cold outside and because it's beginning to get dark. 'We'll get something. Okay?'

Cogagwee

(Walks around the Life of Tom Longboat)

I ran. No one could catch me. Only a few could beat me.

There was a glass jar inside my window, between the glass and the torn screen. It had six sides and no lid. A long black bug flew into the jar and did not fly out. (Could not? Would not? I wonder now. But not then.) I watched it walk across the bottom of the jar and try to walk up the smooth sides. But it slipped off them, sliding or falling down. It tried again, on one side or another. Three or four other beetles – dead, dried husks – littered the bottom of the jar. The walking beetle stepped over and around them.

Mother came into the room while I was watching the walking beetle. Briskly, she upended the jar on the sill and slapped at the contents with a newspaper. Once, twice. Her face alert and irritated throughout. 'Don't watch a trapped thing die,' she snapped. 'Kill it or let it go.' She flicked the scraps up onto the newspaper, balled it.

She left the room. I stared at the empty jar, its movement erased. But still somehow present. It hadn't occurred to me that the insect was dying. But the idea did not seem surprising or important. I had been watching it walk with its six legs.

❦

'Catch me if you can,' Mother said. I never did.

❦

The Globe, Boxing Day, 1906: LONGBOAT ALWAYS WINS
    And that year, my nineteenth on earth, for a few months, I did.

Wins:
    Victoria Day, Caledonia. Took lead over five miles and never lost it.
    'Around the Bay', Hamilton. Caught John Marsh napping on the

Stone Road and opened up three minutes on him before the tape. At the awards ceremony outside the *Hamilton Herald*, Bill Sherring predicted, You won't win pretty but you'll win.

Ward Marathon, Toronto. Fifteen miles. High Park west along Lakeshore Road and back again. Burned out Bill Cumming (and seventy-two others). Won by three minutes.

Christmas Day, Hamilton. Cumming and I duelled on icy, hard-rutted road. Halfway along, about the five-mile mark, a rig trotting beside us skidded on the ice and fell over on us. We squeezed out from under and kept going. My 54:50 broke the old course record by more than two minutes.

First year: 0 for 1. Second: 4 for 4. My perfect season.

❧

'Interesting a study as the world's champion long distance runner makes – as Indian first and before all – with, over those deep racial attributes, the light veneer of the white man's ways and habits, of far deeper interest is the girl he is about to wed. Here the Indian traits are well covered.... Few would imagine that she had been born and raised on an Indian reservation and was of Indian blood. In every way she is a winsome little girl who has, as she says, been educated away from many of the traditions of her race. She does not like to talk of feathers, war paint or other Indian paraphernalia. She is ambitious for Tom and if anybody can make a reliable man and good citizen of that elusive being, Thomas Longboat, it will be his wife.'

Lauretta read it out like a teacher at the Institute, enunciating primly, shoulders back, hand on hip. She cracks me up. I was laughing out loud by the end, and she must've wanted to, but she kept her poker face.

'Lord-a-miracle,' I said, 'how'd you like to get scalped?'

'Is that what we're calling it now?' she said. Still prissy-like.

'Watch out for the tomahawk!'

Her smoky smell gets stronger when she sweats. We were lying side by side. Red lips over her ribs where I'd pinched her hard, made her giggle finally.

'What's "elusive being"?'

She answered after a bit. 'It means no one can catch you.'

'Pietri couldn't anyway,' I said.

We were silent for a bit. Sounds of the hotel, and streets below. New York. My mind went ahead four days to the rematch with Pietri. He would want it.

'And "winsome"?'

'Happy, I guess. Cheerful.'

'Are you?'

'Cheerful?'

I shoved her. 'Happy.'

'Sure. Sometimes.'

'Now?'

'Sure.'

Martha Silversmith was a good wife too, though she lacked Lauretta's mischief and her rebel fun. Then again, Lauretta was younger, and perhaps Martha had more to contend with. All Lauretta had to face was me getting killed and then coming back to life again.

(Spring morning. A robin bulgy with eggs on a stump outside the window, orange on brown on blue. Lauretta's new husband rattling cups and dishes in the kitchen, letting us know he's there. 'Tom, I'm awful glad you're alive,' Lauretta says, 'but I think I'll stay where I am.' That twitch at the corner of her mouth which you never knew if she meant or not.

We were sitting at her kitchen table in Ohsweken.

When the robin flew up and my eyes followed it, I saw a raccoon curled up on the corner of the neighbour's second floor porch, dozing in the sun. Chew marks on the lattice told me the work he was resting from. When Lauretta went to reassure the rattler, I rapped on the glass. The way the coon sat up and sniffed, plus the awkward splay of his fat rear, gave me an idea, and when Lauretta returned, I said, 'I wasn't dead. Just hibernating.'

'I don't need a bear any more than I need a ghost.' Quick, Lauretta, so quick.)

Martha Silversmith. Lauretta Maracle. I only married women with beautiful names.

Sometimes it seemed Martha and I were running, sprinting full bore after something, and sometimes it seemed we were standing still. Hardly ever walking, though I tried to find that pace. Running and standing still are much closer to each other than either is to walking. I saw the plum side of that when I won the marathon in Boston. After I caught Petch on the Newton Hills, I felt like I was standing still. Policemen pushing people back at the end and I could see every face clearly, Rockefeller on a riverboat, watching the faces on the banks float past. Hands brushing me like branches, but still separated from them. By water, by current.

Afterwards, a terrific steak dinner. Then the governor of Massachusetts presents me with a gold medal (for breaking the record) and a bronze statue of Mercury. As I'm hoisting it up before the cheering crowd, suddenly I feel air fanning my face, cheers and shouts lost in a wind roar, and I glance up and see the wings on Mercury's bronze feet spinning to a blur, like hummingbird wings. The faces too all just blurs, smudges lost to speed.

*

When your father dies and you are only five, many people assume you spend your whole life looking for a mentor. Untrue. Advice is overrated; you have to learn everything yourself. Every mistake must be made at least once. And when you do find yourself needing a guide, a teacher, there will generally be one close at hand. Overall, I had more trouble shucking off mentors than I did finding them. I have no memories of my father.

*

Running children.

When I was twelve and finished grade four in the band school, they enrolled me in the Mohawk Institute, the Anglican mission boarding school in Brantford. Two rules: no 'longhouse practices' (which would have made Mother laugh; she always said that longhouse was just the Bible watered down for Indians – 'They know the hard stuff goes to our heads' – and that Handsome Lake should've been paid by the missionaries and maybe he was). No 'Indian', only English. That was a bigger problem.

The hours I spent standing in the corner at the back of the classroom.

Glancing up I could see a painting of Joseph Brant and the poster of Pauline Johnson, which might have been hung there for my benefit. She wore a bear-claw necklace and fringed and beaded buckskin.

Tekahionwake
(Miss E. Pauline Johnson,
The Iroquois Indian Poet-Entertainer)

She was a handsome woman (Lauretta resembled her, though softer-faced and plumper), and the Institute's most famous student. 'If you mock her, you mock all of us,' intoned the fat, laced-up teacher in a dangerously soft voice. It was Art period and she was standing behind me. I stared down at my paper (which in a few seconds she would tear to pieces) –

myself in shorts, raising my lacrosse stick after a goal

Cogagwee
(Mr Thomas Longboat
The Onondagan Lacrosse Champion)

– wondering if something my pencil and a dreaming mood had traced could really have such a sharp point.

No running (except in P E class). No fishing.

The first time I left, I was weeding the Institute garden. Cabbage whites flitted about my head. Bent over in a row between peas and carrots, watching green coil and feather upwards in the sun, feeling myself sink down the other way, muscles pooling like butter. A black bug walked a lime stalk: nothing. The last thought I had before I started running was, *I might as well be weeding Mother's garden* (which would have handed her another laugh).

They caught me, punished me. But the next time, I made it all the way to my uncle's, who said I could hide there if I worked for him.

All the way up the road swinging an imaginary lacrosse stick, snaring passes from blurred wingers on one side, snapping them into blurred nets on the other, stampstampstamp, brain hollering *CogagweeCogagweeCogagwee – EverythingEverythingEverything* – as all the Indian and English names drop behind me in the dust.

* * *

Later the Institute would ask me back, but I declined all requests to appear. The first invitation came after I won the Boston; they came periodically after that, and frequently after Pauline Johnson died in 1913, just before the war. They needed another example. So did I.

Arguments with both wives on this score. Lauretta could recite 'The Song My Paddle Sings' by heart. So could Martha (hell, *I* knew most of it), but with her it was more a matter of don't refuse an invitation: it's unlucky and who knows when you'll get another. A good woman, but fearful.

'I left the Institute,' was all I ever said. Many times. To both of them.

1930. Thirty years almost to the day that I ran from the Institute, I made a guest appearance at the Canadian National Exhibition. I smiled at the spectators, started a race. Afterwards, my eight-year-old daughter ran across the street to greet me and was killed by a car. Her body flew through the air a short way, then fell to the ground with a thud. Like a shot goose, not much bigger.

Later, holding Martha as she cried and blamed me. 'You can't stop a child from running,' I said, and was sorry I said.

But can you? And would you if you could?

Martha's shoulders shaking as she sobbed, my mind running.

Would I? Would I? Would I?

The Globe and Mail, 1937.

Youngsters in North Toronto are fired with a new ambition, not merely to be engine drivers, G-men or even cowboys. Their growing ambition now is to be a street cleaner. That is what their idol is – a man who 30 years ago was the most famous athlete in the world and the idol of Canada.... 'Oh, I'm not news any more,' protested the once famous marathoner when a reporter discovered him sweeping leaves on Lawrence Avenue today. 'I've had my day – and no regrets.'

'You're a pretty important fellow to the children of this district,' answered the reporter.

'Well, I'm glad they like me,' smiled the big Onondaga Indian. 'Maybe all I'm good for now is sweeping leaves, but if I can help the kids and show them how to be good runners and how to leave a clean life, I'm satisfied.'

Note: I was never 'big'. Was five foot nine, maybe 145 pounds by then (I ran at 132).

✿

Evening Walks (1).

From 1919 to 1926, I mostly kept to a comfortable stroll. Others might have worried (Martha did!), but I felt I knew the pace and the road.

Went out west to see if I could scare up a veteran's homestead grant, but no luck. Saw a lot of pretty country, though, moving from town to town. All manner of jobs: digging ditches, mucking barns, baling hay.

Then back to Ontario, since Martha wanted to raise the kids closer to Ohsweken. Worked Dunlop Rubber in Toronto, then the Steel Company in Hamilton.

'Doc' was a janitor at the Steel Company. His nickname came from the rumour that he had been a doctor before and during the Great War, but had returned to work as a labourer. Others found him strange, but I found him to be a true gentleman, courteous and soft-spoken. We'd already been working together three months when Doc showed me a scrapbook he'd kept of my exploits before the war. The curious (and slightly embarrassing) part was that Doc had cut and pasted headlines, pictures and articles not just about my running but also about my marriages, my children's births, the scandals about my 'professional' status, my enlistment (and death) in the army. Mostly from the Toronto papers, but Doc even had the side-view shot of my naked lower half (privates artfully concealed) – 'Tom Longboat's $20,000 Legs' – published in the *New York Telegram*.

Flipping through Doc's scrapbook was like flipping through my life. Reliving it in shutter clicks.

The last article was only a month old. From the title, 'Walking into the Sunset', I got the gist and knew it was a cornball piece. My eyes skipped down and found the phrase, 'falling from the limelight into obscurity'. I guess nobody'd told the reporter everyone does that.

'I've had a good run,' I mumbled, closing the book.

And now Doc – who normally you had to crowbar words out of – told me that he and I had the same birthday. Same day, same year. That shook me more than his scrapbook had. I stared hard at him a few moments. He looked at least ten years older than me. Broom-bent,

73

veiny-bald, his eyes starting to film. But then I've kept in shape, never stopped walking.

It was about six months later that I got my layoff slip. Production was slowing down. Doc was safe, of course – he had eight years in, and a janitor is always needed – but he seemed to take it hardest of all. I was emptying my locker after a long shower, the rest of the gang already cleared out, when I heard a gulp behind me. Doc was sitting hunched over at the other end of the bench, crying almost silently. One hand over his eyes, his shoulders shaking. Hardly any sound. I didn't know what to do other than move down closer to him. I was standing behind him, my hand floating toward his shoulder, when Doc blurted, 'I saw you run in England.'

I pulled my hand back. This little man kept surprising me. It was certainly possible. I ran races with the 180th Sportsmen's Battalion in England, then with the 3rd Reserve. Races in France too. With the 107th then, the 'Red' (or 'Injin') Battalion. February. June, I think. August, near Vimy. I didn't know anything about Doc's life.

'I *saw* you run.' Quieter and fiercer now. His wet eyes glaring, his hands white-knuckled on the mop handle. If there ever was a picture of a man running *and* standing still, it was Doc just then. Which told me what to do.

I leaned the mop against the wall and led him by the elbow out into the wide clanking night. We walked around the Steel Company premises, among and between all the hulking black shapes. Men in sooty shadows, smoking or hiding. It was a pleasant cool night, the air decent and fresh, thanks to a west wind blowing the bad smells east. Doc kept peering upwards, but the yard lights and flames killed the stars. I walked him along the coke oven tracks and we saw a 'push' just ahead of us. Red glowing coke tumbling out of the oven into a waiting rail car, orange sparks flurrying upward. Better than fireworks because it meant something. Further on, where the track ended, we had a good view of the dark bay with two freighters, black oblongs, moored in it. There were two huge hills, dark silhouettes, humped up to points, with soft sides rounding down. This was the iron ore and coal the ships had left behind. Right between the two peaks was a little curl of moon, bright white.

'Egypt,' Doc said, his voice almost a whisper. The piles did look like pyramids, their edges gentled by centuries.

That's the way, I thought, and I clapped him between the shoulder blades in encouragement. That's when I felt it. A tingle, small but unmistakable, like a current passing through my fingertips into Doc's back. Mother's words came tumbling back to me: 'Spirit's just like food or money. You can earn it, spend it, lose it, hoard it, give it away.' She recommended the first and the last as the best courses, and I knew I'd just followed her advice and passed on a little soul bread to someone who needed it more.

᠅

Hibernation (or: My Activities While Deceased).

It was like the end of a long, lost marathon. Like the end of my Olympic dream, 1908, in London, when, as I was running a strong second, almost without warning, my legs turned to slush and I dropped. False accusations later that Flanagan, my manager, had drugged me (after running up the odds in my favour, then counter-betting). Flanny only gave me a stimulant when I was already twitching on the ground, bleeding from my nose and mouth. No, something poisonous was in the air that day. Something that took men out of the race. Hefferon's lead died – he finished, but they carried him off in a stretcher. Pietri staggered into the stadium, turned the wrong way round, collapsed, was helped up, staggered, collapsed, fell again, got up … there was a film of all this and I could hardly believe it when I watched. Finally Pietri fell and didn't move. Hayes entered the stadium. That's when the officials panicked, I guess. Picked up Pietri by the elbows and escorted him across the line – it looked like two burly, well-dressed bouncers giving the heave-ho to a half-dressed drunk.

(Question for the Press and the New England AAU:

If I was not an 'amateur' – accusations that my managers, Rosenthal then Flanagan, took more than expense money and/or kicked back some of it to me – why did I turn down Alf Shrubb's 1907 offer of five races, at $1,000 per race, just so I could go to the Olympics?

Five, ten, fifteen, twenty, twenty-five miles. Seventy-five miles for $5,000. Do you think I got more than that to smash the American ten-mile record?)

It had to hurt Pietri, being disqualified. But Dorando was a runner, unwilling to overlook one yard, let alone forty. On December 15 we had our first rematch, at Madison Square Garden, also (note to Press) my first 'pro' race. Twenty-five thousand people stormed the Garden doors; firemen drove ten thousand away. Pietri had beaten Hayes three weeks before. We traded leads, back and forth, but this time Pietri collapsed with six laps to go, and I didn't. They brought him in by stretcher and we spoke in the locker room. 'Tough miles, Dorando,' I said to him. 'Tough eenches, Tom,' he answered. Only a week later, in Buffalo – and Lauretta and I just married in between – we ran a return match. Dorando stepped off the track at nineteen miles. *Eenches, Tom,* I heard as I walked-jogged home.

It was conceived as a ladder tournament. Now I got to tackle Shrubb.

January 26, 1909. The Shrubb-Longboat Marathon at Madison Square Garden was watched by twelve thousand people. Flanagan had just quit as my manager, selling my contract and puffing some smoke, which the papers (typically) blew into flames. At the worst, Alfie had eight laps on me, but eventually it was he who tottered off the track. I tick-tocked in the roar for sixteen laps.

Professional Champion of the World.

What a season of races that was! None of us willing to leave anything on the track. Like boxers who won't settle for a decision. Knockouts only!

Nine years later, in France, it was a different game. As a dispatch runner, I covered short distances, but the organizers had added in obstacles of bullets and shells and barbed wire and craters. Mud and fog. You lost the field and ran entirely alone. If the fog got too thick, you were welcome to sleep overnight in a soggy field, no penalty except an aching back. And the goal was reversed from the golden years: since there were no winners, you prayed just to cross the finish line.

I ran hunched over like a gnome, due to back wounds and the presence of guns.

Then one day, in Belgium, there was a magic like the spell that overtook me in London. Only with a much happier result. I had just jogged into an officers' communication trench when a shell exploded and buried all of us. It took me a few minutes to realize this. At first all I felt was my knees buckle, my eyes go milky, and my head roar. *London,* I thought. Then when I came to and shook free of the dirt, there was blood – something warm and salty anyway (it was pitch black) – running from my nose.

London.

But it was Belgium, and here was the miracle. No one in the trench was hurt, though we were good and buried. (It took some time to convince two boys that they hadn't been killed. They were clutching each other in a corner, moaning and shivering. Later they put their hands down each other's flies and spent the next six days that way, still moaning and shivering.)

'Are we dead?' whispered a voice in the dark.

I started laughing. 'No, boys, we're out of the race, and with any luck we'll stay out for a while.'

We were getting air somehow, and we had provisions for weeks. Of course, the smell of six men, close, got a little rich, and an overflowing latrine and the lovers carrying on … all in all, it was like most trenches. We slept twenty hours out of twenty-four and ate like hogs. When they 'rescued' us, after six days underground, we must have looked like winter groundhogs, blinking unwillingly at the light.

Still, that 'death' cost me Lauretta, who for once believed the newspapers. I was already demobbed when, in 1919, I ran my last military race. Kicked out to win against Bill Queal in a three-miler at 'The Grand Army of Canada Sports Show'. I was thirty-two years old, and for fifteen minutes, the decade just past rolled back and never happened, or got ready to happen again.

✦

On Training Methods, and my decision to quit the YMCA and join the Irish Club.

The Y felt that liquor and the company of women, even in moderation, were weakening for any man and disastrous for a runner.

I disagreed.

As did Tom Flanagan, hammer thrower and owner of the Grand Hotel.

As did Lauretta.

✦

Evening Walks (11).

In the photo of Alf Shrubb and me, taken before our 1931 exhibition race, we look like what we are: a couple of old coots who used to be pro runners. Alf looks skinnier than ever, maybe sick. Me, in my white shorts and sleeveless undershirt, I *look* like a city worker who has just woken up and is leaning out his front door. What the paperboy must see Sunday morning when he comes to collect.

I don't remember who won.

It flashed on me that I'd agreed to enter the four-mile Jubilee run in Hamilton only on the condition that the first prize be a second-hand car, a '26 Chrysler. I was forty, just hired on by the City. Martha and the kids and I liked to drive out of town on the weekends, out to Ohsweken or just around. To lacrosse and wrestling matches. And it hit me in the moments after she fell – looking down at her and sprinting like hell – that probably none of that would change. That seemed very strange and awful: that this death could not alter our habits.

☙

The Onondaga Wonder

The Streak of Bronze

The Caledonia Cyclone

Wildfire

☙

My best run?

Hard to say. It might have been *almost* beating Higasadini's record for twelve miles.

Higasadini (Deerfoot), a Seneca, ran in moccasins in the 1850s and 1860s. Mother remembered hearing about him. In Hamilton he and his partner Steep Rock won $1,000 by outrunning three horses in a ten-mile relay race. On his tour of England in 1863 he set a record for the one-hour run that would last for ninety years. In my training runs I sometimes took a poke at it. Grinding concession road into 3,600 second-grains, and draining them through the most pinch-waisted hourglass I could find. Telling no one, I found a white farmhouse that was exactly eleven miles distant from Mother's house, standing by itself in a field. Reaching it would have given me Deerfoot's record, plus a few yards to spare. But always, always, at the end of my run, my watch-hand jerked to 12 with the farmhouse still up ahead, starting to loom, but still a good ways off. I kept walking towards it as I cooled down, but out of superstition I always turned back before I reached it. Of all the roads I walked and ran, it was the only one that stopped me at eleven miles. In a way I'm just as glad.

*

Evening walks (III).

In one way 1946 was like 1906, except that now it was Martha, not Mother, who disbelieved how far I walked.

When I checked myself out of Sunnybrook Hospital (they'd already told me I had diabetes, which was all they could do), I phoned Martha. A mistake. She was almost too angry to come and get me.

'What road are you coming in on?' I inquired, trying to make the question sound innocent.

My second mistake. She was as sharp as Lauretta in most ways.

'You stay right there,' she hissed. 'Don't move.'

But I put down fifteen miles before I saw the Studebaker approaching. Henry Greene, our neighbour, was at the wheel; Martha no longer drove. Martha made a show of checking Henry's pocket watch before she'd let me in the car.

'Good. You hitched a ride,' she said, smiling grimly.

But if she really believed that, why did she make me sit in the back? 'You're too sick to drive,' she declared. And shot a glare at Henry who was grinning at me in the mirror.

'Drive,' she told him.

*

A runner's strides are all to reach himself. That thought's occurred to me more than once, usually while running. As if, with enough speed and stamina, you could catch the front-runner who decides things before you know or act on them, and tap him on the shoulder. *Hey.*

(And suppose he turns his head: do you recognize him?)

Like when I wrote my protest letter to the *Hamilton Spectator* 'to declare war on the cheap two-bit imposter who has been capitalizing on my famous name for the last fifteen to twenty years, by calling himself Tom Longboat for the purpose of obtaining free drinks in various beverage rooms.'

I'd heard the story for years. At first it made me chuckle; rumours were nothing new, and they generally come in one shade: black. As time went on, it nagged a bit, something I'd have to get around to fixing, though there seemed no hurry.

What surprised me, when I finally put pen to paper, was my anger. Swiping the envelope flap across my tongue, mashing it sealed with my fist.

Naturally I thought of Doc. It was twenty years since we'd taken our midnight ramble through the Steel Company, along the tracks at Hamilton Bay, seen the pyramids of ore and coal, Doc whispering 'Egypt'. And Doc, I figured, who had the soul of a panhandler already – with his boy's scrapbook and old man's tears – maybe the tingle of spunk I'd slipped between his shoulder blades was all the push he needed to make him an aggressive one.

Roused up, I started rifling through the other pictures in Martha's cedar box, where I'd found the recent snap I'd sent the paper. She kept everything (unlike Lauretta, who was content to let the moment slide by), in a jumble of no particular order. Picture of me in a Maple Leaf singlet, hands loose-fisted at waist, looking more like a boxer than a runner. As a body under a blanket on a cart, being wheeled off the field by an official after I collapsed from sunstroke: Chicago, 1909. (And it occurs to me – for the first time, strangely – that Martha must've been keeping her own scrapbook, because we hadn't even met yet and I never saved these.) Alfie and me, lining up for 'Auld Lang Syne'. Ghosting Shrubb in greener days. Flashing my 'smile that won't come off' after beating Pietri in the indoor marathon. *The Indian Made a Pace the Italian Could Not Hold. 'Bring on your next champion,' dared the Canadian redman.* Grinning as I buy a newspaper from a kid in a trench in France – remember nothing of the day, the kid, or the big rangy guy grinning between us. Only the kid unsmiling.

Here's Lauretta and I on our honeymoon, looking starchy. The photographer was a prim and fussy individual whose flashbulbs kept popping. Plus we weren't giving each other much sleep.

The two at the bottom must be thirty years apart. From my pro days: I relax in a wingback armchair, dressed to the nines in a fancy suit, sucking a fat cigar ($17,000 in winnings my first three years as a pro; Lauretta kept the accounts, entering it all in a slim red book with blue lines). Right behind it a more recent clipping from the *Star*: we see a placid old fellow in suspenders, smoking a thin-stemmed pipe, smiling benignly under a straw hat. One gloved hand at his side, the other reaching up to the heap on the truck, as if to pat some stray litter back into place. *Tom, Tom, the Garbage Man* – one neighbourhood kid kept trying to get my goat.

I stir through the pictures a while, to no particular purpose. But feeling restless, jazzed up. I keep coming back to the last two, holding them one in each hand and slightly apart, like bookends on a short shelf. It's not just that they look so different. Mother always maintained that anyone who looked the same in every photo was not a human being. I know that's so. But she also said you gain spirit by spending it, and here I'm not so sure. There I have to pause for a second. Because the fact is, the young lion at his ease in 1909, and the obliging codger circa 1940, not only don't look like each other, but I don't think they *are* the same man. And neither of them resembles the face I shave. For a few moments, sitting in our living room in Ohsweken, Martha off visiting somewhere, there is this mystery in the air that can't be explained or dispelled.

❧

After the Boston several thousand people met my train at Union Station. They gave me a torchlight parade, in the competing blare of three bands, up Bay Street to City Hall. There Mayor Coatsworth presented me with a gold medal and a promise of $500 for my education. (Controller Hubbard had told the reception committee: 'I have been thinking of the silver cabinets, etc., which other runners have received, and I have decided that they are not fitting for the young man who has practically no home but a boarding house.')

The *Daily Star* added this praise: 'Canada makes no bones about gaining a little glory from an Indian. In other matters than footraces we have become accustomed to leaders from the Six Nations. We give the Boston papers notice, one and all, that we claim Longboat as a Canadian.'

An additional $250.05 was raised by public subscription.

Later in 1907, I asked if the money, instead of being saved for my education, could be used to build a house for Mother. At first the board of control agreed, but when the American AAU started grousing about my amateur status again, the city treasurer decided to withhold the money until after the 1908 Olympics.

November, 1908. Flanagan requests the money be paid. The board of control authorizes it, but issues no cheque, and gives no explanation.

1909. I write. They cannot do it at this time.

1910. I write again. I am paid $50.

1911. I write again. The city sends $165 to Lauretta. (She agrees – privately – to buy me a box of cigars.)

1912. I hire my first lawyer. He chases the city around the legal track. The city pays me the $35.05 remaining from public donations.

I never received the $500. Though it could never be said that I did not get an education.

꧁

Surprised Frank Montour, the wrestler and band councillor. He stopped to give me a lift on a cold night just after Christmas.

'No thanks,' I said.

'Where have you been?' he asked.

'I've just had a nice walk to Hagersville.'

Frank's mind going as he figured the distance. Close to twenty miles. He drove, I walked, back into Ohsweken.

I would be dead of pneumonia within two weeks.

In 1949, after a sojourn of sixty-one years, eleven years before my People got the vote, I was buried according to the dictates of the Great Spirit.

The women of my family hand-stitched the cotton and wool they dressed me in. Two white fringed shirts and dark blue beaded trousers: Onondaga colours, the colours of my tribe. They tied a blue silk ribbon across my chest and draped a blue silk shawl over my shoulders and tied a silk bandana around my head. My daughter slipped new buckskin moccasins on my feet. The service was spoken in Onondaga, my sons leading the chants.

Henry Greene whittled a V in the top of the coffin to permit my spirit to escape. V less for Victory than for a runner's legs, upended, still.

He kept it small, mindful perhaps of Mother's favourite lesson: *Be a prodigal soul.*

Cogagwee.

⁂

My Greatest Race?

Maybe the one I lost to George Bonhag.

It was a three-mile match race in 1907 that I had no business running. Bonhag was the U.S. five-mile champ and he held the U.S. indoor three-mile record. I'd won my four races in 1906 in Hamilton and Toronto. I'd never run a short race before and I'd never raced indoors.

Nine thousand people paid to watch us.

Bonhag beat me by eight inches.

We both broke his record.

(Bonhag at the finish line beside me, both of us bent over double, hands on knees: 'Goddamn, kid. God *damn*.' His gasp of breath urgent as a lover's hiss.)

⁂

For a runner there is only the official version, the truth of legs, the clock's verdict. But a committee, composed of hereditary chiefs, speaks with many tongues, none of them ideally correct. Officially, the council of the Six Nations at Ohsweken refused to join the war. As a sovereign nation, historically allied to the British crown, they held out for a request for assistance from London. They were patient men.

Unofficially, women on the reserve raised money, knitted socks and sweaters, and made bandages. Men who enlisted were not disdained.

I was of two minds too. I raced myself, alone, but when I chased Alf Shrubb, the Maple Leaf hung low over my diaphragm, a flaming at my middle. Alf wore the Union Jack higher, a cross with rays below his neck, on a dark singlet.

Attempts to shame were crude, but hardly ineffective.

The Issue is One of
CIVILIZATION vs. BARBARISM

If civilization wins, Canadian people shall enjoy their rights
and privileges as heretofore.
If barbarism wins, Canadians will be placed in German shackles.

THE DUTY OF CANADIANS

The participants in outside Canadian sport are mostly unmarried men with
few responsibilities, and with years of vigorous athletic training, are the
logical individuals to defend the honour of the nation.

'Logical?' Lauretta jeered. 'Ask the women what's logical. They might say leave the young fit men here. Send the fat married ones first.'

'I'm married.' I tried a grin.

'Yes, *you* are,' she said softly, but with that sternness. Like Mother, I could see then. I don't know how I missed it before.

Six months later, when I enlisted, I was trying to get up nerve to tell her. We were sitting in the house at Ohsweken, smoking and drinking. Clock ticking. Lauretta's talk had a more corrosive edge than usual, brittle, like she'd touched acid or frost. She was a sensitive woman. When a bee passed she felt the shock wave, a tiny slap of honey or death.

The worst of it was, I didn't have a reason I could tell her (which needn't have bothered me, since *why* paled beside *what* to Lauretta). The pro running circuit had been drying up since 1912. I was twenty-nine. Near the close of youth (I realize now), men are prey to wild crusades, a target for that poised nerve and muscle.

'This is just stupid,' Lauretta said.

I crossed the living room, a long distance it seemed, and stood beside her chair. Looked down where her thumb, hard-shelled like a beetle, lay alongside another advertisement.

'WHY DON'T
THEY COME?'

WHY BE A MERE SPECTATOR HERE
WHEN YOU SHOULD PLAY A <u>MANS</u> PART
IN THE REAL GAME OVERSEAS?

Lauretta snorted softly. 'They spelled "man's" wrong.'

Did they? It seemed Lauretta had even more contempt for the minds behind the war than for the war. But I thought the minds were adequate. They did not dissuade me through foolishness, made foolishness irrelevant. In my mind I'd already moved closer to the soldier in the picture, with his pack and rifle and boots and bandaged head, silhouettes of artillery cannons puffing smoke behind him. Had already shifted from the fantasy blooming in the smoke from his rifle barrel, fans waving hats at toy figures playing hockey. I was ready to go, had gone.

Lauretta looked up and saw. She didn't say anything. Just opened her brown eyes wide and looked at me, long and hard, then narrowed them. She did that several times, as if her eyes were a camera and she were taking my photograph. My perspective whirled, and I felt she was looking down at me. And I felt that she was measuring my face to remember it after it was dead and still.

Truth was stranger. I would come back from the dead to find her married happily to another man. 'Tom, you're back,' she said. It was an accusation.

⁂

Walking. The sportswriters used to marvel when I told them my training consisted of daily walks of fifteen to twenty miles, with a couple of fast timed runs per week. Even in this, they suspected me of lying. One scribe waxed eloquent: 'Could this modest regimen really produce those prodigious feats of stamina and speed we have been privileged to witness?'

Answer: yes.

But he wouldn't have believed me. And – in a way – perhaps he was right to be sceptical. For me walking went far beyond a key to success in sport. It was my way of life, my life.

I discovered it accidentally, and in defeat. The way most true things are found.

After I left the Institute I was a running fiend. From twelve to eighteen, I ran every chance I got, my legs two long itches only speed could scratch. I'd run from crosses and pale droning spinsters, painted Saints and sour-smelling scribblers, hours spent communing with the ghosts of Pauline Johnson and Joseph Brant, my farting rear to the classroom. Running could take me away from everything, I believed. And this was true.

Heading out to jobs as a farm labourer in houses off the reserve, I tore up road. I walked only with the greatest reluctance, a penance I paid to scorched lungs and swampy legs. There were canneries in Caledonia and Hagersville, Hamilton, Brantford and Burlington, where I picked up seasonal work. I ran (and walked), ran (and walked), to and from all of them.

I watched the road races on field days and in the Highland Games. Knowing – knowing-dreaming – I would be part of them soon.

Bill Davis was my hero then. A Mohawk from Ohsweken, he'd won races all over Ontario. In 1901 he'd finished second in the Boston Marathon. 'That close,' he said, his hands straddling a length of air.

In the spring of 1905, just before my eighteenth birthday, I decided it was my time. My legs wouldn't let me wait any longer. I entered the annual Victoria Day five-mile race in Caledonia.

When the starter's gun cracked I sprang into the wind, the Institute behind me. The rest is easy to tell. I ran too fast, burning myself up, and in the last half mile someone passed me.

I was unhappy and happy. I had run my first race. My second-place silver medal, which I fingered in my pocket as I walked home, could not but turn to gold. I was eighteen. More strength lay ahead of me.

The walk home was almost five miles too. I walked it fast, and sometimes I broke into a scornful sprint, just to show the speed I had to waste. After one such run I stopped, gasping, beside a field of tall grasses. From the field came a giant hum, a churn of rampant life, which I could not separate into the sound of individual insects. It seemed more the sizzle of growing, of life itself. Breezes passed through the grass like blushes through skin. Clouds sent cool bobbling shadows over the field and me. And there was the buzzing, like a tiny roar, the crackle of a fire breaking out, everywhere.

Cogagwee, I thought. Me, my name. *Everything.*

Excited, I leapt over the ditch to be closer to the buzzing grass. I stood in it, the sharp blades scratching my legs. I passed my hands over the frizzy, flowering tops, wondering if the pubic hair of women, which I had not felt yet, felt this way, soft yet dry, pleasantly prickly.

I saw a black dot near the base of a long stalk of grass, and stooped to look at it. It must have been a type of beetle, it was black, but though I peered at it closely, no other details of its appearance have remained with me. Only its motion. I remember touching it with my finger. It stopped climbing. I touched it again, a gentle nudge. Now its six legs scrambled forward – it ran – but only for a short distance. Then it walked again.

Several times I did this – touched the black beetle to see it stop or run – while I felt an idea growing inside me, my stomach prickling with excitement from the beetle's lesson.

Running and stopping are the same, you do them *from* something. Walking is life, is time, it takes you *towards*.

The secret churned my stomach, ached along my limbs.

⁂

I walked to Dunnville and back, fifty miles. 'Don't lie,' Mother said, 'or you'll find another house.'

My brother took a horse and buggy to Hamilton. I gave him a half-hour lead, then met him on King Street. His jaw fell open. 'Does Mother know?' he asked. I think at that moment he believed me capable of anything: of flying, of telepathy, of spirit-walking. I just grinned at him.

Next Victoria Day, at Caledonia, I walked to the start line. Felt the touch, a tap, a flick, between my shoulder blades. Ran a short way along the stalk and won easily. Resumed walking, and walked slowly home.

Karaoke Mon Amour

Foreign Shapes

Taiwan is shaped like an egg, an ovary, a tear. Korea is a stubby uncircumcised penis, one million soldiers stationed at its base. Japan is long and gently curving, tapering from a central mass into a chain of ever-smaller islands: it is the seahorse, tail unfurled, floating on ocean currents to the east.

The seahorse (*Hippocampus syngnathidae*) is a marine fish found in shallow tropical or temperate waters. The male develops the eggs and bears the young, incubating them in a brood pouch.

The hippocampus forms a ridge along each lateral ventricle of the brain. It is part of the limbic system, which is involved in the complex physical aspects of behaviour governed by emotion and instinct. The activities governed are those concerned with self-preservation and preservation of the species, the expression of fear, rage and pleasure, and the establishment of memory patterns.

The Two Sisters

English only! was their strict rule at the start, but George soon saw the sense of bending this a little. June, the younger of the two women he tutored on Tuesday, could speak English haltingly – the Taiwanese school system had drilled her mainly in grammar – but her sister, May, could barely speak at all. As they sat around the carved cedar coffee table, George working with first one sister then the other, it was only natural for June to help out in Mandarin whenever he and May reached an impasse.

The house was May's. Or the first floor was. The basement was rented 'to China boy' and the upstairs 'to mother, her girl', which partly answered George's puzzlement at how two thirty-year-olds, one with five small children, could immigrate and right away purchase a house in North York. Not all of the mystery evaporated. The family business in Taipei seemed modest enough – 'We are selling hats,' June explained – and May's husband had no regular employment. He practised a martial arts discipline George had never heard of and couldn't pronounce. His trophies stood on the mantel and medals and diplomas hung above them, the only furnishings in the living room except for the table and the heap of children's toys in a corner. He travelled throughout Asia giving demonstrations. For free? George wondered. He had been gone on one of these junkets since George had met the sisters. Tomorrow he was due back.

'Husband … pick up.' May made driving motions in the air.

'I am picking up my husband,' George said, writing it at the same time on the paper he would leave behind. 'Try.'

'Try to say?' May made a comic song of the three words. She said something to June. They both laughed.

'What did she say?' At the question, June blushed and glanced at her sister. May was still laughing, her black eyes glittering.

'He say, your voice sound like music.'

George smiled dryly, to show he didn't believe that.

Paper Cranes

Some of the paper cranes could sit upright, correctly balanced, but most lay over on one side; some were upside down. It was as if a strong wind, which neither of them could feel, blew gusts through their apartment. Or perhaps – George had been taken duck hunting as a boy – a flock of the coloured birds had been flying through and had met a hail of gunfire, launched by miniature marksmen hidden among the furnishings.

He showed one to Sonoko, his Friday morning appointment. Shelley made this, he said proudly, bringing out the lime green crane from a zippered pouch in his briefcase. It was only slightly crushed by his sandwiches.

'Shelley? Ah … your partner.' Sonoko spoke with slow precision. She had studied traditional tea ceremony at an institute in Kyoto. Once when George asked if she would work at that when she returned, her eyes went wide. 'I have not served tea for six months.' *Out of date?*

George thought, before remembering that the whole point of tradition was *never* to go out of date. What did she mean, then? That the motions of performing the ceremony were so complex – he imagined slow sequences of turns, clockwise, counter-clockwise, bows, subtle hand gestures – really, he couldn't imagine it. He and Shelley poured water over Lipton.

'This ... is ... very ... lovely,' Sonoko said, turning the crane delicately. 'Origami. We made in junior school.'

'Elementary,' George corrected, his armpits flaming for himself as well as Shelley.

Karaoke

I am in love with someone. He is foreigner. It is impossible to think. I will be insane.

All the way home on the subway, he pressed the pocket of his shirt, feeling the message on the slip of paper burn against his heart.

But climbing the fire escape stairs to his apartment, he remembered his friend Howard's words. *These Asian women, they're like Western women forty years ago. Marriage is everything to them. If they don't find a man, they're nothing.* Howard was sexist, reductionist, casually racist; partly for these reasons, George found his company bracing. He pricked balloons. Snug in a regular teaching job, he found George's ESL gigs more amusing than exotic.

Once, in a Forkchops on Bloor, George pressed him to try kimchee, the Korean national dish of aggressively spiced cabbage.

Howard, a curry devotee and foreign film fan, was not fazed by the fiery red flecks in vinegar. He chewed a large mouthful judiciously, sweat beading on his forehead.

'They bury it in a pot in the backyard,' George told him.

'I believe it,' said Howard.

There was a name printed in a bottom corner of the note, so tiny it looked like a fly's footprints. *Kil Eun-Jee.* He liked the fact that the Koreans seldom picked a Western moniker to avoid embarrassing struggles with their names. They let you try. Sometimes, mouthing substitutes like 'May' or 'June', he felt he was addressing a ghost self, like a hologram, shimmering between himself and the real person.

Losing Babies

George reckoned that he and Shelley had lost three children in six months. Shelley felt the same way, though George knew she went too far when she said, as she sometimes did, 'It's just like they died.' It wasn't *just* like that. As a language teacher he was sensitive to the dangers in the overly literal as well as in the overly metaphorical. Whatever sense he had of a higher power – and it was a very hazy, flickering sense, like early TV – he was sure that it involved at least a fine ear. Talk like that was dangerous. It could get you smacked with some real bad luck.

Not that he and Shelley hadn't had their share. First, they had thought Shelley was pregnant. Finally. Six weeks since her last period, and they had been tossing around names, when her doctor informed her that what she was growing was in fact an ovarian cyst, not a fetus. After her surgery she was down, lower than even George had ever seen her before. At thirty-nine, and with her history of tricky menstruation, her doctor put her chances of another pregnancy at slim. It was George who first contacted the adoption agency. Four years, he was told, if everything went smoothly. Four *years?* He would be forty-five. Without mentioning it to Shelley, he made further inquiries and finally found an agency that got – their blunt word – babies from Russia. An agency in Moscow took in homeless babies from all over that vast country, as well as from the former republics, Kazakhstan, Belarus, Georgia. 'A clearing house,' George thought unwillingly, and saw a van, like an old-style dogcatcher's van, roaming the muddy side streets. 'Good health, parents and children,' said a crisp young female, who was no less impressive when George met her in person.

Shelley was too depressed still to be very dubious or excited. She acceded.

'Igor? Vasily? Vladimir?' George joked gently, trying to bring her around. He still came home most nights to find her eating nachos in front of *Jerry Springer*. 'Good-Time Grannies: My Mother Slept With My Son.' She had gained twenty-five pounds and was still gaining, even after returning to her part-time hours as a data entry clerk with a survey firm named, unfortunately, Matrix. Their sex life was nil, but had been dwindling for a long time.

'Katerina,' she said one night with a weak smile. 'We can shorten it to Kate.'

Good Fortune

George was disappointed when, after the return of May's husband, May and June cancelled their next two appointments. It was business, partly; they were the last two sessions left in the package of hours they'd bought. But also, he missed seeing them. He had come to think of the two sisters as an oasis of calm in his week. Peace, and something more. A hint of mystery, and promise of the most relaxing kind, since it need never be fulfilled.

They gave him cups of tea, green or black. Ginger tea once, when he was sick; it was sweet and spicy, the pale root slices floating in the pot, and after each sip it filled the head and chest with a surprising surge of delayed heat. And new food too: red bean soup, which he found too sugary. Delicious warm buns filled with green onion or pork bits in a sauce. The house was always silent, strangely silent for a home to eleven people. But the husband was demonstrating his martial art abroad, the children were at school; even the three tenants had vacated the premises, perhaps in deference to the arrival of 'tutor-man', as May sang out when he rang the doorbell. The sense of stolen moments was what made him think of an oasis. The small delight of water and a palm tree, an hour of shade before the march again.

They sat cross-legged around the low carved coffee table, he on one side, the two sisters on the other. The silence felt to him like another language, a third tongue that murmured between the English and the Mandarin. They laughed a lot. Giggled at mistakes, at deformed vowels and ribald consonants; at bad grammar. Words popped and fizzled and flared like a backyard fireworks display in the air around their heads.

There was an undercurrent. Of course he knew that. It came most forcefully from May, the married one. June was shyer. May would rattle off a string of Mandarin, several sentences worth, which at George's prompting June would translate as 'She feel tired.' May, black eyes dancing, looked anything but pooped. He kept asking just to watch June squirm, mumbling the double translation into a safe lie and then into English.

'Teacher hit,' May suggested, holding out her hands when she had failed to do her homework. Her fingers were long and slender, pink from kitchen work, the nails clear and shapely. He felt a buzz of tingling energy in what Howard called 'the lowest chakra'.

They taught him a Chinese character which they translated as 'Good Fortune'. Its difficulty surprised him, sixteen strokes in a precise sequence. But then there were quite a few strokes involved in printing 'Good Fortune' in English. During lulls in the lesson he sometimes practised it, May and June laughing delightedly.

Naturally he had fantasies of sleeping with them. Taking the two sisters to bed in the echoing house. Such thoughts never occupied him for long; he enjoyed them in passing. During the first bald patch in their sex life, he and Shelley had visited a therapist, who asked them – five minutes in, which George recognized as a shock tactic – if they 'got off on other people'. George admitted he did occasionally (often by that point), and Shelley, tearing up, said she thought she had 'once'. 'Once, schmunz,' the therapist, a tough-lover, jeered. He said, 'Who cares where you get your appetite, as long as you eat at home.' After three sessions they paid their bill and discontinued recovery. They went back to irregular snacking, from their own, or each other's, hands.

The day May's husband returned, there were sounds in the house at last. Deep breathing sounds from the kitchen, like breezes in a poplar grove. George felt nervous. At the end of the session, a squat young man in a burgundy track suit, with a serene boyish face, planted himself in front of him and announced, 'I am Dave. I'm happy to meet you.' His English was fluent, lightly accented. George wondered why he didn't teach his wife himself. 'I would like to speak with you soon.'

Soon, George promised.

Out of Business

Often it happened, an almost-expected miracle. 'Nature's blessing,' the doctor said, then wincing at his own corniness, added that it was probably hormonal. Happy expectation led to the release of endorphins, which stimulated the production of other, ah.... George heard confusion and perhaps ignorance in the too-rapid delivery. But it didn't matter. Shelley was smiling. Suddenly, two babies were on the way. Vladimir-Katerina would be joined by Michael-Rebecca.

They would love them equally.

But actually, both babies took a detour and wound up somewhere else. The Russian baby agency, or Canada's branch of it, went out of business. *This number is no longer in service*, said a sexy female voice each time George called. Then they received a registered letter from a lawyer's office saying that their deposit had been seized as evidence pertaining to a police investigation and would be returned when, and if, etc. Vladimir-Katerina was stuck in Vitebsk or Kustanaj or Batumi. George didn't know why, but it made him feel better to find these names in the atlas, give him/her a dot in the countryside at least. Michael-Rebecca went down the toilet, a spontaneous first trimester abortion. 'Go down the toilet' was one of the idioms he taught his students for a project failing; 'go down the tubes' was another. It was the horrible accidental exactness of language, no less than our fumbling attempts to control it, that oppressed him often.

Shelley didn't cry, not once that he saw. Her gently sorrowing face frightened him more than a Hallowe'en mask. She watched *Seinfeld*, *Springer* and *Sally* with an unwavering attention, but was often hazy on details when he asked her the retention-testing questions he had developed in his work.

Eat Snow

When he asked his students what they had done on the weekend, the answer, if not 'study English', was usually 'karaoke'. George had once joined a group that bellowed 'Proud Mary' at a smear of cheering faces in a northern roadhouse serving half-price draft and chicken wings. That was fifteen years ago. Shelley had been one of the other drunken singers, swaying in a line with arms linked about each other's waists. He hadn't known her name yet. Six months later they were living together.

But the Asian karaoke experience was, he gathered, different. 'You must join us on a weekend, I insist,' said Dae-Jung, a stylish architect from Seoul whom he met for 'grammar refinement'.

George was drunk by midnight when they reached the bar. Pitchers of draft were sloshing on top of a slithery supper of noodles topped with a fried egg and a glutinous black bean sauce. Tasty enough, though a bit much for his chopstick technique. The six Koreans, three of them clients, laughed good-naturedly. Shelley had begged off. Outside Christie station, George saw signs in Korean, the oblongs and circles less angular than Chinese characters. 'Korean town,' said the slight girl with the sombre, almost grieving expression who had been sitting next to him at dinner. He had forgotten her name, but at the hint of irony in her voice, he smiled.

Concrete stairs led down into the karaoke bar. Opium dens, George thought. It was not officially licensed, but at a word from Dae-Jung, the manager dipped below the counter and came up with a twelve-pack of Coors. An assistant showed them to one of the rooms. It was small, with clean white walls; an L-shaped black mock-leather couch faced the electronics stand in the corner; between them, a coffee table with the songbooks, a remote and two microphones. Faint thumps and laughter could be heard through the walls. Sex hotel, thought George, renting rooms by the hour.

The three girls were giggling as they flipped through the Korean and Chinese songbooks. He opened the English one. 'Moon River.' 'What's New, Pussycat?' 'Do Ya Think I'm Sexy?' Obviously selection was going to be a problem. 'I insist you choose,' pressed Dae-Jung, standing with mike in hand. He hit the dimmer switch and a small mirror ball in the corner began spinning, spraying dots of primary colours through the dusk. The lights spattered over and around the stand with its winking numbers, not quite reaching to where they sat. Electronics are the star, George thought; we have to emulate them.

Dae-Jung punched in the numbers of a Korean song. He blended seamlessly into the mix. So did the next two singers, each of them delivering a song without a glitch. That spooked George. He had been expecting a sing-along, but this was more like lip-synching. Another problem was the accompaniment, not the original tracks minus the vocals, as long ago in the roadhouse, but a peppy Muzak, heavy on synth and programmed rhythm tracks. The videos featured beautiful Asian women in filmy clothes, striking poses in front of a backdrop of stone columns, ocean sunset, or floral wallpaper.

Dae-Jung was pointing with the mike. George scanned the titles hopelessly. That was when he spied 'Come Together' and remembered its tonic weirdness.

96

In the far corner of the black couch, the thin sad girl was staring at him. Grief and longing sloshed behind the mini-portholes of her glasses. No one sat very close to her. She had not sung, would not now.

With a sigh amplified into Apple wind, he began. Chanting the Lennonese, he was bolstered by the thought that it could not mean much less to his listeners than it did to him. When he reached the title phrase he was shouting.

For once the group didn't laugh or clap loudly. After he finished rasping, a smattering of polite applause dispelled the silence. Dae-Jung slapped him on the back and launched into 'Don't Be Cruel'. He had a nice light tenor.

Sometime toward the end of the evening, George had sung a few songs and drunk a few more beers, he was getting into it, not caring any more, when he heard a voice in his ear, at first he thought it came from inside his head, a woman's voice murmuring, 'I like your deep voice. I wanna –' Was he hallucinating? Around the urgent whisper, he heard a thin male voice, climbing an alien melody over a pounding beat.

He looked to his left and saw the grieving girl staring at her hands folded in her lap. He thought he saw her lips move – a silent prayer? She got up suddenly and left the room.

A short time later he found himself on the street. New snow had fallen. The other faces looked as dizzy, as reeling under the streetlights, as he felt himself. The thin girl was looking away. She seemed impatient now, like someone waiting for a ride that is late. In the shuffle of going she had slipped a note into his pocket that he could feel with his fingers. A girl was scooping up snow and pushing it at her boyfriend's face. 'Here, eat snow!'

737

Shelley had learned to make the origami cranes from a home decorating show on the Life Network. The show's host was a sort of Canadian Martha Stewart, less finicky and less impressive; often her instructions trailed off in a hazy ' ... or whatever'. After she taught the viewers how to fold them, she showed the finished cranes to her gardening specialist, who happened to be Japanese.

'Ah ... lovely,' he said, as Sonoko had told George. He went on to relate the Japanese custom of making one thousand of the cranes as a form of prayer, for someone who was sick, for instance. He didn't mention that the technique was learned in elementary school.

'Wow! Well, if you're not up to a thousand, you can always enclose one in a Get Well card, since they flatten right out, or on a gift, or whatever,' bubbled the host.

Shelley bought sheets of coloured paper which she cut into two-inch squares. She had sheets of many colours: grass green, cedar green, ruby red, sky blue, cobalt blue, cotton candy pink, butter yellow, tangerine, burgundy. Deep, rich colours. She made a special expedition to the Japanese Paper Place to get sheets of gold and silver. These were George's favourites; they glittered like treasure trove.

When folding the cranes, Shelley worked her way through all of the colours before returning to the first one. It was her own superstition. She did not use white or, of course, black.

At first, George knew, she was folding the cranes as a prayer for a healthy baby. She had seen the decorating show when her period was four weeks overdue. When that baby turned out to be a fibrous growth, he thought she must be folding the cranes for herself, substituting her name for the baby's in her prayer. He reminded her of the doctor's lack of concern, which they should interpret as reassurance. Finally he got up nerve to ask her.

'No,' she said, folding deftly by now. 'I want a baby.'

All through the successive fiascos that followed, the loss of two more babies, each loss more actual and thus more painful than the one before, Shelley kept folding the cranes. By now George was confused about the reason, and to pray without purpose made him vaguely uneasy. Coloured cranes perched on the bookcase, the table, the fridge. They filled glass jars and bowls. Inevitably, with the wind of someone passing, they littered the floor, snagged in dust balls. George began to worry that they were unlucky.

'You didn't actually "lose" the babies,' said Howard over lunch one day. Then, remembering, he added, 'Except for the miscarriage, of course.' He didn't blush at his gaffe, though George winced inwardly. In his private sociology he had noticed that film buffs were not as easily embarrassed as most people.

'We didn't win,' he said, demoting his feeling to irony. He thought that he had gone further than Howard in plumbing the meaning of loss. Loss was any missed chance or opportunity. It was the perception of absence, specific or generalized. It carried with it feelings, not only of sadness and anger, but also of guilt and confusion, blurred identity. Sometimes he felt he must have misplaced the babies; they would turn up if he only looked hard enough. Other times he felt that the babies were right where they belonged, and he was the one who had got turned around. He was a wanderer in a vast labyrinthine city, and he couldn't find a map or properly ask for directions. He couldn't even remember where he was staying, or who he was supposed to meet. Had the babies sensed that in advance and avoided such a befuddled dad?

'You don't have to see it all the way through,' he said to Shelley one night. He had decided she was in superstitious thrall to a number, 1,000, and maybe he could help her free herself.

'No!' Her face filled with a foreboding he had never seen in it before. 'I don't want us to lose any more.'

So she did have a prayer. Not for gain, but against loss. Any, all, loss? And when she finally gave up folding, was that, he wondered, final resignation? He preferred to think it was boredom. Boredom was the commonest kind of bad faith.

But he wished she had given up earlier or else finished the job. Seven hundred and thirty-seven miniature coloured cranes, constituting just over two-thirds of a prayer: that seemed like a definition of bad luck.

What happened at that theatre?

Some events are stubbornly surreal. It is as if they exist in an alternate universe and resist all our efforts to drag them into this one. All we glimpse here are odd, off-kilter limbs, sudden gasps, bits of a reality that somewhere else, perhaps, is correctly proportioned and breathing comfortably. It was like that the time George took Sonoko to the movies.

It began the night before, when he phoned to ask her. 'Hel-lo … hel-lo?' she kept saying, as if they had a bad connection. Then, dubiously, 'George?' They had been meeting once a week for three months, but this was the first time he had phoned her. Occasionally she called him, to cancel or reschedule.

After a pause, Sonoko said, 'It would be … Dutch treat?'

'Good,' George said, 'yes.'

They met outside the Cumberland theatre. Sonoko's normally pale face was chalk white, her black hair pinned back severely. She wore a long black wrinkled raincoat. He thought of Pound's lines: 'The apparition of these faces in the crowd/Petals on a wet, black bough.' She had also studied kabuki theatre. Not performing it, of course, only men did that. But as they paid for the tickets, he looked closely at her face, believing he saw a layer of fine white powder blend with warmer tones at her neckline. A sweetish smell rose from around her.

The ticket-seller and his companion – the manager? – were middle-aged men who George assumed were gay. They were well-groomed and they spoke in quiet voices, their heads close together. It made the bare lobby strangely cosy, so unlike the brisk hetero exchange – a boy or girl barking 'Next' – at most box offices. The ticket-taker also seemed homosexual, perhaps just by association, but his personality was rougher, less composed. A high-school dropout beside university graduates, thought George, configuring things. He was also a bit younger.

'Ah, you're going for the real stuff.'

The ticket-taker spoke so quickly that Sonoko frowned in puzzlement. Even George barely understood the blur of syllables.

'If it weren't for live flesh none of us would be here.'

The comments seemed torn out of context, and George was sitting down before they made any sense. The movie they were seeing was *Live Flesh*, directed by Pedro Almodovar from a novel by Ruth Rendell. Waiting in the dusk, he smelled Sonoko's perfume, stronger at close quarters, a cloying scent with something faintly metallic, a faint iron smell, underneath. Sonoko was too fastidious ever to permit body odour. George thought idly of sleeping with her, her strong legs – she rock-climbed as fiercely as she memorized verbs – cinched around his back. Partly this was automatic, having sexy thoughts before movies. It was the dark, the screen about to come alive, the nearby strangers.

A woman's scream began the movie. Briskly an older woman bundled her into an off-duty bus where she gave birth to a baby boy.

Sonoko leaned close to whisper something.

'Erotic?' he guessed.

'No!' Fiercely. 'I know "erotic". Exotic.'

The helpful woman used the driver's shoelaces to tie off the umbilical cord, and then, having nothing else sharp, she bit through it with her teeth. She sat in the seat behind the mother, her mouth red-smeared, like her hands and the baby she cradled. Tennyson's red-toothed, red-clawed nature. That was unusual in movies; usually newborns were shown pink and glowing, as if bathed and talcumed prior to entry. The mother groaned deeply. 'Keep pushing, it's the placenta,' the impromptu midwife advised. George heard another soft gasp.

It was Sonoko. He turned to see her face floating ghostlike, drained and stricken. At once he understood her perfume with its ferrous undertone and the enhanced pallor of her face. It would be like Sonoko, with her blended masochism, to cover the evidence of her period with ministrations that actually drew attention to it. Mishima, he recalled, was her beloved author.

'Excuse me.' Sonoko squeezed past without touching him. She never returned.

Afterwards he felt disjointed but refreshed, which Howard had told him was standard for an Almodovar movie. Shelley was in bed sleeping when he got home. He climbed in beside her and began stroking the small of her back. She responded slowly, with sleepy moans. Guilty but horny, he persisted. He came to a vision of Sonoko wearing a strap-on, fucking the sad Korean girl in the ass.

Who cares where you get your appetite.

'What happened at that theatre?' Shelley murmured before returning to sleep. He had told her that much.

Asshole

Dave was doing his breathing exercises in the kitchen next to the living room. George could hear him as he finished with the two sisters. He sounded like a soft engine starting up. Husbands, George thought, and wondered who would be more hopeless: a TSN addict who spent his days on the couch, or a martial arts expert who stood in rooms flexing and breathing. June poured more tea.

'My country is beautiful, yes,' Dave was saying. George had asked about his trip. 'It is my country. But it is crowded. Con ... compressed? No. Congested?' George nodded. 'Europeans called it Formosa.'

Dave smiled as he spoke, a winning, boyish smile that lit up his handsome face. But George knew that he put too much stock in smiles. He always had; it was a weakness. He couldn't recognize aggression easily unless it came accompanied by scowls and grimaces and glares. But usually it didn't.

'I always called it Taiwan,' George said.

May and June had moved back discreetly from the table. They were standing a few feet away, their faces meek and expectant.

'You are a great language teacher.' George grinned at the exaggeration. 'I am also a teacher. I could show you something.'

Which is how George found himself standing rock-still in the centre of the living room for several long minutes, trying to relax and 'go heavy' as instructed, feeling stiffness and soreness and restless energy migrate around his body. Feeling aches and pains. Feeling idiotic as he stared straight ahead out the window at the street, catching blurs of May and June and Dave moving around him, observing him as one would a museum exhibit: *Toronto man, 1998.*

Dave had showed him the place on the balls of his feet where the weight was supposed to concentrate. He told him the name, which George pronounced and forgot. By now he had great difficulty learning anything he knew he would never use. Dave's instructions were to 'relax … go heavy,' let all his weight flow down through the balls of his feet. Back into the earth. George tried. Then, having read some Zen in his time, he tried not to try. Dave moved around him like a tailor, prodding him in the shoulder and stomach and thigh and buttocks. George was shamed by the mushiness of his muscles, but Dave muttered 'Not tight … let go.' Finally George succeeded in the sense that his various aches and pains merged into a general discomfort, and the energy of his body was concentrated mostly in his brain. He wondered if the froth of pink in the yard was a cherry tree. That would be almost as good as a lotus blossom. He also wondered what the best word would be for the way he felt, standing still in a living room among moving, watching people, his mouth falling open whenever he forgot about it.

He decided the best word would be 'asshole'.

Finally it was over. Dave looked at his watch. 'Five minutes. Okay. Do it every day until you can do fifteen minutes. Very relaxed. If you feel pain, sudden pains, stop immediately.'

'I will,' George promised.

May and June were watching him seriously. It was a pleasure to be able to move his head again – *that* relaxed him. Soon he would leave and that made him feel warmly about May and June, the times they'd had together. He looked back at Dave and almost gasped. Dave's mouth was open, his eyes glazed. His arms hung limply at his sides and he leaned forward at a dangerous angle. He looked like a corpse tied to a stake. After a moment George realized that he was being shown the correct procedure. He felt his own posture sag at the thought that the demonstration was not over.

'Feel my chest,' the corpse murmured.

George put his hand on Dave's chest. It felt plump and still. 'Through your stomach?' he guessed.

'Feel my stomach.'

More plump stillness. Despite himself, George was curious.

'I'm breathing through my ——.' The word for the balls of his feet. George nodded, as he did when a street person told him he could fly.

After watching for another minute or so – seeing nothing more – George said that he had to go. He bent to get his briefcase. 'Let me show you something,' he heard as fingers gripped his upper arm. Anger spread like a rash over his skin. Now he was being detained.

'Stand there,' Dave said. He turned George's shoulders and positioned his feet so that George was advancing on him partly in profile, like a boxer. Standing very close, an inch away, he snuggled up with his head on George's breastbone. He adopted his limp posture, breathing through ——, his hands falling like soft plumb weights against George's forward thigh.

'Now push me,' he mumbled.

George knew what was coming. Any man would. But he pushed anyway.

The result was still amazing. It was like pushing a rag doll weighing three hundred pounds. Dave felt soft and slippery, George could barely get a grip on his shoulders, as if he had been rolled in butter and then bolted to the floor. Despite himself, he pushed harder, straining. The head lolled against his chest, the small massive body rotated barely. The two sisters snickered. George felt duly humiliated and also, strangely, that this was deserved. 'Push harder,' said the other man. George stopped pushing.

Slugfest

'What kind of a name is Kill?'

'Just one "l".' George usually did the laundry, but Shelley had been emptying his shirt pockets – why? he wondered – and had found the note Kil Eun-Jee had passed him at the karaoke bar.

'Whatever.'

'It's just a name. Like Smith.'

'Smith is like Kill?' They were looking at two different names in their heads, and he couldn't change her spelling. She had her hands on her hips.

'It is if you don't know the words.'

A simmering silence followed. They retreated to opposite corners of the small apartment. Like most long-time couples, they argued with the practised rhythms of boxers, in rounds with inviolable rest periods in between. The combat itself took many forms: dancing, feinting, jabbing, slugging, hugging and resting. Or someone could drop his or her gloves inexplicably, inviting the knockout punch.

'What do you think of me?' She was standing in the doorway. Why does she have to be in a doorway? he thought, with a sudden opaque fear. He put down what he had been doing, writing cheques to various creditors, while she repeated her naked question.

What right did he have to speak the truth? Lying seemed more defensible at the moment. But he began anyway. 'You've let yourself go.' An emptiness, a soft vacancy, came into her face. 'At times you seem to have given up already. At thirty-nine.' He could feel himself using these complaints as ladder rungs to climb toward an impossible statement. Finally he reached it. 'I don't love you any more.' It had to be the truth.

She went to her sister's in Brampton. At least it was closer to where she worked. Her new smile was soaked in irony. There had been no more scenes after the last one.

Word of Mouth

Dave was smiling broadly. 'Each of us is a master of his own –' He sought for a word and then gestured at June. She knew it. 'Discipline,' Dave repeated.

They were standing by the front door. George had his coat on.

'You can learn any language,' Dave declared, with how much intentional absurdity George could only guess.

He groped behind himself for the doorknob. Then, on impulse, he opened his briefcase and retrieved a piece of paper and a pen. Quickly and accurately he made the series of strokes May and June had taught him. 'Good fortune,' he said, handing it to Dave.

Dave was a controlled man. His only reaction was the abrupt extinction of his smile, as though a candle had been blown out. It came back, but flickeringly, beset by an inner breeze. He turned and went down the hall.

George felt the brass of the doorknob, a cold globe; he just had to turn it. May and June were whispering, darting hurt glances up at him. Well, he had betrayed them. He knew, in a general way, what the character must mean, even if he couldn't translate it exactly. *Fuck? Fuck me?* Probably it was less aggressive, almost innocent. *Sex. Make baby.*

Then Dave was coming back, his face dense as a stormcloud. He advanced swiftly upon them. George assumed he was about to be given the complete demo.

What Dave did, in fact, was hand him his business card. Characters and numbers on a cardboard rectangle. *Fax* and a number added in pen. George inclined his head, but had nothing to give in return. He had no card. His business was strictly word of mouth.

With a groan of relief, he sealed himself in his car and switched on the ignition, windshield wipers and Mix 98 (Oldies and The New). The Eastern peace. He had to admit he didn't understand it. The comfortably slumped body, the calm eyes, took on another aspect as he watched them in memory. What he was seeing looked very much like what he would call stubbornness. Could it be a basic difference between East and West? He considered the possibility cautiously. Prejudice and stereotypes lay that way, but perhaps some truth as well. He was a Western man, desperate to fly by any means, guile definitely not excluded, and as he drove down the drizzling road he puzzled over why anyone would deliberately court the forces pulling him back to earth.

Friends

Howard had been a lot of things. Had started being a lot of things anyway. A film studies major. A law student. He was one of those who
become a teacher in order to have a steady platform from which to make
leaps into the unknown, certain he will land somewhere safe. Grey-
haired now, he was thinking of applying for medical school. 'Before the
door closes.' These days there were some Doc U's that counted life experience almost as much as marks.

One day in May, George met him for coffee at the Manulife Centre.
They sat at a wobbly little table with their cappuccinos. 'Okay, so play
doctor,' George said.

'What do you mean?'

'C'mon, I know you. What've you been reading?' George did know
Howard. 'Reading up', in its preliminary phase of dreaming and loose
associations, was what he did best, what he started things for.

Howard looked sheepish. 'Geez.' Then, with a frown of retrieval, he
was off. 'Well, I've been doing some reading on neurology. Brain
anatomy and function. There's this little gizmo called the hippocampus
which is sort of a mystery. I mean, it's involved in higher and lower func-
tions in ways nobody understands exactly. The name comes from the
Latin for seahorse. Actually, the Greek: *hippos*, horse, and *kampos*, monster. Some of those early anatomists must have been pretty wired to see a
seahorse in a little bulge of grey matter.'

Howard paused, and took a long sip of coffee. 'You sound like a
doctor,' George said, untruthfully. A doctor would have bypassed the
whimsical etymology and the wired anatomists for the serious memory
work. Howard relaxed visibly. His shoulders sagged with a naturalness
that would have pleased Dave.

'How's Shelley doing?' he asked.

George hesitated, then confided in the pseudo-doctor.

'I feel guilty somehow.'

'In what sense?'

'In the sense –' What was the sense? 'In the sense of collaborating
with the forces bringing her down.'

'That sounds pretty abstract.'

'It isn't. Not at all.'

They left soon after that. Howard had himself on a schedule and had to get back to studying. George walked along Bloor Street; paper litter was eddying in semi-tropical funnels of air. Leaving friends, he often felt vaguely depressed. He made friends quickly, had found them wherever he lived; but after seeing them, his dominant impression was of not knowing, or being known by, them. At times this could feel invigorating. It was like the bitter freedom he had sniffed reading Camus for the first time. But that was twenty years ago, and nowadays the scent was more elusive, its hints more apt to frighten than inspire.

Homeland

The coloured cranes, which he moved to safe places but did not discard, were like confetti thrown at the marriage of need and speed. He thought of the jets whizzing overhead, full of tourists, businessmen, students, the intercontinental flux. Seekers in their early twenties who thought nothing of stopping in Toronto *on their way* to Europe. The planet was small, but wind-swept.

He took out his datebook. The last page was graffitied with phone numbers. He looked at them, not sure which was the one he needed. The numerals swam, changed places. Finally he tried one:

Hello. I have returned to my homeland. If you want to talk to me you can reach me there. I hope you will contact me.

The hiss of tape unspooling after this was not a mistake. George realized this as he listened to it. The moving silence was full of whispers, of ghost voices, a conversational wind, decipherable if one had the key. Patience was the key, as was desire. What else? No one had forgotten anything.

Meat

In the dragged-out afternoons that first fall, after he had dropped off his résumés and before Debbie came home from work, Tom used to sit at the kitchen table with a beer and wonder seriously when the city would give them a break. This would be after he had decided on supper and maybe rinsed the vegetables, and he would be sitting with a Coors in the last glow of the setting sun, enjoying the graininess of the October dusk and looking forward to the moment when he would dispel it with a flick of the light switch, bringing yellow light.

'C'mon,' he would mutter, 'cut us some slack!' with a crooked grin at hearing his own voice in the empty kitchen.

By a break, or slack, he mainly meant a job for himself. For Debbie, since she was already working at Donut World, he wished for peace of mind. Calm. She was having even more trouble adjusting to Toronto than he was. Her hands no longer shook so much in the morning, before she rode the subway, but she still made little groans and yelps of panic in her sleep, starting awake from nightmares that she couldn't describe and that made her cry softly for a long time afterwards, Tom holding her and patting her back and shoulders.

'We've been down here before,' he would remind her. 'What about all those trips to the Ex?' Six or eight of them in a borrowed van, pounding down the 400 from Oro, hooting and drinking, cursing as they circled the vast plugged parking lots, plunging into the cotton-candy crowds. They used to have a bet on who would puke first, the hurler getting an ironic cup of coins.

'That was just fun,' she would murmur. And he would nod into her back, not quite alive to the distinction she was making.

Sometimes the frayed nerves, on both sides, flared into argument. *What's a crowd? Get used to it. I will when you get a job.* But they'd been together five years, since the end of grade twelve, and, after a simmering silence, the heat could still merge easily into rushes of apology and desperate lovemaking, burning itself clear.

In the cooling aftermath, they discussed calmly the possibility of returning to Oro. What kept them here, they both agreed, was the certainty of what awaited them there. There was a room, unchanged since childhood, reserved for each of them at their parents' homes, on small berry farms behind Gasoline Alley. 'You're always welcome back,' Debbie's boss had written on the card they gave her, along with a cake, on her last day at Tim Horton's. And Tom's father, who owned one of the Alley gas stations, where Tom had pumped and rung in sales since he was little, had gruffly said much the same thing.

Always welcome: to anyone under thirty the phrase was bound to have a mixed and faintly toxic ring.

One of those early evenings, Tom was so busy at the stove that he didn't hear Debbie come up the stairs or open the apartment door. Unemployment was at least teaching him to be a better cook. He did stir-fries mainly: frugal breasts of chicken, diced and mixed with vegetables, garlic, soya sauce and spices. He had the rice bubbling, and onions sputtering in oil in the wok, when he turned and saw his love standing right behind him.

His heart bumped with shock. He might have lashed out, he could feel adrenaline zinging along his muscles, but he saw how white and stricken Debbie's face was. Her meek eyes frightened wide, hands twisting together at her waist.

'What?' he said. 'What happened?'

She didn't answer. Her face was as blanched and drained as it got at the start of her period, though that wasn't for another two weeks.

He set the wooden spoon he was holding down on a plate and took the wok off the heat. Covered the rice, turned both elements off.

As soon as he put his arms around her, as soon as he touched her, she began crying. She cried as she did sometimes at night, with soft wrenching sobs, pain sloshing in a deep well. He felt his shirt front getting wet.

'What is it, Deb?' he said. 'C'mon, you can tell me.'

He knew he had to wait until she was ready, but it was hard at such times to keep impatience from creeping into his voice. Partly it was his helpless feeling, hearing her sorrow and wanting to erase it, but also it was a fear that they were missing the chance to take action. Seconds were slipping by when they might be phoning someone, chasing someone.

'Deb, what happened?'

Finally she said, without lifting her face from his damp chest, 'I lost our money.'

'What?'

She took a step back to face him, swiped at her eyes. 'I think I lost our money.'

Tom was more confused than alarmed. First off, they didn't have much money. Second, the few hundred dollars they did have were in the bank; neither of them carried more than coffee coins.

'Debbie,' he said. 'I need to know what happened.'

And she told him, dry-eyed but gulpingly, as if the story kept punching the breath out of her. A young man had approached her in the subway. He was panicky, on the verge of tears. He said he was a member of an Argentinian soccer team and had missed the team bus to the airport hotel. He had no money and he had to get back before the plane left.

'He begged me to give him the taxi money. He said his wallet was at the hotel and he would leave the money in an envelope at the front desk. He wanted to mail it to me but I wouldn't give him our address. Just my name.'

Tom stared at Debbie as she told him this. His mind was blank. He seemed to see her through busy fizzing dots, like TV static. She gulped, and said,

'I'm sorry, I gave him sixty dollars.'

Tom groaned. 'From where?'

'From our bank machine.' Another groan creaked out of him. 'I'm so sorry.'

'You know how scared I am, how paranoid. But everything seemed to fit. He seemed so upset. Well dressed. He wore a gold chain, a nice watch. He looked like an athlete. He had a big bag.'

For his loot, Tom thought. He had a picture of himself tackling the thief from behind, pummelling him senseless. But where in the vast city was he by now?

'How was his English?' he asked.

'Terrible. Broken. It took me five tries to understand he was saying "Argentina". That's what I mean. It wasn't until later, when I was riding the subway that I....'

Mingled with his anger and dismay – sixty dollars about a fifth of their holdings – Tom felt a creeping admiration for the brazenness of the con. Not: *I'm broke. Could you spare a loonie?* But something so bizarre that, like a headless ghost in a mystery, it made you overlook all the improbable details of the plot. Why not carry a wallet? Why *sixty* bucks? Why not a quarter to call the coach and have *him* send a cab?

'What was the name of the hotel?' he said. They had to play out the script the thief had given them.

Debbie fished a scrap of paper from her jeans. There it was: a name in blue ink, a phone number. Tom dialled it, surprised when a hotel clerk actually answered. Hope flared up in him. He asked his questions, was answered, and hung up.

'Nobody by that name. No soccer team,' he said, staring at the blue ink which connected him to the man's hand, his fingers. This time he saw him and Debbie hanging around that subway station until he came back to work it again. Debbie pointing him out and the two of them pounding him bloody, an avenging team.

He looked up from the couch. Debbie's eyes were red. He saw – connected still by the paper scrap – what the thief had seen. What he'd waited for. Someone scared but guileless, tender-hearted. He had seen the same thing.

'I'm so, so sorry.'

'It's all right. It is. Really.'

And they set about putting it behind them. Tom resumed fixing dinner while Debbie sat in a chair nearby, keeping close together as they always did in a crisis. As the loss receded he began to glimpse its positive side. It seemed to restore a balance, reassert a truth, that he'd felt slipping away. He considered himself more worldly than Debbie; that was why it was so galling to be the one still out of work. At first he'd told himself it was because his sights were set too high. After high-school Debbie had gone on working at Tim Horton's, merely switching from part to full time. But he'd taken computer programming at Georgian College. He was known locally for his Web pages; he'd designed two for pick-your-own farms in the area, and one for a bed-and-breakfast couple. But only a few of the computer ads he'd answered down here had let him fill out an application, and none had called back. After a month he'd broken his resolution and begun applying to gas stations. Time to give Deb a hand with the bills, he thought. But he was shocked to find that even in that field his experience didn't seem to count, in fact seemed to arouse suspicion and hostility, as if he might confuse his cash register with the actual running of Petro-Can.

He didn't fit into anyone's plan. Debbie's story reminded him of the bright side to that.

But the city had many surprises and reverses, more sudden switches of fortune than seemed possible in rural areas. It was only two weeks later that Debbie came home with her face made pale by another unexpected event. Tom's heart dropped again, but then he saw a ghost smile flickering over the discovery in her hands. She had found a wallet.

She handed it to him.

It was a thick black leather wallet, bulging with credit cards and cash. He counted out $300 in fifties and twenties. The cards covered every possible purchase contingency: Scotiabank, CIBC, Visa, Mastercard, Canadian Tire, The Bay, Sears, Esso. The only two articles not directly related to finance were a Canada Health card and a driver's licence. There were no family photos. The picture on the driver's licence showed a thirty-something face, balding, with round glasses.

They spent a silent minute surveying the items spread out on their kitchen counter, like doctors at an autopsy of the consumer life.

'We've got to give it back,' he said at last.

'Yeah,' she said.

He glanced at her. Her instincts were purer than his, she had a better heart; what made him their moral leader was his greater decisiveness. But she also believed vaguely in the occult, in magic and destiny, karmic chance. She probably felt this was fate compensating them for the earlier theft. But if so, it could only be by another theft.

'We've got to give it back,' he said. 'We know who he is.' He had a vague notion of sacrifice. A propitiation of the gods that had let them down. *The end of our bad luck.* This was not contradicted by the hope of a reward from the grateful owner.

They found the name and address in the phone book. He watched as she dialled the number and told her news. 'Uh huh … oh, really? Yeah?' she kept saying, the wallet's owner talkative. When she hung up, she told him that the owner lived just around the corner from them. 'I'm just going to run it over to him,' she said.

'What? Okay, sure.' He felt a tick of worry. 'Do you want me to come with you?'

'No, why? It really is just around the corner. I'll be right back.'

As soon as she'd gone he realized what was bothering him: someone finds your wallet and you want her to *deliver* it too? A bloated sense of entitlement was the least of the dangers he saw lurking.

He went down to the street to wait for Debbie, growing more anxious as the minutes passed. It was forty-five minutes before she appeared at the corner. She was strolling along, as if the good deed had calmed her.

'What happened?' he called before she reached him.

'You know how he lost it? You won't believe it. He was putting his kids in the car and he set his wallet on the roof. Then the kids were making so much fuss that he drove off without remembering it. It must have fallen off, probably just before I came by. That's how lucky he was. He said it wouldn't have lasted long on the street.'

'What's he do?'

'He's a lawyer.'

A lawyer. 'No reward for the Good Samaritan?'

'No.' She winced. 'I have to admit, I was thinking the same thing. But he was very grateful. He kept thanking me over and over.'

You're welcome, Tom thought.

The next morning, they were having breakfast when the phone rang. Debbie answered it. It was the lawyer asking her if she wanted to deliver some papers from his office to the courthouse. She could do it on her way to work. It would pay $75.

'That's like a day's pay,' she said after she hung up. But Tom was affronted.

'Isn't that cheap?' he muttered, clearing the breakfast dishes in his housecoat. Debbie was gathering up her things to go. 'Christ, that's cheap.'

'It's a job,' she said, pecking him on the cheek.

After that the lawyer became a minor but growing presence in their lives. Over the next few days he phoned to offer Debbie two more delivery jobs. Rush jobs, he said, that he would have had to pay a courier for anyway. Tom imagined the lawyer keeping the accounts in a little ledger. 3 x

$75 = $225. One more errand and he'd have paid Debbie back for the cash she'd returned to him. In tax-deductible wages, of course.

But the next job the lawyer offered Debbie paid $100. It involved Debbie serving a summons to a client who owed the lawyer money. The summons had to be served at a precise time; they arranged for Debbie to go in late to work.

'Serving a summons?' Tom said. 'Couldn't that be dangerous?'

He saw Debbie walk up to a chipped grey door, a bearded guy open it.

'Colin' – that was the lawyer's name – 'says the guy's a pussycat. Not dangerous. Just broke and lazy.'

Hearing the lawyer's smug words in Debbie's mouth made Tom frown. He glanced at her as she sat beside him on the futon, mending a tear in her orange work uniform. She seemed less nervous lately, more purposeful and assured. Fewer nightmares shredded her sleep. Running around for the lawyer seemed, more than Donut World or Tom's midnight pats, to have convinced her that she could stride into the city confidently, knowing she had a place in it. He didn't feel jealous of the lawyer, exactly. He knew it had more to do with being inside a city as opposed to on its margins. Walking into an office building with an envelope you knew someone was waiting for – that could put you at ease. Making a *latte* for people who had the leisure to sip it, or else slurped it on their way to a meeting – that had a different, more tangential feel.

It was only when the lawyer stopped calling that Tom felt jealousy of a more familiar kind. The kind he used to feel in Oro when he sat at the counter in Tim's in his oil-stained jeans, sipping a coffee while Deb finished her shift, and a well-dressed man from the highway would joke with her and make her laugh and blush. Tom wasn't very experienced with women – he'd only dated two girls before Debbie – but it didn't take much experience to recognize the lawyer's sudden silence. It was the seducer's pause, the 'space' that even the simplest man learned to grant a skittish woman before pressing the point. He realized these suspicions had been floating in bits and pieces inside him all along, and were just now coalescing.

'What's he like?' he asked one night. Debbie was soaking her feet in a basin of warm salt water; the standing at work was killing them. He had brought her a beer and was sipping his own in a chair across the room.

'Who?'

'Our lawyer. Colin.'

'Colin?' Debbie was bent over, rubbing her feet in the basin. 'Kind of weird, actually. Super nice and polite, but dead quiet. For a lawyer he doesn't seem to have much social skills. I think he's shy.'

None of this fit with the voice Tom had heard on the phone. A clipped, firm voice that asked for Debbie and, if she was out, left a message for her to call. No small talk, no fumbling.

'Has he ever come on to you?'

She laughed. 'Colin? Good God, no!'

'It's not ridiculous.' He stared at Debbie's lowered head, the part in her brown hair that showed white scalp. She raised her face.

'Believe me, if you knew Colin, it is.'

If I knew Colin. Tom's job search had been dwindling slowly down to zero. Instead of hitting the pavement every day, he saved the ads and dropped his résumés off in bunches once or twice a week. He used the Perly street guide that had been their first Toronto purchase to zone his deliveries, like someone dropping off flyers, junk mail destined for the nearest garbage can. He didn't tell Debbie how his real search had ended. Daytime TV, and conscientious shopping and cooking, still left plenty of time to mull over the lawyer. He was a symbol as much as a man. Of the city beyond, of smooth street threat. Sometimes his thoughts would veer from the lawyer back to the pseudo-soccer player, turning from the maybe con to the known one. How would he, Tom, have reacted to the tanned imploring face, the heavily accented tale of woe? He gave himself different answers.

Finally – it was late November now – the call came that Tom had been waiting for. He watched Debbie on the phone. 'Mm hm … yeah … right.…' He was glad she didn't agree at once, made him talk it up. 'Can you hang on while I check my schedule?' she said.

Covering the mouthpiece with her hand, she turned to him with a quizzical frown.

'He wants me to go in on Saturday, to copy and collate some documents.'

Collate? Tom thought, then he remembered.

'Do it,' he said, an idea coming to him.

She was to meet the lawyer at noon on Saturday, when the law office was closed. The collating was supposed to take an hour. Tom told her that he would pick her up at one. Present the living fact of a boyfriend, rather than just a voice taking messages. Debbie looked relieved.

On Saturday Tom got to the office ten minutes early. Debbie was waiting outside the door. Alone. 'All done?' he said. As they started walking away, they met two men coming out of a restaurant. Tom recognized one from the driver's licence he'd seen, only in better colour, with pink cheeks and wisps of blond hair fluffed by the breeze. The men were pudgy, a head shorter than Tom. They wore lawyerish beige trench coats, with crossed belts. Debbie introduced them.

'Well?' he said as they walked on. Behind him he heard a snicker, and turned to see the lawyers sharing a joke as they entered the office.

Debbie shrugged. 'It was easy. Colin and his partner left for lunch, and I finished the job in half an hour.'

'Why is he still giving you this work?' Naturally he'd asked the question before, but not for a while and not with so much force.

She shrugged again. 'He says he has to pay someone.' She glanced at him. 'He knows we need it.'

Tom felt suddenly sluggish, slow, ox-like. He felt like a large crude boat, manoeuvring awkwardly in the wake of a much lighter craft.

'Are you hungry?' he said.

Soon after that, the lawyer offered Debbie her biggest job yet. More rush copying and collating, several hundred pages' worth, which had to be done this Saturday, and paid $200, whether it took three hours or six. Debbie checked with Tom again, perfunctorily he thought. He shrugged. Whatever angle the lawyer might be working, it seemed too subtle – too fussy – to take seriously as a threat. What mainly struck him was the bogus sense of urgency the law needed to surround itself with, and the amounts of paper it generated. Forests had to be felled for a routine divorce or appeal.

The day after this arrangement was made, he finally found a job. It wasn't hard in the end. He just woke up knowing he *had* to find work. Any work. The dull deep ache of the conviction, a throb like a bruised muscle, was new to him. How long can you fart around without knowing it? he wondered.

He bought a *Star*, circled the possibilities, and began calling. After several answering machines, which he knew by now to ignore, he got a live voice and scheduled an interview. It was for a 'telephone representative', which he gathered meant sales. He took the subway and two buses to a low brick building in Markham. After a brief, irrelevant conversation, he was hired. The interviewer took him to a doorway, through which he could see seated people working headsets in a room patrolled by a chain-smoker. He was to show up Monday at 4 p.m. for training and orientation. His shift would start at five.

This was Friday. That night, though, he didn't tell Debbie his news. He wanted to hold it inside himself a little first, incubating his changed circumstances like an egg, before hatching it to her at the proper time. Unemployment turned you inside out, advertising the bare hours to anyone who cared to look. It felt good to nurse a secret of his own again.

He made supper, and soon after, Debbie, bagged by the work week, went to bed. 'You shaved,' was the last thing she said, feeling his cheek with a smile. He almost told her then.

He channel-surfed for a couple of hours, drinking Coors on the couch. Relishing the idea of a job before he had to stomach its facts.

After breakfast Debbie went to the lawyer's office. Tom shaved again. He gave the apartment a quick clean-up. Then he went out and bought two large steaks. Also salad fixings, wine, a loaf of sourdough bread. *Tonight's the night...* Neil Young hummed him home.

The afternoon seemed even longer with good news to tell. The egg crammed full of feathers and little bones, yet still bounded by the infinite thin shell. It was better when the early December dark dropped down and he could turn the lights on. He put on some blues, John Lee Hooker. 'Crawlin' Kingsnake.'

He took the steaks out of the fridge and laid the raw red slabs on adjacent plates, drizzling a marinade of soya sauce, wine and garlic over them, turning them as carefully as babies. In the pause between tracks, he heard someone buzzing the front doorbell. Leaning on it hard; they must have been trying for a while.

Downstairs, he opened the door to a deliveryman of some sort. A tall, middle-aged man with dark skin, a toque snugged low on his forehead, two large paper bags held in front of his chest. Tom couldn't make out his face very well in the cold dark of the porch. At the curb a little car was running, two wheels up on the sidewalk.

'What number is it?' Tom asked, leaning forward to see the bill stapled to the bag. This had happened before. But there was no bill.

'Nummer five,' said the man. Tom could see his face a little better now. Small black eyes like holes below the toque, pudgy brown cheeks pitted by purplish acne scars.

'I'm number five,' Tom said. 'But I didn't order anything.'

The man pushed the bags towards him. Tom kept his hands at his sides, avoiding the consensual touch. The man smiled: brown, gappy teeth.

'Is paid for. Is your food.'

'No, I'm not –' Tom started, but as he brought his hands up in a gesture of refusal, the bags got placed in them. They felt heavy. The man was walking away.

Tom shut the door and examined the bags by the dim vestibule light. Near the top of one was his address and apartment number. No name, though.

He mounted the stairs slowly. A heavy, barbecued meat smell leaked out of the bags, which felt damp. In the kitchen he opened them. Each bag held two white boxes. Two contained barbecued chicken quarters, eight in all. One had a rack of pork ribs cut in sections. The other had pieces of a small animal, a rabbit perhaps. They all exhaled the moist, sweetish fug of charred meat. There were no side orders of fries or salad or bread. Just meat.

Arrayed around the marinating steaks on the counter, the containers made up an archaic picture. He saw the remains, cooked and raw, of at least five animals. He had to close the styrofoam boxes and sit down.

He thought of the woman in Oro who came around every September and November to take Thanksgiving and Christmas orders for her free-range chickens and turkeys. She carried a clipboard and wrote down the orders. There was never any mistake. One house, one bird.

The city, though, was a confused and wasteful place. He saw this with more force than ever. It had been oppressing him, he realized. The confusion, the constant spin of possibilities. It could sap your energy or add to it. Debbie, after a frail start, seemed to be gathering strength from the muddle.

Had she ordered the food? Surprised him with it from her $200? The impulse wouldn't be like the Debbie he knew; nor would the pile of meat, ungraced by fries or greens. But did he know Debbie any more?

That – the shiver of uncertainty – brought the lawyer hovering into view as the other possibility. He had paid for the meat. Rattled off a credit card number and a list of dishes. Enough food for several people. But who was coming home to eat it with him? If Debbie and the lawyer both arrived, he had a speech ready: *You're not welcome here. Your meat can stay or you can take it, but you can't stay.* He wondered if he could deliver the phrases in a properly cool, urban tone. And if Debbie would admire, or resent, him for it.

Or maybe it was a pure mistake. An order foul-up, someone mumbling on a cellphone. Would the restaurant sort out the problem and return to claim the meat?

Each scenario grew to plausibility, like a bubble, then popped. He had no idea what had happened, and each guess seemed both reasonable and random.

While he was sitting there pondering the matter, he heard the phone ringing in the bedroom. As he hurried to get it he realized the music had stopped. He reached the phone just as it gave a last half-ring. He didn't pick it up to check. Looking at it, wondering if it would ring again, he thought of the hours of his new job. His shift would run 5 to 10:30, 6 to 9 being peak time for catching people in for telephone sales. Debbie, who worked 8 to 5, and he would be running exactly counter to each other, together only when asleep.

He looked at his watch. It was 6:05 now.

He sat down on the edge of the bed, but the phone didn't ring again.

He went back to the kitchen, aware of the first pricklings of hunger. He poked through the meat in the styrofoam boxes, picking out a chicken leg and sections of ribs. He put them on a plate. But he didn't like to look at all that meat. He turned off the overhead light, leaving just the lamp in the living-room corner. It cast long, friendly shadows. Standing at the counter, he began to gnaw at the ribs. The meat was juicy and tangy-tasting, some hot mixture of spices in the sauce. It tasted much better than he'd expected. He chewed slowly and steadily. The room got darker as he ate. He didn't turn on another light. He stood there eating patiently, not bothering to turn on another light. He tried the chicken and the 'rabbit' too. It all tasted much better than he'd expected.

Reno

Reno lived in the basement, but he'd heard that there were naked people up under the roof. Kendra told him about them. She used to rent Apartment 1, and even though Reno had picked her out over a dozen other applicants for her green eyes and roomy hips, she'd ended up driving him crazy with midnight knocks to fix things: dripping taps, wiggly doorknobs, blown fuses. She was rough on things, and despite her sexy looks, Reno wasn't sorry to see her go.

Now she lived in the attic of the house behind Reno's. She said she could look across the two backyards and see the couple in Reno's attic walking around naked.

'Stark naked,' Kendra said, wrinkling her nose with a prudishness that amused Reno. He used to lie awake on his basement cot, listening to the booms of Kendra's bed against the wall (Polyfilla'd twice already), like distant artillery thuds ending in screams and groans.

Kendra wasn't wearing much herself. Cutoffs with frayed hems feathering her thighs, a scoop-neck lime-green tank top that showed the slope of milky breasts and, in a band of midriff, a pouty little navel. It was her get-Reno-to-do-something outfit – a clogged drain this time – and it went with a Little-Bo-Peep voice dissing her present super and lamenting the whim that had driven her from Reno's good graces. Reno knew of course he was being puppet-played, his waning sixty-seven-year-old lusts pandered to, but watching Kendra stroll away, her buttocks bobbling like a juggler's weighted balls, he didn't consider himself *under*paid.

An old fool. It was the one accusation all his wives had agreed on, the one that rolled off him easiest and that he disputed least. There were worse things....

Kendra plied him with liquor too – catering to his other known vice – though he had to finish the chore first to get it. This time she let him take home half a mickey of Jack Daniel's, which he swigged out in the April sunshine, playing ball hockey in the parking lot with some neighbourhood cats.

Another former tenant, a law student who let off steam with weekend shinny, had left behind three old sticks, the blades worn down to stubby scythes. Reno slapped at a fuzzy old tennis ball, caroming it off the tool shed and the fence and the maple tree that reared up beside the house, while the cats, pets from the neighbourhood that mostly ran wild, darted around after it. Sometimes Reno, getting rambunctious, would slap or spear their furry sides, plump with mice and birds and garbage scraps, and get scratched on the calves in return, his pants ripping over trickles of blood, man yowls and cat yowls mingling in high-spirited fun ... while at windows in the surrounding houses neighbours would appear, shake their heads, swing away....

The way Reno liked to drink – and he supposed he was an alcoholic, without stopping long on the thought – was to lay down a haze around his thoughts and then stay at that level, a kind of mist he could wander about in, bumping soft-edged things. He hadn't married until forty-five and then had tried it three times, three quick pulls of the bandit in a fun, though overpriced, casino. The three wives had been married before too, and all of them knew how to get off a Greyhound that was stalled. Though Reno sometimes wondered what they'd expected from a middle-aged bachelor whose two longest jobs had been as school custodian and Sears security guard. In the early days they'd liked his easy ways, the trick he'd learned of letting life come sidling to him rather than chasing after it. But soon after, *low-key* had been downgraded to *lazy*, to *weak* ... to *an old fool.* Eight dollars an hour Reno's top lifetime wage, yet he denied himself nothing: these simple habits and pleasures going, in the wives' eyes, from marvellous to pitiful in a bunny skip.

Reno guessed the ladies – the word, with distance, hiding its sting in a talcumed grandeur – had needed him as a break, a pause in their busy lives. Two had remarried, professional men, one of whom had obligingly died of a coronary soon after. All three kept vaguely in touch, through occasional late-night phone calls when both parties were in their cups. They talked to Reno as to someone they'd met on a cruise somewhere, bonded by a once-shared ease that threatened to dissolve without occasional updates. They'd had a pleasant interlude together, which had only turned sour when they tried to extend it into daily life.

Reno could appreciate the need for a temperamental counterpoint. Why else did *he* stock the building with young go-getters: students, professionals on the start-up, house-scrimping couples? The landlord – averagely shrewd, but busy and preoccupied – shaking his head that they couldn't fill up the place with good cash-cow retirees or long-term wage slaves. Types which applied in droves; Reno turned them politely away. The truth was, it rested Reno – further rested him – to be among citizens on the move. He was like a drowsy, suited-up beekeeper, working at a tenth the speed of the clouds around him, soothed by and separated from the humming. Or maybe – he'd considered this – he just needed a certain minimum of activity to focus on, or else he might drift off one night for good. *Corpse Found with Coors in a La-Z-Boy!*

One sunny afternoon in May, Reno was sitting on a lawn chair in the parking lot, after a short but zesty scrimmage with the cats. The felines were still frisking about, their energies not yet exhausted. 'Dig in there, Isis! Don't let him run you off!' he called to the ginger kitten, who was being bullied off the ball by the larger tabby. Not knowing the cats' true names, Reno gave them his own: monikers like Bossman, Spice Girl, Aladdin, Mr Universe, which, since they didn't answer to any of them, he could change at will, as the mood took him.

Lounging there, he thought of what Kendra had told him about the upstairs couple. *Bare-ass. Letting it all hang out.* Reno had forgotten the story soon after hearing it – flushed it away with the rest of Kendra's snarled drain – but now it came bubbling back at him. He glanced up at Kendra's window across the yards, where he'd been known to catch his own spicy flash. Nothing: the blinds snugged down. Reno felt a soft deep tug in his groin, like a tap root jarred. Good luck, bud, he thought.

Kendra had a relaxed relationship with the truth (not unlike his own), but Reno had never caught her in a bald lie. Nor could he think of a reason why she'd lie here. Still, it was hard to match the nudist-camp scenario with the skinny, strait-laced couple on the top floor. Math students at U of T, they had bitten-down fingernails and rode mountain bikes from March to November, quick-stepping in the winter months. The man had the same close-shorn black beard as the landlord, like a facial glove, and his girlfriend had long stringy hair stiffened with gel. They kept to themselves, leaving the house early and returning after dark. On Hallowe'en Reno was surprised when they came down to the front step to help him hand out candy. They sat on either side of Reno's jack-o'-lantern, jumping up to pass out the treats, but – this was what floored Reno – in between visits they worked on a school assignment, pens scratching at pages of signs and numbers. 'No need to stay ... I've got it covered,' offered Reno, but they shook their heads soberly. They had a duty to their homework *and* the kids, it seemed. Reno had got a kick out of it.

Letting it all hang out? This time, he thought, Kendra had stretched it to the snapping point. He went in to get another beer.

A couple of weeks later, on a Saturday, without having visited him in the meantime, the question tapped at Reno again. The circumstances were the same: Reno and the cats, a bright May day; the only difference being that everything had itched a little further into spring. Maybe it was the sun, beating a little higher and hotter, or the cats rubbing themselves languidly against fence posts, but the idea of nakedness near the roof came back to him with a little more juice, nudging him closer to action. Each of Reno's mysteries got dumped into the equivalent of a jumbled mental closet or fridge, somewhere so cluttered that by the time it surfaced again it had turned into junk or a godsend. This rumour felt like a bit of both.

Yawning, he decided to settle it. He'd never got around to cleaning the refuse out of the eavestroughs last fall; rain fell off the house in sheets. The big old maple that grew next to the house sent out branches that grazed the roof. It made for a solider perch than a ladder for roof or eaves work, or, now, in a cloud of new leaves, to hide. Reno also remembered the dead branch that the landlord nagged him about. A measly thing, but the absentee owner saw peril in it. He'd take the saw up too with his garbage bag: two excuses usually better than one, unless they cancelled out.

Recalling that Saturday was also the one day the mathematicians took it easy, seldom appearing at street level before suppertime, Reno felt events coalesce graciously.

Five minutes later, working quietly but not suspiciously so, he had the aluminum ladder extended up against the tree, and was up in the roomy crotch with his Glad bag and saw. The ginger kitten jumped up after him, its claws scratching on the shaggy bark. Reno looked down at the curious white-whiskered face, tried to frown it back. But after a moment it seemed to realize that this was a purely human errand, and jumped down. The three cats slouched mewing around the base of the tree.

The maple had any number of thick, sloping branches and, for a reasonably spry senior citizen, posed no problem to climb. Reno got himself up to level with the attic apartment's rear window, just off to one side. He put a justificatory hand out towards the eavestrough, while peering down the length of the apartment. Nothing he could see yet contradicted Kendra.

The mathematicians were surprisingly sloppy housekeepers. Newspapers and laundry littered the floor, dirty plates on the coffee table. Green plants, ferns and spider plants in need of watering, hung from the ceiling in macramé baskets.

At the far end of the living room, framed by the bedroom doorway, two pairs of calves and feet were moving in a lazy rhythm on a mattress, one pair of legs inside the other. The inside legs stayed tight together and slid in slow kicks back and forth. Meanwhile the outer legs, bowed to accommodate them, curled and arched. Reno, watching, thought of frogs hopping; he thought of cats rubbing. Curiously, he did not think of people, or even animals, mating. That was just the end result. Ants building. Moths flapping.

It went on so long that Reno actually did stuff a few handfuls of mucky black leaves and twigs in his bag. He stood on a thick branch, his arm around another. He peered through a froth of foliage that smelled tangily fresh and clean. If he inched ahead he would be able to saw through the dead stick that hovered above the roof and absurdly worried the landlord.

Meanwhile the languid fucking in the bedroom continued. The feet and lower legs slid and curled. Reno, wanting to see more, got bored with what little he could see. He kept looking away; at the houses to either side, behind him at Kendra's room. He counted on seeing a final jerk or stiffening, maybe a kick, but he missed even that, because suddenly, a naked man was walking towards him. Reno almost dropped his bag in shock.

The bearded mathematician, skinny and hairy as an underfed ape, strolled towards Reno, scratching the balls below a pink shrinking pecker. Reno put his face partly behind leaves – a delicate balance, working *and* hiding – but the man turned into the washroom.

A few moments later his mate emerged from the bedroom.

Reno watched her with interest. He felt curiosity and a mild, rashy kind of lust. Curiosity, mainly. He favoured plumpish women, and this girl's build was almost as bony as her man's; only less hairy, and with small pointy breasts and a concave matted crotch.

She walked slowly toward the window – *Kendra's right*, Reno thought, as if the situation were evidence merely – and stopped just in front of it. Reno could still see most of her. She stood amid her hanging ferns and spider plants; Reno crouched in his cloud of leaves. He'd already missed his chance to make a noisy show of working, and he couldn't believe she hadn't spotted him. The sun was slanting in her eyes, though – the swath of light that gave Reno such unfettered sight. Or maybe she did see him. Three marriages hadn't revealed much of the female essence to Reno, but one thing he had been convinced of was woman's essential slyness, a guileful subtlety unapproximated by men. Her hand came up and she scratched under one breast in a natural-seeming way. There was a mole near the nipple.

A toilet flushed – Reno's knees wobbling on his perch – and the man came out and stood beside her. They looked out together – straight out at Kendra's, Reno peering in from the side. Their hips and shoulders almost touched.

Adam and Eve, Reno thought, with a fuzzy blooming warmth that reminded him he'd had his quota of beers so watch his step. Once he'd been on his way to the corner Mac's to pick up the landlord's Lotto tickets, when he saw a squint-eyed midget walk by – by and under – a girl from St. Vincent's, just as a gust of wind flipped up the hem of her plaid skirt. Reno recalled the midget's sly and grateful look now, because he figured he must be wearing a similar one.

Many things happened at once just then. A meow came from somewhere close by, startling Reno. He dropped his bag of gunk, heard it plop on the parking lot concrete. Confused, he reached out his saw toward the dead branch. But he leaned too far – the beer, his knees, sixty-seven years, everything, plus peeping-Tom chagrin – and had to grab at the branch to stop himself.

The branch broke. Snapped with a dry click. Reno fell.

It all took only a few seconds, and Reno didn't know, at the moment he started falling, whether his naked, spied-on tenants had even seen him yet. Throwing out his arms he clutched wildly. He got something firm with each of them, grabbed hold for dear life.

The saw hit the concrete below with a wavery Chinese twang.

Reno was suspended awkwardly three stories above, hung between the eavestrough and a branch like an old ape paralysed in mid-swing. His skinny old arms trembled with the strain. He kicked his legs feebly a couple of times. That was a funny feeling, kicking air.

Would the mathematicians – violated but duty-bound (Reno hoped) – be fast enough to haul him in before his slack arms gave out? Could they even reach him?

Time, though very short, stretched long. Thoughts sparked in his lazy mind.

He closed his eyes.

An old fool.

Opened them. Leaves. Sky. Bits of houses.

The thought that Kendra might look out and see him dangling made him grimace in embarrassment, twist his mouth up in a panicked grin. Behind him the kitten mewed again, but he didn't dare turn far enough to see her little pointed face.

Doctors

Scalpel

Now it was Thanksgiving and Cate and her grandpa were sitting on the porch on Mill Street, waiting for the knife sharpener to arrive. He comes on holidays because that is when most people will be home and needing sharper knives for whatever they're cooking. Grandma Sterne calls him a lazy Italian. Grandma's house makes Cate think a little bit of school and a bit of her birthday. Somebody was always trying to tell you something – that was the school part – but if you waited long enough you might get a nice surprise. A candy kiss. A goldfish in a bag.

Like the old grey-and-brown horse, with big shiny eyes that bulged, a sunken back, and long grey prickly whiskers – Grandma called him a *nag* – that pulled the milk truck up Mill Street. She'd seen that one morning when they visited for breakfast. A milk truck with a horse. She'd never seen that before. Her dad told her Hamilton was too big to have them any more and Waterdown wouldn't for much longer. Not because it was small. Just because. 'Because it's 1969,' her dad finally answered. With a big silly grin that made her slap him, something she couldn't do if her mom was watching. The red mark on his cheek felt warm.

The milkman came up the walk with his white bottle. He patted her head and said 'Hi, Doc' to her grandpa, who nodded and smiled. Cate watched the horse out on the street. He never stopped walking, but it was the slowest kind of walking she'd ever seen. It looked like his four big feet were lifting in slow motion, in one spot almost, yet this motion carried him forward. By the time the milkman had taken the empty bottle from beside the front door and left the full one, mussed her hair again and made another joke to her grandpa, the horse had pulled the milk truck to about even with the middle of the next lawn.

Cate ran after the milkman. She skipped down the steps with the apple she'd half eaten. The milkman turned at the sound of her clickety heels. He looked over her shoulder at the little window above Grandpa. That was where Grandma's face was most likely to appear.

'Did you ask like a good girl?' said the milkman.

Cate nodded yes.

'You're a new little girl. I haven't seen you before,' the milkman said.

Cate knew why too, but she wouldn't say. He must bring milk on weekdays, and usually they visited on weekends and on holidays. Christmas, Easter, Mother's Day, Thanksgiving. But today was Grandma's birthday and her dad was on call that night. All that veered through Cate's mind like bright bats and she decided how much of it the milkman needed to see: none of it.

'All right then, hold your hand out flat,' he told her. 'Don't curl your fingers when he pushes down. He might bite them right *off.*'

The horse had stopped now but his feet were still lifting. The milkman held his collar. Cate held out her hand, palm up, with the half-eaten apple on it. It looked like a giant apple on a little plate. She could see her teeth marks in the white flesh and red skin. Her hand was steady, the milkman noticed. Sometimes even the older boys got nervous.

The horse's nostrils flared, his head jerked upwards. Cate saw him shiver, a ripple under his skin, even though it wasn't cold. Then the head – big as a cooler – dropped down to her held-out palm. Cate felt the prickle of his whiskers, then slubbery wetness as the thick tongue sloshed her hand, pushing it back down. She watched the horse chew gnashingly, his lower jaw slipping sideways. She saw big yellow teeth, and white froth, mixed with apple bits, bubbling out. Some of the froth was on her hand. It looked like dish soap. She rubbed her wet hand on the side of her dress.

'What's his name?' she asked the milkman.

'This old boy?' said the milkman, laying a hand on the horse's wide brown neck. 'Doesn't need one, do you boy?' He smiled down at Cate, who looked back at him. 'Glue, maybe,' he said. The milkman chuckled to himself. 'Just about, eh, old boy? Okay, then. Glue.'

Cate looked down at her shiny black patent leather shoes. She knew Glue wasn't his name. Glue was stupid. The milkman was stupid.

Something fell with a splat behind the horse. In the shadow before the truck Cate saw a pancake of lumpy brown pooh, flecked with yellow bits.

'Mind your manners,' the milkman said. 'Ladies present.'

'He likes you,' he told Cate. 'Feed him again, if you want. Just ask your grandma first, all right? Come on ... Glue.'

Cate ran up the steps. The milkman was stupid. The horse's heavy head had startled but not frightened her. It had dropped like a heavy box into her hands. A filled box, with soft brown, slightly fuzzy sides.

Her grandpa was waiting with one of his scrapbooks open. He was nodding and smiling. A week ago she'd started kindergarten, but she'd been playing school for years with her three older brothers. *Go stand in the corner. Put out your hand.* Real school had naps, milk and cookies. A plump, white-haired teacher, Mrs Robson, who cried at songs and fights. Cate wasn't sure yet if she liked it as much.

She knelt down by her grandpa's chair. He had a basement, or a closet, smell. He smelled like cough syrup, and something else she couldn't name. Slowly, one at a time, he turned the crackly yellowed pages, thick with glued-in pictures, waiting for the one he'd choose. Men running, a race. Groups of people, dressed up. Army men. A big boat. He stopped at a picture. He laid a wrinkled finger, like a fat lined stem, on the page. Cate looked.

Two statues. Sand. He'd picked an easy one.

'Egypt,' she squealed, so loudly she surprised herself.

Her grandpa smiled a bit, and nodded slowly. Which didn't mean yes necessarily, it just meant Grandpa. She had to make up her own mind if she was right or not. She was, she decided.

'Something's got to be done, that's all I know,' Mrs Sterne said as she ran water into a pot filled with peeled and quartered potatoes. Her daughter-in-law, Lucy, was peeling carrots at the counter beside the sink. *Riding shotgun,* was how she thought of it.

'Something's got to be done about him,' Mrs Sterne shouted over the gush and hiss of water. Others might have turned the water off to make their point, but Mrs Sterne wanted you to know that this *and* this were her afflictions. No responsibility made way for another, they just piled on. She banged the pot of potatoes and water onto an element and opened the oven door to check on the turkey, which was fine.

'What's he done now?' Lucy asked. She had to wait until Mrs Sterne was done fussing at the stove and had turned to face her again. The candid-seeming lurches of their conversations were due mainly to Lucy's never having found a comfortable way to address her mother-in-law. To avoid using her name, she had to wait for the moments when they were facing each other. 'Call me Mom,' Mrs Sterne had said when she and Dick had moved in. That was fourteen years ago; they'd been married just two weeks, but Dick was beginning his residency in anaesthesiology and they had no money. Dr Sterne – whom she already called 'Dad', just copying Dick – was still working then as a janitor at Stelco. But 'Mom' had never felt right; she'd only tried it once or twice. 'Alice' was never offered. And after a while 'Mrs Sterne' seemed too cold. Lucy had pushed Dick – who, after some initial awkwardness, seemed comfortable in his old bedroom, able to eat his mother's cooking and sleep with his new wife – to borrow the down payment on a house in Hamilton. 'You're a straightforward girl. That's good,' Mrs Sterne told Lucy one day shortly before they moved out, her pale blue eyes sparking, in one of their brief face-to-faces. *Lying on both counts*, Lucy thought, while lowering her eyes to murmur 'Thank you.' She never underestimated Mrs Sterne when it came to details. She might ignore the big picture, but she would never miss a speck of dust on the frame.

'Done?' Mrs Sterne's eyes popped in surprise. She could never believe her trials were not self-evident to every other consciousness. 'He's drinking again,' she said as she opened the fridge door and rummaged clankingly among the bottles.

Lucy didn't consider the charge seriously. Her father-in-law had never *drunk*, no more than most men drink. He sipped his afternoon beers and enjoyed his glasses of wine with dinner. A year ago, when Dick – unconvinced, but acquiescing to his mother's tearful pleas – had gone over to empty the house of every last bottle, anything that might tempt an *alcoholic* – including some dusty, unhidden and untouched sherry bottles in the basement – his father hadn't protested. No one had expected him to. He hadn't said anything in several years. A silence that hadn't struck anyone, even his wife, very forcefully, it was so gradual and inevitable. He'd been a strange, elderly man who seldom spoke when Lucy first met him. Now he was a strange, old man who never spoke. There hadn't been a turnaround, only a progression. A deepening channel or groove.

No drama, Lucy thought, scraping the carrots. *You've had to make up in melodrama for what you missed in drama.* Considering her dislike of her mother-in-law – 'Dick's *mother*,' she would moan, rolling her eyes, when her neighbours, other doctors' wives, came over for coffee and

Sara Lee cheesecake – it was surprising how often she thought of her, and how often those thoughts took the form of sympathetic recognition. Lucy liked that she couldn't recognize her husband; his unknowable *difference* was a blessing to cling to, a kind of anchor. If she could ever fully predict and understand Dick's reactions – and, with time, she *was* getting better at it – she thought it might make her scream.

'How do you know?' she said, when Mrs Sterne had closed the fridge door and was facing her again, jar of Bick's pickles in hand.

'Lucy.' Dick's blue eyes – but paler and sharper, in veiny pouches in a small woman's face – stared up at her in reproach. 'We've been married fifty-four years.'

They stood side by side at the double sinks. Mrs Sterne held each carrot Lucy handed her under the stream of water, then shook it dry and placed it on the cutting board to her left. She had a way of drawing out simple tasks while appearing to be overburdened, which might, Lucy had considered, be her natural manner or else the solution to the too-simple routines of looking after one silent and undemanding man to the age of thirty-nine and then one well-behaved child. Nothing took long enough. The window above the sink looked out into the sunny October yard. Dick was throwing a football to the three boys, waving and calling patterns at them as they scrambled about, competing for his pass. The passes went to either side of the hawthorn tree, which stood like a gorgeously useless, red-and-yellow lineman. The grass shone a fresh, wet green. The leaves Dick had raked earlier stood in a glossy mound in one corner.

'How's Richard's appetite these days?' Mrs Sterne gave a mirthless chuckle. 'Craigie's I'm not worried about.'

Lucy kept her eyes on her boys. What Mrs Sterne was alluding to made many people ask about triplets. Richard was small for his age and Craig was big-boned and plump, making them both about Danny's size. She'd had them bing, bing, bing. Thirty-four months from first to last. Then, four and a half blurry years later, just as Craig was about to start school, Cate came along. Where Craig was bold, bluntly pressing for advantage, Richard was timid. Timid and talented. He ran at arm's length from the swiftly spiralling ball, which sometimes resulted in miraculous, leaping and one-handed, catches. Danny was middle-child steady, a bit blank and cipherish. Now bossy, now bossed. Neither change in status seeming to affect him much.

'How would he get it?' Lucy asked. 'Dad doesn't leave the house now, does he?'

'No, of course not. Not in eight blessed years,' Mrs Sterne said, spacing the last three words precisely.

Lucy watched the football game in the gleaming yard. A soft gang tackle in wet grass.

'How then, do you think?'

'That's a puzzle.' Risking a sideways glance Lucy saw her mother-in-law's eyes brighten, her mouth purse. She'd had it with mysteries, craved only puzzles now.

'Our bell-ringer?'

Again that pop-eyed surprise.

'The knife sharpener. An *Italian*.'

It had never alarmed Lucy to think of her father-in-law as strange, and lately, probably senile. But now the thought that Mrs Sterne might be insane slid up her spine like an icy drug.

'You can't have any idea what it's been like for me. No one can.' Mrs Sterne's low, singsong lament meant that she was comfortable; she lapsed into it rarely. 'I married a man I thought was a doctor. But he turned into a janitor. Like something out of a fairy tale.' Cool fingers flicked out to graze Lucy's arm. 'I'm glad you'll never know it. You wouldn't have a clue what I'm talking about, dear. Thank God.'

No? Lucy thought. Putting people to sleep. That's not exactly a real doctor, is it? Not quite. But it would be too cruel to voice such a thought. Like complaining of your small snack to someone who is starving.

Cate heard the bell before she saw the man who was ringing it. A crisp, round jangling that took her off her knees by Grandpa's chair and out to the edge of the porch. Far down the street, at the end of an arched corridor of orange and yellow, a little man was walking slowly toward them. He held one arm behind him, like he was pulling a wagon. Cate couldn't see what it was yet. His other hand swung his bell, back and forth, in slow arcs.

A man up the street came down off his porch and the bell-ringer stopped by his walk. Cate's mom came out the door. 'How's my little afterthought?' she smiled. Cate pulled out the hem of her yellow dress and dipped in a curtsey, black shoes crossing glossily below pale, stick-like legs. She turned again to watch the bell-ringer.

'Hi, Dad.' Lucy put a hand on his shoulder, feeling bone under the worn Viyella shirt. His finger was still on the picture like a wrinkled stem. Lucy bent down. *The Colossi of Memnon* she read below it, the letters printed in neat black fountain pen ink, half a century ago. She saw two huge stone figures, crumbling at the face and elsewhere, seated on thrones. Amenhotep? Lucy thought. When she'd come to live here on Mill Street, she'd taken an interest in the scrapbooks that her father-in-law pored over – not constantly then, not permanent lap companions, but far too often for his wife. After a few pages of wedding photos and shots in his new army uniform, the troop ship at the docks – all of which seemed preliminary – the pages began to fill with a profusion of pictures of old runners and races – Tom Longboat was one, she remembered ... and then Egypt. Egypt, Egypt, Egypt. Temples, statues, sand, columns. Sphinxes. All labelled in the neat black script. Only a few soldiers, funnily enough. Mostly standing grinning beside the monuments, to give scale she supposed. But no soldiers in beds, bandaged men, half-men, even though Gallipoli was happening nearby and the medical corps was receiving shipments of its casualties daily. No nurses.

Lucy had been interested by it. But frowns and mutterings from around her had informed her that interest was not welcome. This was not a pastime to encourage, only to tolerate. It was an offence somehow. An insult. But to whom? Dick's feelings had long since lapsed into a permanent mild embarrassment, the slight dip in his voice whenever he said 'my father'.

'Can I take our knives out to him?' Cate, her clear-eyed daughter, was looking up at her. Her bent knees looking like she wanted to spring, to run.

'Ask Grandma,' Lucy said.

Cate made her 'monkey lips' face, which could mean anything she wanted it to mean and usually meant nothing at all. Just a bunched tightness in her mouth that could make grownups laugh or frown.

'Go now,' Lucy said, and Cate sprang to the door in a cricket leap.

Lucy looked down at the tanned dome of skull nodding below her. Brown and smooth, rimmed with a crescent of grey fuzz. It *looked* the way it had for fifteen years – for twenty, thirty years, according to photos – but Lucy guessed there *was* something new happening inside it now. Not just a deepening – of silence, of immobility, of inwardness – but a skewing too. An addling. She had friends who said they found bald sexy – almost always women whose husbands *were* bald – but she was glad for Dick's shock of thick red hair. It swept up from his sharp features in a way thrillingly like posters of Peter O'Toole. Bald was *companionable*, though. Lucy had always been totally comfortable with Doc. She was fond of his mild brown eyes – moist like chestnuts just pried from their casing – and of his long, unstrained silences. Part of her comfort was a certainty that she would never, could never, end up marrying a man like him. Much as she liked being *around* him, she couldn't quite deny a creeping contempt for any woman who would be *with* him.

'Okay, Dad?' She patted the hard ridge of shoulder. The slow nodding of his head, like the vibration of an idling motor, didn't alter or stop.

'*Yes*, darling?' her grandma said sharply, shocked by the sudden little face looking up at her. She spent her days in a kind of muttering somnambulism – *Can't cope with this, He's got to go somewhere* – and occasionally woke up to these plain, intolerable sights – man nodding in a chair, granddaughter's curious amber eyes – that made her gasp and almost clutch her heart.

'Mom said to get some knives. For the man.'

'The – oh, the Italian. Why didn't you say so? Stand up straight, Cate.' Sticky webs of dream began to drag her under again. She yanked a drawer open hard, all its length, and brought out a shallow cardboard box of knives. She shook the box; the blades clanked dully together. 'Here. Take these to ... your grandfather.' *Doc,* she almost said.

Cate looked up at her with bright, flinty eyes. Held out her hands for the box. Terribly *keen* eyes, Mrs Sterne thought with a comfortable, sinking fury. Grey-bright, streaked with yellow and gold. Like rock, like quartz. When she cried – which was seldom, and then softly and steadily – they were pebbles glinting in a clear, cold stream.

'Go on, now.' Cate hopped away. The poor little thing seemed to be trying to skip.

And then, without further distraction or delay, Mrs Sterne fell swiftly down into her half-century-old plot, gnashing and flailing. *Getting to be too much … too much for one person to handle* – when in reality things were getting to be too little, slipping below a threshold of necessary response. The too-little she'd had to deal with for so long was dwindling down to zero, the dark core of her nightmare.

And it *was* interesting, Lucy told herself as she walked down the flag-stone path beside the brick house, passing the two fanned trellises where Doc's roses, untended for years, still climbed in summer. Gardening had been his hobby, his one hobby really, discounting TV sports and his scrapbook.

And silence … as pruned and well-tended as a garden. Doc – his steel company nickname – the one word Mrs Sterne couldn't stand to hear. He was well liked, as any mild and faithful man is appreciated at work. Doc-*ter*, Mrs Sterne always said when she couldn't avoid the word. *She went to the doc*-ter. Giving it an odd, foreign twist.

A man leaving for war as a new MD – just graduated, just married – and returning to work as a janitor. Thirty-six years, until he retired at sixty-five. 'Shellshock' was the only explanation Lucy had ever heard – though not from Mrs Sterne – for the dramatic about-face. But there was a dismaying lack of visible trauma to support this view. Dad seemed tranquil enough. Maybe a little bent. But not broken. Not shocked. Not even surprised, actually.

So what had happened, really? He had stopped … stayed?

Turned?

The war, people said. Or, more occultly, *Egypt*. But maybe that was just where it happened. Where and when. It was not more, or less, accurate than the way people said *the weather* to account for major swings in public or private mood.

A story. With a firm beginning, a long dull middle, and a fuzzy but certainly approaching end. A key piece missing. Something that would lock it all into place. Secretly, Lucy hoped no one ever found it. She was pretty sure they wouldn't, that maybe there was nothing *to* find.

The rush of sound around her – the intermittent, clanging bell, nearer now, the shouts from the backyard – made her happy and hungry for more stories.

*Bring 'em on. The weirder and wilder the better. Hairy, messy ones.
Ones that never end.*

'Catch, Mom!' she heard, and got her arm up fast enough to deflect the
hard stinging leather.

She walked to where it lay in the grass, picked it up, and, after a
feinted calm, drilled it in a perfect hard spiral at Craig's soft – Mrs Sterne
right again – belly. He folded up over the impact like a cushioned lawn
chair, sat down with a thud.

'Mom!' Richard and Danny, secretly pleased.

'Luce!' Dick.

She delighted in giving them these little shocks. Last week she'd taken
a pan of brownies they'd been complaining about and dumped it on the
floor beside their black Lab, Jenny, who'd popped her own rheumy eyes
before starting to gobble.

The boys chuckling now, plotting revenge. Dick coming to her side
with a concerned look that was already evaporating. It was one of the
things she loved about him, the fleetingness of his power to fret. In some
way she didn't care to examine closely, it reassured her. The Sandman
was *his* obvious nickname at the hospital. *Sweet dreams*, she imagined
crush-ridden nurses murmuring behind the handsome, languid
redhead who put people to sleep.

'How's Dad?' he asked.

Lucy shrugged, nodded. *Ischemia*, Dick said, when the question of
his father came up. *Transient cerebral incidents ... vascular interruptions*,
he said, then *little spells*, as if she hadn't been married to a doctor all
these years. He offered these phrases at intervals – *shellshock* too, a relic
of his pre-medical boyhood – as if injecting them into a mystery that
threatened to jar awake. Lucy thought that he hadn't learned anaesthesia so much as perfected it. And he was still the only one she wanted.

The subject came up more often lately, now that his mother was
phoning nearly every night. 'We'll place him, Mom ... we'll get him
placed,' he told her. And Lucy was surprised Mrs Sterne didn't know her
son well enough to have confidence in him. When the time was right he
would push the plunger.

Often Dick rehearsed the diagnostic possibilities – in 1969 people
didn't reach for Alzheimer's automatically – after they'd made love and

could consider things with a detached calm. Their sex, which happened usually when they woke up together, as if synchronized, in the middle of the night, was mostly oral and always, still, intense. Lucy loved to suck on a spike at the centre of him while he juddered and moaned. Then he buried his face in her, lapped at her expertly. They came with glad shrieks that sometimes woke the children. *Cock-a-doodle-doo,* they kidded after settling them.

Cate carried the small knife down to the man waiting at the foot of the walk. He had dark skin and a stubble of grey whiskers, a cloth cap pulled down low. He made her think of the milkman's horse; she liked him better than the milkman. He took the knife from her and then the dollar bill she handed him. He pushed the dollar into his pocket and held up the knife to inspect it. Then he stepped beside the thing he dragged. It had two rubber wheels on the ground, a ladder of metal, and a stone wheel with a handle at the top. It was like a strange, three-wheeled wagon that he'd tipped up into the air. Cate stepped closer to see better. But he held out his arm and pushed her lightly back. When he turned the handle and held the knife to the stone, blue-white sparks sprayed out in a brief fountain of light. Then the other side of the blade. He handed the knife back to Cate, handle-first. With a wave at the porch he walked slowly on. He never said a word to her, and she liked that fine.

Back up on the porch, her grandpa did a funny thing. He closed his scrapbook and lowered it to the table beside him. Usually Grandma had to take it from him; sometimes she had to tug it out of his hands, which shook but were still strong. They trembled until they found what they were looking for, then they clutched. He took the knife Cate was holding out to him and he held it up in the air, as the bell-man had. Cate saw pretty white lines along the blade, etchings from the wheel, that made her think of sun rays scratched into stone.

Grandpa used his fumbly hands to position her between his knees. She felt them, bony, against her sides. Like he was riding her, almost. This was different but she didn't mind.

She did feel a little thrill of fright when he grabbed her by the ponytail, then realized he just wanted her to be still. She looked into his filmy brown eyes as he nodded: *All right. All right, now.* She heard the words inside her head. From outside she heard the bright, well-spaced rings of the bell.

Out of the corner of her eye she caught a flash, a scratch, of light, and saw a brown, unshaking hand. Not her grandpa's.

Mrs Sterne was watching out the porthole window beside the door, wiping her hands, which weren't wet, on her apron. She saw her husband fumbling in the box of knives, all of which were dull as sin. She saw him select a paring knife and hand it to the girl.

Imposter, she said under her breath. It was one of the recurring words of her half-century nightmare. Unhitched from actuality, the word was free to roam and haunt, slurring its sticky accusation over one man's face then another's. Who was the imposter? The small, lean, dapper man in uniform she'd married, with his soft brown hair and doctor's future. His eagerly considerate hands those first few nights together. Or the small, lean, dapper man in uniform who'd returned to her in 1919. Balding when he took his cap off. And not very different at night either, only a little shyer and more tentative. Though she didn't often let him after he became a janitor. When her doctor – after a spell of quiet sitting, which all the veterans were granted as a courtesy – hitched a ride to Hamilton one afternoon and came back as 'Doc'.

Or the man who wrote her letters from across the world, pages of neat writing that she read as code inside of ordinariness. They were not quite letters, since they were pages from his diary folded inside the briefest of affectionate notes to her. Getting news of him this way, she was troubled faintly by a perception of economy and indirection in their new marriage. *Arrived Alexandria. A hospital ship unloading wounded made do as a Welcome Wagon ... Hard to believe that I am greeting the new year in Egypt ... 'It's sure hell down there': Even the worst patients from Cape Helles find breath to say that ... 9 operations this morning. Ewert nearly killed the first man and had trouble with the other 8 ... Went to the museum. The statues etc. are very fine, the mummies very much as described ... Walked all day. Played cards most of night.*

What she especially resented – and resentment could be ravenous as a shark some days, big enough to swallow disappointment and shame and confusion, every other feeling – was the homelessness he'd forced her into. Other girls had dead husbands, new beaus, returned men, healthy or crippled. There was every shade of powerful feeling, from grief to joy to mixed relief, to festering bitterness. More than reason enough for any of these. But she had a man, passably like her husband, and well enough, who'd returned to her. What emotion was hers to rightfully inhabit? In another era she might have become an obsessive reader of fantasy fiction, seeing her own life in its devious, trivial warpings of time and reality.

Imposter.

He must've seen some terrible things. Too sensitive to be a doctor. Friends murmured solacing suggestions. Which she'd had to accept graciously, while uttering to herself private reservations. *Just because terrible things are happening around you doesn't mean you see them.* And: *Maybe not sensitive enough.*

Another spirit had invaded her husband's body (leaving her this alien, this imposter), and not being able to seize the interloper, which she would crush if she could, she must hate the body that had offered itself as host, moved aside meekly, surrendering its own claim.

A single, high-pitched scream had just split the air when she turned to walk back to the kitchen.

༄

Cate's *accident.* After a brief period when it wasn't mentioned at all, it would always be referred to in this way. One of those reliable, starred days in the human calendar.

Lucy sat on the edge of Cate's bed, watching her sleep. The white mound of bandage on her temple seemed to pulse with a sinister life of its own, a white heartbeat that contracted in Lucy's eyes and then blew out large, the little girl's face a dot in its glare. She felt herself winding up again. Dick had phoned a while ago to say that after he'd looked in on Dad an emergency had come in, and was she okay for a few more hours? Of course, she'd said, her biggest lie in ages. Dick was in control now, in gear. Had been ever since he'd pried her bloody fingers from Cate's temple to announce, 'Superficial ... thank God.' 'It's superficial,' he said, and she hated him. That's when she'd lost it and raised her hand to swing at Doc, nodding in his chair, ruby-tipped blade still in his hand. *Kill him.* Not even the glimpse of the three pale faces cowering below the porch slowed her. Only Dick – who was everywhere suddenly, a hyper-awake Sandman – had caught her wrist on the downswing. Cate had already stopped crying. Such a good, brave girl. Lucy heard laughter, high barks or bleats of sound, that slid quickly into a deep, oboe-like sobbing.

Mrs Sterne, who hadn't gone to the hospital on either trip, took her time putting away the uneaten Thanksgiving dinner. There was an entire turkey to slice, cool, wrap and refrigerate, for starters. It was after eight before she'd finished.

Dick was good about phoning. First about Cate: just three stitches, and not as near her eye as the blood had made it appear. Then about his dad, who would stay on the psychiatric observation ward long enough for them to place him. Dick said the words *place him* very slowly, made sure she heard them clearly. 'I'll make the arrangements, Mother,' he said. Fine, fine, she told him. The last time he'd called was to ask her if she wanted him to drop by with something to help her sleep.

After that day, she told him, I'm dead on my feet.

Though after her work in the kitchen was finished, she did permit herself a medicinal glass of the wine Dick had brought. A room *could* be more silent if you subtracted a silent man. That was her first surprise. Blinking, hearing the clock tick and the furnace come on in the basement, she imagined more surprises up ahead, waiting for her.

She had a few more sips of wine. A non-drinker mostly, she felt it tweaking, not settling her.

Dear little thing. After a pause Cate's face swam up to go with the words. Eyes alert and wide, sniffling in her father's arms.

The wine was dry. No, sweet. A bit of both. Pale gold.

Brave Sam. Generous Sam. The use of her husband's name, even in her private thoughts, startled her, and she had to peer around the room to reassure herself that she was seeing things in a plain, if sentimental, light. She was awake, not dreaming. In the precision of the injury her man had inflicted – terrifying yet unserious – one sure, damning flick at a girl's temple – she saw the touch of the surgeon she'd thought she was marrying fifty years before. The doctor behind the Doc she'd been saddled with. Never gone, at least not irretrievably.

And that – that taunting glance as she slipped back under – just made her angry all over again.

* * *

A little later, when she was calmer – Dick had phoned between cases and she was drinking Scotch – Lucy remembered the philosophy elective she'd taken back in her undergraduate years, when she was eating at the restaurant the interns frequented, telling herself she couldn't care less if she met one. The professor, a skinny bearded man she had a feeble crush on, told them about Ockham's Razor. William of Ockham, a fourteenth-century philosopher, called it his Principle of Parsimony. His Razor. 'Entities are not to be multiplied beyond necessity.' Which meant – explained the twitchy black beard and sleepless eyes she imagined shocking – that one was to cut away extraneous ideas and accept the simplest hypothesis that can explain the data. Lucy saw right away that the method could as easily describe an intolerance of ambiguity as a path to certainty. She understood its appeal, just as she understood that some wishes come true. But to set up neatness as a guarantor of anything except itself seemed to her simply wrong. Worse than wrong, foolish. At the time it had struck her as wishful thinking, a very male thing, as if neatness and truth had any essential connection to each other. But the thought came back to her now, Scotch-softened, liquor-luminous, and she wondered if she'd seen, they'd all seen, the flash of Ockham's Razor today. And the Gordian knot, was it? Slicing through a tangle of cords with your sword. That was the same thing, wasn't it? Solomon? No. Alexander the Great. Who also died, or was buried at least, in Egypt. She was drunk now, she supposed.

Decoys

'Decoys.'

'I know decoys. Carved birds. To lure the others.'

Lure, she thinks. He does know everything. Vocabulary, idioms, grammar. This truck driver, she thinks.

❧

It was the summer of her *pills*. When her mother swallowed twenty of them, two weeks after Cate had aced her pharmacology exam in second year meds. *Have some fun. Get some rest*: the Sandman, shrugging unpaternally as he handed her the plane ticket.

After a few days in Switzerland, eating milk chocolate and walking beside blue lakes paved round with concrete, like giant swimming pools, she headed for the highway, intending to hitchhike north.

The truck driver picked her up just outside Basel. A wide bend of empty highway, like an asphalt rainbow. He was Dutch, he said. His English shadowed by the merest accent, maybe only a little too precise. It was common in his country, he said: English all through school, and compulsory military service after graduation. Cate sensed he lacked confidence.

❧

She climbs up three big metal steps – so great to *climb* into a vehicle, biceps and triceps hauling – and then she is in the spacious cab, big enough that she can stretch her legs out full under the dash, with room to slide her pack in under her knees. So free, this kind of driving, being up, up and over the frenzied lights of the autobahn. Like the prow of a great ship cleaving through blackness, night whirring with lights. Soft clashing music, drums and synth, issues from the dial-lit dash.

'How old are you?' Then he guesses: 'Nineteen?'

Off by four, Cate thinks, it must be the schoolgirl braids. She nods.

'Not married.'

'No. You?'

'No.'

Too late, Cate thinks, as he drops a white-flesh-ringed finger into the shadow below the wheel. The steering wheel is larger than a car's and tilted nearly horizontal, like a bus driver's. It must feel strange and good to crank on it, she thinks, or sprawl across it on the straightaways. She settles in for a good time.

'It's an all-night drive. Six hours to Bremerhaven. You should tell me about yourself,' he says earnestly. But has the grace or cunning to smile when Cate can't quite stifle a giggle. She steals glances at his square shoulders and lean waist, the nose firm and large like the profile on a Roman coin. Wondering if the request for information comes from trucker boredom, or the probing of a seducer or serial-whatever, scoping her out, or the simple innocent avarice of an info-geek. His short brown haircut, sleep-tufted at the back, fits each scenario.

And it is tempting to tell her story to this stranger, fill this black speeding techno-bubble with her life. But the simple truth, especially the recent truth, fills her with ennui. Her mother tiny in her hospital gown, sniffling after they'd pumped her clean: 'This isn't what I meant, dear.' And Cate's sure it isn't. The meltdowns her family has been experiencing ever since she can remember never seem to have meaning in themselves, so much as they give meaning – lend meaning – to some ongoing chaos that punctuates itself in periodic catastrophes. Mad, gay and dangerous to know: those are her three brothers, though she can't always remember who is which, and sometimes uses it as shorthand for her whole family. Her grandpa stabbed her in the temple with a paring knife when she was five – left side in school meant the keloid bulb behind her eye, her 'horn' or 'worry bump' – which had finally settled the question of whether he was mad or senile, or just a weird old duck who'd gone to Egypt as a medic in World War I and come back odd and silent. He'd pushed a passive broom in the steel company, his MD unused, to the everlasting rage of his wife and the mystification of everyone else. With a knife flick he'd cut through that half century of speculative murk: the *fact* was, he was dangerous. Into the Home he went. Followed a year later by his wife, who soon after being liberated from her famously unhappy marriage – which was all she'd ever claimed to want – stopped eating, bathing, going out. Stopped living, to the best of her passive-aggressive abilities. They were both dead now. And Cate had never found it odd that they'd occupied separate but adjacent rooms in AltaVista: the management said that many old couples preferred it that way, and the arrangement seemed to approximate their former life together. They were like the photo in her grandpa's scrapbook of the two statues in the desert, the one his trembling finger had always rested on when he flipped the pages. Two huge figures seated on adjacent thrones, separate but inseparable, crumbling in tandem. *The Colossi of Memnon.* Doc and Mrs.

Indirection her family's curse and course. Seepage, trickle, subterranean swelling – then meltdown. Flood. 'Her name is Lindy. *Lindy!*' her mom had moaned. And Cate had understood that that was as precise an autopsy as was warranted on her dad's affair with a ward clerk thirty years his junior. A couple of years *Cate's* junior….

All too much, much much too much, for this hawk-nosed, Cato-headed techno-driver. But after banks and chocolate she craves talk. So she improvises.

'We have a game called Tangents.'

'In Canada?' He turns his head minimally. Not bad, she thinks.

'Where I'm from?'

'A line touching a curve.' Quick, this driver. A little voice inside, a quiet one, reminds her to be careful. An engineering student slumming for the summer? she wonders. But the only engineers she's met, and the one she slept with, would have been aching to do a beer run on this chick talking tangents. Maybe he is. Anyway he's not that young. Thirty, maybe. The education is better here.

'That's a mathematical tangent, yes. But this is a talking game.'

'Truth or dare.' He shows square white teeth, and pink moist lips that she wouldn't mind sucking at all.

'Truth *and* dare. What happens is, you talk about your life by talking about one – only one – character in it. It can't be a major character either. No parents or lovers or best friends. Someone further out. That's your tangent. The listener can get as much, or as little, as possible from that.' *He can get into your pants if he's not too good.*

'That's interesting.' Deadpan Dan. Watch this guy, she reminds herself again.

'Do you know what inference means?'

He shoots her a righteous glare. He barely has an accent. And Cate relaxes a bit, knowing he can be teased. *Your serial-whatever couldn't be, could he?*

.ℐℬ⌐

'I'll go first.' *And last,* she knows, stretching out in the spacious speeding cab. She'll never learn anything, not really, about this driver. There is not a sensation of speed so much as of power in a vehicle this size. Hurtling *mass.* She thinks for only a few seconds before a face appears she can riff on.

'Jack McAllister.'

The driver just driving. Hands on the wheel. Plying his gearbox.

'A Jack McAllister story. I can't remember when our house wasn't full of them.' Actually his visits were not that many, but they made such an impact, seeming to encapsulate whole eras of her life, that she will always forget their true frequency and duration. And how many of them she'd failed to witness but come to believe she had, so much brio did her dad invest in retelling them. Never Mom, she thinks now, rolling her tongue inside her cheek, as if the thought were a candy she could suck, probing its tart-sweet centre.

'A relative? An uncle?'

'Uncle? A colleague. He was this gonzo surgeon my dad idolized. He was an anaesthetist, my dad.' She does a vocab check on the driver, but he's cool, eyes fixed and dilated on the unspooling autobahn. 'The Sandman.'

'McAllister stories filled our house. He was this mad outdoorsman too, but the weird thing was that his hunting and fishing stories sounded the same as his medical stories.' McKiller the U of T fullback who preferred to run over defenders, though he had the speed to go around them. The man who left a New Year's Eve party at midnight, saved two lives from a car wreck, and returned at dawn to finish the Scotch and make eggs Benedict and Bloody Marys. Who'd hand-picked Dick to be his chief assistant – *on all the really tricky cases* – walloping her dad on the back. 'McAllister diving into rapids to retrieve his wife's bracelet. Bringing a boy back from clinical death, the Emerg team already starting to put away the gear. It all sounded exactly the same.'

'Macho man.'

A worrisome comment from the Dutch driver: it sounds too dumb. Every McAllister story came from the same recipe: recklessness and danger and amused self-recognition that was only mock-rueful. He might have been the first person Cate met who liked his life.

❧

'I can still hear him praising my father, telling me how great he was at, like, putting people to sleep. "This is a guy who has the touch. He knows just how far to take someone down. Too deep and their fluid balances get out of whack, plus you depress heart function, and so on. Technical stuff."' The driver nods. '"Too shallow and they might wake up on you. I've had that happen. Every surgeon has. See, surgery's mostly nuts and bolts. But there's a *feel* to what Dickie does." And I was maybe eleven, but I can remember thinking: But you don't need to feel, do you? You *know*.'

'Where was this?'

'Where?' *Where?* Okay. It's funny, she can feel the rumble of the truck beneath her, a thrum like she's straddling a wide live wire, but already she can forget it for long stretches while she's talking. Already it's a given. 'I guess that was up at his cottage. My dad was getting really tight with him and we used to go up weekends. For a while I felt like I had two sets of parents. Two fathers anyway. A couple of summers my brothers even lived there, working at this lodge down the lake. When we visited I'd pick them up in the boat after work. I used to like to do something wild with the boat. Hit a big wake, or swerve suddenly. Almost swamping us, knocking them around. "HEY!" they'd yell, scared by a girl and pissed by that.'

'Got you,' the driver says. She looks at him. 'You said no family. No you.'

It's possible she said no family, but she knows she didn't say *no me*. She wouldn't've. 'Gotcha,' she says. 'Not got you.' The driver purses his lips.

❧

'He had this broad hairy chest. Very hairy. I mean hair on his back, tufted with black fur like a bear, hair on his knuckles.' And she thinks of the first hairs she found, dark brown, blue-black where they entered the skin, little quills, on the white of her pubis. Her curiosity about them, her pride and boredom, some accessory to a plan unrolling on schedule. That was at McAllister's too, sitting in his outhouse, poplar leaves flipping in the breeze.

'So one day, out of the blue, I'm going past him and he grabs me by the wrists. He's a lot older than my dad, late fifties then I guess, but with the strongest hands. Wow, some bedside manner, I'm thinking, but scared. He's leaning into me and staring at my face. He gets this real serious look and his eyes narrow' – like he's going to come, which she won't tell the driver – 'and then he drops my hands and says to my dad, "That's a nasty keloid, why don't you get Stan Pieps to scrape it off." Pieps was this plastic surgeon, kind of effeminate, who my dad and McAllister used to call Mrs Pieps.' But now suddenly he's good enough to take a knife to my face, their eyes gooey with admiration, praising him as the best.

'Take what off?'

'Yeah, right. This. This.' Saying it harshly – people go myopic, hard of hearing, just to get a better look, make you show them twice – before she reminds herself the cab is dim and he's watching the road, just sparing glances. And hey, it's a small defect, an oval raised scar, a speed bump. But on her *face.*

'My dad's dream was to retire early. Stocks, real estate deals, calls from his broker. Big thick envelopes, statements, you know. Freedom fifty-five.' Maybe he doesn't get that one, but it doesn't matter; it works without the commercial, she sees, a bit amazed. 'And he actually made it. He did. Last year he retired. And, you know, McAllister was always encouraging him, like, Get out, Dickie, get out, man. Canada's health care is going to the dogs. He went on cutting people open until he was seventy, but he was concerned, it was going to kill my dad to put people to sleep past fifty-five.' She goes quiet for a bit, all the small whizzing cars on the autobahn, light-clusters out the sides. A hundred and forty kliks on the gauge beneath the driver's wheel, and they just keep flitting by.

She laughs. It sounds like sobbing over the truck throb. 'You know the word nihilism? Nihilist? Nihilistic?'

'Turgenev,' the driver says. 'Nietzsche.' He straightens in his seat like a student.

Hauling freight, she thinks, then silently scolds herself for something, gives herself a mental slap.

'It's all bullshit.' His expression is mulish.

'Yeah, well, I don't know where I picked it up.' She peers at the driver. 'But I used to think it when they were talking, just say it to myself as I was listening. *Nihilism*. It gave me power, a weapon or something.' Big Jack with his consuming passions, Dad just a doc. 'It's funny how much I got into words then, 'cause I wasn't much of a reader. Maybe words meant too much to me. I didn't need thousands of them, one good one would do. Last names. That was another thing. I don't know when I discovered it, but the difference it made to call adults by their last names. Or anybody. No more Dr McAllister. Jack McAllister, Uncle Jack. Just McAllister. Saying all this stuff to myself.'

'And one more thing. And don't tell me the rules again.' He nods. The only flaw in his handsome face, she thinks, is how tightly he presses his lips. Like someone's holding a spoonful of his least favourite food up to his mouth. 'For the longest time I couldn't remember his wife's name. It was Doris, but I kept thinking: Lois? Martha? Irma? It got to be a real problem. It just wouldn't stick.'

⋙

She had a Kingdom in her eyes. If she thinks now of her adolescence, teen years, coming-of-age – all those euphemisms for that cyclone – that's how she remembers it. As a simple weapon, one she discovered in herself. It was a Kingdom of sand and light and endless time. If she opened her eyes wide at someone – feeling the cascade of light and searing heat – she saw their features go large and dizzyingly clear, then shrivel. The Kingdom sun X-rayed then torched them. 'Don't stare!' the kids had cried in elementary school. Boys and girls, both. 'Bug Eyes!' They'd drawn pictures of her, insectile, mantis-eyed, on notes they'd passed. Penned cootie vacs on their arms against her fatal magic. Her scar on a special stalk in this one sketch, David Coombs, this nerd cartoonist she had a shameful crush on. And she had learned to hood her scrutiny. But by grade nine she knew how to let out some of the Kingdom light without staring. She could just look, like easing a door ajar. It looked like she was just looking. People got strange facial tics, ducked away, their self-confidence curling in her heat like crackerjack prizes.

153

The driver was fine with periods of silence. Prolonged ones even, he just drove. Which she was glad and grateful for, figuring that had to be part of Tangents too. Had to be.

❧

The driver slides in a tape ... soft grinding industrial, a music she's never been in the right zone to get into, but here in their spaceship-cabin it is perfect, soft clashing and chanting over a hypnotic beat – true *background* music – tension built on rage perhaps, but codified to a kind of grimy lullaby, strangely peaceful and permitting.

She unzips a pocket of her pack and brings out some crackers, cheese and chocolate. The driver shakes his head. She wonders if he is pissed off, decides he is just busy. Traffic has clotted around them, whizzing little cars. Four a.m. The jostling on this small continent. *More room!* For centuries now. She puts her head back and sleeps.

'Where are we?' she says when she opens her eyes.

'Hanover is just up ahead.'

'Where's Berlin from here?' It's 1987, the Wall still forever. Its cool half-life as Jeopardy echo – Pink Floyd on the retro mix, Richard Burton's best role – still an unimaginable two years away.

He points an arm past her out the window. 'East. That way, over there. About 250 kilometres.'

Europe is stamped on his brain, she thinks. Webs of routes, lines. Distances.

'The DDR.' He's shaking his head. 'Shitty place. Shitty people.'

She studies him out of the corner of her eye, pretending to scan through the windshield. The thickness in his words, intimating mental slurriness, makes him sound stupid again. She wonders if he's glimpsed any of the curve grazed by her tangents. Then remembers that she made the game up anyway, why should it make sense? She yawns, goes on.

'The last time I saw him I was out running. We hadn't seen him for a couple of years. I think he was finally semi-retired or something, up at his cottage. I was hell on running then. Flat out, for about five years or so. Then I just quit. Haven't even jogged since.'

Driver: 'That's not a tangent.'

Cate: 'It's my life. I can't leave myself out completely.'

Driver (sternly): 'You could if you wanted to.'

Okay, Cate thinks. Okay, okay, okay. But she doesn't really mind. It's just the old problem, the guy never awake or sleepy enough, not at the right time. Not when you need him to be. 'I *was* out running, though, just scene-setting here, and I sprint after this big bottle-green Lincoln that's making this big showy turn into our driveway.' Like the *Queen Elizabeth* deigning to enter a private bay. Running a series of cruel truths. You know right off you lack the power muscles for the sprint. But it takes time to learn you don't have the endurance, or focus maybe, for long distance, though the pared-bone physique attracts you powerfully. Belatedly you set yourself a middle goal, to run the 800 or 1,500 metres.

'Doris was with him this time. She was something else.' But how to explain what she means to the driver? This driver with his habit of reminding her he's listening, just when she's settling into talking to herself. 'Imagine a bull dyke crossed with a prom queen.' She says this to the window, a muddy reflection of herself, not wanting to see the driver's lips clamp tighter, or God, grin. His forearm tendons twitching on the wheel. McAllister liked his women at the extremes, black and white: powdered and perfumed and demure – or nasty with dirt and sweat, hoisting one end of a muddy canoe, gutting a fish, squatting over a log in the rain. He could have partial admiration for a woman who could be either, but he could only have married one who could be both. She used to wonder if Doris had been able to be both before they got married, and which part she'd had to learn or fake.

'How's little Cate?' McAllister says.

Big enough to bite your hairy old balls off, she thinks. And knows he hears her, because his eyes fill with a queer light. Telepathy she takes for granted, is always amazed when others speak of it as exotic or hypothetical. None of us could get along without it, she thinks.

'Cate runs,' her mom says.

'Oh?' McAllister looks her over, up and down. 'Come here,' he says. He stands beside her and presses down hard on her shoulders. 'Up on your toes,' he says. Cate lifts up against those hands. He smiles thinly. 'Okay, I think so. Yes,' he says, with real approval. Stands back and appraises her, head to toe. 'Not sprints, not distance. Eight hundred metres maybe?'

Which is amazing, really, truly impressive. Her grandpa ran long distances – at least she gathers he did – she has dim memories of stringy men with warped faces in his scrapbooks – but then his Egypt pictures are in there too, statues and sand dunes, with no clear connection, but an obvious importance, to his own life. Hair is a question at the moment, with running. (Another thing she likes about running: the way it subjugates your life but makes all its details matter, arranging them around its core.) At the moment she wears braids, likes to feel them slap her back when she runs, two lank arms patting encouragement. But she is thinking of cutting them off – going totally aerodynamic with a short buzz. She pictures herself with perfect speed and wind, and tries on each head to see which fits, like switching faces in a collage. Each detail matters. *Hundredths* of seconds, her coach keeps muttering, the word ancient and forbidding.

'Where're the boys?' McAllister asks, and Cate wants badly to tell him. Richard's in a psychiatric ward, has been for three months. Danny's living with a stripper ten years older than himself and doesn't phone or call. Mom's hair is falling out. Craig is fat, really fat, and might be gay. She has vivid earlier memories of them all, the three boys and herself on their periphery, hundled around McAllister reverentially, sucking up his 'tall tales' with a child's credulity.

'Oh, out gallivanting,' her mom says. Craig *was* out. At a movie, he said. With his friend, *Gordon*.

'Awww,' McAllister groans, and laying claim to their sofa with splayed arms and legs (Doris tucked into a corner hugging a cushion) he launches into fond memories of fishing trips with *the boys*. Hearing them, Cate measures them against her own memories and decides they *could* be true ... the weekend McAllister is recalling with such relish was three years ago. Her brothers were sixteen, seventeen, eighteen then. They could still have perched around McAllister's chair, listening with rapt faces. *Just* could have, she thinks. For their dad, maybe. For Mom? Now such a performance would be impossible. Three years *could* mean that, she decides.

Three years could also mean a time when she had confusing pictures of her mom. Cate was twelve, almost thirteen then. Some of the memories of her mom from that time are normal. Others seem dream-like, fantastic. They seemed so at the time. She hadn't known whether to believe them then and didn't know whether to believe them now. The thing was, the fantastic pictures in her head got stronger – stronger and clearer – while the everyday kitchen snapshots were going blurry and weak, like photographs left in the sun. It was a time when her parents gave big cocktail parties (something they never did now); they would pay for caterers and young men and women in black pants and white shirts would move through rooms, refreshing drinks, handing out hors d'oeuvres. Cate and her brothers would help to serve. On one of these glittering, crowded evenings, Cate rounded a corner and surprised her mom taking a bottle out of her pocket and upending it with a little shake into her mouth, capping and pocketing it. It was so quick and fluid, like a bird ruffling its feathers or a dog shaking itself. There was furtiveness in the act, but two more steps into the bathroom would have made furtiveness unnecessary. Another evening (though the Party Era was really one long evening) she passed a linen closet – walking on tiptoe, something her running coach had said was good for balance and the calves – and saw, through the parted door, McAllister and her mom hugging. Her mom's back was to her, and McAllister's hand was down her stretch pants, moving over her bum – Cate's eyes widened as she passed until she thought she could see each wiry black hair on his forearm, the wiggling bunch of his fingers under her mom's silver lamé slacks. But the hair turned red and sparse in her mind, her dad's arm, she couldn't keep the pictures separate or in focus, and she went to the bathroom and sat on the fuzzy toilet seat for a long time, so she could enter the living room with everyone seated again and not have to decide if it was her dad or McAllister whose fingers made that silver sack of wriggling eels. Her mom's car accident ended the Party Era (though with a flurry of phone calls, awkward visits, cards and gifts that seemed like a funhouse extension of it). She banged into a bridge abutment on the Queen E, her dad said, but 'bang' made it sound like bumper cars. Cate shook her head, and her dad gulped and left the room. When Cate visited her in ICU she looked little and old, her hair fanned out in damp grey tufts on the pillow, tubes in her arms and nose and mouth. The nurses kept saying 'She's lucky she had the best' – and Cate remembers her dad and McAllister coming home together the night after her mom's long surgery, one long car gliding into the driveway after the other. Drinks in the study, sunk in deep leather chairs. 'I'm glad you were there.' 'I'm glad *you* were.' And Cate had stood for a moment in the short hall connecting the kitchen with the study, hearing two generals, or a general and a captain, discuss a costly but ultimately successful campaign. Rules had been bent, her mom told her later, because *Jack* wouldn't operate on her – 'I was a tricky case,' her lips tilting toward a smile – unless he had Dick beside him as his anaesthetist. Cate imagines her dad and his master stitching her together – McAllister stitching, while the Sandman kept the sleep drugs flowing. She had crashed the car into a concrete slab on a clear day on a dry road. 'I must have been in la-la land,' her mom liked to say, and Cate noted and filed away the length and loudness of others' laughter at this falsity.

๛

'Let's hear one of his outdoors stories. You said there were outdoors stories,' the driver says.

Not how the game's played, she's about to say, you asking questions. And then thinks, yes it is. Of course it is. Why not? 'I think I'm too sleepy,' she says, an excuse that is suddenly true. Her body feels like lead.

'There are some pills in there if you want to stay awake.' The driver nods at a door just to her side of the big gearbox. When she opens it, it is not shallow and curved, like a car's glove compartment. There is the same little light, but it is a square box with two shelves; it reminds her of a squat medicine cabinet. Sure enough, she sees toothpaste, a toothbrush, breath mints, a drinking mug. Chipped white enamel, this mug, it probably came from his mother's kitchen. In the glow that spills out she sees the outlines of other compartments on either side of it, their catches raised. Safety deposit boxes, she thinks. Cupboards in a tiny kitchen.

'Pink pills,' he says. A touch impatiently? But she has her hand on the unlabelled bottle. With two fingers she nudges the mug and sees a bottle of blue pills behind it. *Drink me. Eat me.*

'What are they?'

'Just beans. Pretty mild actually. Probably just caffeine. You'll need a couple.'

'D'you want one?'

'No, I'm good. I'm fine. Maybe later.'

With her little finger she crooks the blue pills closer. Pharmacology was an interesting course, all those ingenious tinkerings with internal chemistry. The little door, open to the driver's side, screens her anyway. She feels like a magician working behind a curtain.

'What about sleeping pills? You must need downers too sometimes.'

He shrugs admission. Heavy, good shoulders. Really ace, she thinks. 'Sometimes my night starts at noon. I've got to sleep when I can.'

She palms two of the blues, caps the bottle and pushes it behind the mug again. Knocks the tiny pills back and clicks shut the door. The pink bottle safely stowed in her pocket.

'Nighty-night.' She leans her head back, closes her eyes.

'They don't work that quickly.' In the crisp retort she hears the pedant, the tightass control freak that would emerge more each day you knew him, a robot stepping out from the shadows in its program. It would drive her crazy. Mad. Mad, mad, mad.

*

The truck's horn booms, like a high foghorn … but this is a good driver, he takes his own space and doesn't have to use it often. No sleep, very little food. Practical calculations, she thinks; maybe the Sandman is right, pharmacy would be a better meal ticket than medicine. Already she feels the beans' crude buzz unspooling in her – her body seems to press an inch beyond her skin – or it must be her mind is starting to canter out in front, this lumpy grey organ now an exoskeleton, hard and bristling … but invisible. She chuckles.

'What's funny?' he asks.

'I don't know.' *Why did the serial killer cross the road? Because he did.*

And the bean, the magic bean, puts the right sliver, the necessary wafer of space, between here and there, now and then, you and not-you, she and I. All the farcical severings of the good story become possible in the light of it. O Holy Bean!

*

'How'd the fall shoot go this year?' her dad asked.

'Should we tell them, Doris?'

Doris rolled her eyes. We *always* tell them, she might have meant. She said, 'Jack almost got himself killed. *Again.* Almost got us both killed, I guess.'

She smiled as she shook her head. McAllister was beaming. 'It was stupid, I guess.' He hung his head and peeped out from under thickly woven, lush black eyebrows. Then he straightened and said bearishly, 'But there was no choice. Absolutely none. It was go in or we'd still be out there on that point.'

This was the familiar arc of a Jack McAllister story. Stupidity that sprang from urgent necessity and led to heroic risk. Gallant stupidity.

'What happened?' Lucy said. Everyone said she'd made an amazing recovery from her injuries, and Cate supposed it was true. *Only two months ago* got said a lot in her presence, and it made Cate bristle though she had no evidence to contradict it. Mrs Pieps had done a good job with the windshield lacerations, just a few fine rays around her eyes and at the corners of her mouth, whose slightly startling whiteness she tamed with foundation into crow's feet and laugh lines. And she was not at an age when many more people would see the zipper-like scars on her middle. She wore a pink blouse with a bright red tulip embroidered on its pocket, over grass-green shorts (her legs had been spared) – the same sort of clothes she'd always worn on summer visits to the McAllister cottage, though her colour sense seemed to have lurched toward the lush end of the spectrum.

Doris poked a fist at her husband. 'Genius here took a skinny dip in November in the North Channel. Swam a mile.'

McAllister spluttered his beer and set the glass down rockingly. 'A mile, Doris. It was a hundred yards. And I had on my long johns. Don't let's give Cate the wrong idea.' He winked at Cate.

'It felt like a mile,' Doris said helplessly, 'watching you.'

'It felt like ten, doing it.'

Doris's role in a McAllister story was to be an unreliable witness. Someone whose presence at an event, and whose errors remembering it, added to its authenticity and suspense.

'You went over,' Dick suggested languidly. He was sprawled in a big stuffed chair at one corner of the carpet.

'Not exactly.' McAllister took a swig of his beer, a big swallow to carry him through, and then he told his story.

'It was a beautiful sunny day. But cold. Ice crystals forming on rocks around the shore. Slippery as hell. Jesus. When I woke up at four I could hear this sound, like thousands of little bells – but faint, like wind chimes – and it took me a minute before I realized it was the waves rocking the crumbly shore ice. Pitch black, and all these tinkling bells on every side.'

'You know he never needs an alarm clock,' Doris said. 'Not for hunting or fishing anyway.' Her husband winked at her.

'Well, of course, with all that good weather, nothing was flying. I knew that when we were loading up and saw the stars. Like a planetarium display. And only a little wind. And slippery. God, that dock was slick. I thought for sure one of us was going in, eh, Doris?'

Doris set her lips and shook her head.

'So we went way, way out. Out past Jackman's Point by the last set of islands. I didn't think we had much chance of scaring up anything, even out there, but I thought if we set out all the decoys, spaced well apart, a stray looking for some company might steer in for a look. Give us a long wing shot, at least.'

McAllister paused. He raised his hairy, big-knuckled hands up in front of his face and seemed to regard them with satisfied perplexity, turning them back to front and back again. 'You tell them, Doris.'

Doris said, 'We're sitting in the sun about eight o'clock on this gorgeous morning, drinking our Irish coffee and not a duck in sight, when suddenly I see this boat sifting along out near our decoys. "My God, Jack," I said, "Whose boat is that?"'

'"By God, Doris, it's ours," I said,' chuckled McAllister.

'But how did – ?' This was Dad.

'I think whoever tied it up was in a little too much of a hurry to get to his thermos.'

'Now, c'mon, Doris, I think I've tied a few knots in my lifetime. I *secured* that sucker.' This blustering tone gave way to a sheepish, little-boy turtling of the shoulders.

Doris took up the tale; they were trading it now. 'Well, our *secured* boat was drifting away from shore. Right in front of the blind, sailing peacefully through the decoys.' She made a sign of waves, water moving, with her hands; there was something absurd and graceful in the gesture, like the movements of Hawaiian dancers in movies. 'And weren't we having a fine old argument about what to do about it.'

'I *knew* what to do about it. Knew instantly,' McAllister said gruffly. Listening from her place on the hassock, Coke in hand, Cate felt herself quicken with unwelcome excitement at the surgeon's decisiveness, black and white imperatives that could make the world a chessboard. She caught herself leaning forward tensely, then, with a frown, slouched back and stared at the floor. 'Doris thought maybe we should just build a big fire, hunker down and wait for someone. Maybe shoot our guns off once in a while, toot them like flares or something. But I knew no one was coming out that way. Not that far. Not till freeze-up and they could use their snowmobiles, anyway. And what were they going to find then? A couple of frozen mummies under the snow.'

'I still think we might have –'

'All I *knew*,' McAllister boomed, 'is that I could see the boat drifting farther away every second, our only way home, and once it got past the point there was only water between it and Detroit. So I just peeled off and swam for it.'

'Doris, weren't you scared silly?' Mom put her hand on the other woman's arm.

'I was *concerned*, yes.'

Everybody laughed. In her quieter way, Doris enjoyed a story too, and could tell it as well as her husband.

'All I could hear as I stripped down to my long johns was her crying and blubbering. Then this unearthly scream – "No, Jack, NO!" – just as I did my half-gainer off the rocks.'

He paused for dramatic effect, letting everyone see that airborne red figure, and hear that echoing woman's scream.

At this point in her story, Cate has to pause too. Telling this last story, it wants to come out in a gush, the exoskeleton is striding impatiently ahead of her like an armoured warrior – she has to force herself to put in gaps, loll her head a bit, space out occasionally. The effort of the performance, having to tell it *and* the story – consumes some, not enough, of her excess energy.

'"How cold was it, Jack?" my dad asked.' It was often his contribution to the story. Helping to bring out, through offhand curiosity, the factual scaffolding of events and actions.

'Well, I'll tell you, Dick. A second after I heard that bellow I was feeling it along every inch of me. The family walnuts were, let's say, peanuts.'

'Jack!'

'I would have screamed too, if my mouth hadn't been shocked shut. But that only lasted a few seconds, maybe my first few strokes. Then a numbness set in, and I started feeling weak all over. I'd known it would be terribly cold, of course, but arguing with Doris, I really hadn't doubted that I could make it. The boat was maybe fifty yards out. A pool length, say. What's that? Two dozen strokes flailed out, pull the cord, and back to Doris and the fire.'

'Well, that version of things lasted maybe ten strokes. After that I was in real trouble. Real trouble. My arms and legs just went on me. Lead weights. I mean it was touch-and-go. Close as I've come yet, maybe.'

All the audience, veterans of McAllister disaster stories, knew what that meant.

'When I finally touched the sides of the boat, I couldn't even pull myself in. I was too weak. Tuckered right out. *Out.* I just hung on to the side, gasping. Then I thought, *time.* Time. Every second you hang here you're one second less likely to make it into the boat. And somehow, I heaved myself over.'

'And then?' Mom asked, sitting up straight. Close calls were her field, after all; she was a recent graduate.

'Then nothing, Luce. I just dropped into the bottom like a sack of shit – sorry, Cate – and lay there. I was done in.'

Mom turned to Doris. 'What did you think?'

'I thought, the damn fool's given himself a coronary and left me alone out here and now his body's on its way to – where'd you say, sweetheart? – Detroit.'

'Doris, I'm telling you, I … couldn't … move. *Couldn't* move. Couldn't speak, couldn't raise an arm to wave. Could only lie there, gasping. I was *done in.*'

'What did you think?' Mom again.

'What *didn't* I think,' said Doris.

McAllister grinned at everybody, swivelling his head slowly around the room. The same grin for each of us as he turned, like a present he was giving us, along with the story.

'I don't know how long I lay there. Shivering and shaking in the bottom of that boat, staring up at blue sky, my teeth chattering. It could have been a minute or fifteen minutes. I have no idea. Then I heard this whistling sound, so sharp and clear – and I guess my brain wasn't working right – but I didn't associate it at first with ducks. But then I see them go overhead, low, six of them – six white bellies and these flapping wings against the blue sky – God, what a sight – and *sploosh*, I hear them land in the decoys.'

He looks at his wife like she's supposed to carry on. This is her part of the story. But she just looks back at him. Smiling, though.

'So I'm waiting for Doris to take them.'

'He's waiting for me to take them,' Doris says, 'and I don't know yet if he's still alive.'

'Aww, Doris, six beautiful birds,' he whimpers, actually squirming in his chair. 'So I'm waiting, but I don't hear anything. I think of those whistlers just swimming around our decoys, not a care in the world. So I haul myself – quiet as I can – up over the side.'

'What I see is a white face like a corpse, a couple of red arms.'

'Red?' someone says.

'My long underwear. Penman's, top and bottom.' He looks at me again.

'Well, those cagey old whistlers must've been sun-drunk, or senile or something, because they were all lined up in a sweet little bundle, and didn't even spook. Quiet as I could, I tried to give Doris a sign. I could see the top of her head in the blind, and I imagined she was bawling. God, what I wouldn't have given for a gun.'

'Were you?' Mom.

'Bawling? Not just then. No.' Everyone laughs.

'I think I could've got all six with two shots. Finally I just up and bellowed, "Take them, Doris! Take the fucking ducks!"'

'Up Doris rears, gun blazing.' Now he's on his feet, living the story as he tells it. 'You never saw such a ruckus. Wings flapping, Doris's twelve-gauge banging and blasting.'

'Did you get one, Doris?'

'Here's what she got, Dick. Her first shot tore the head off my best decoy. Hand-carved, an old patient up in Sudbury. Which was out *beyond* the whistlers to begin with. They were that close to her. Her next shot sprays across the water even farther out, it looked like hail slashing towards the boat. That's when I hit the deck. Instinct. Right on my belly in the bottom. Just in time too. Because there was a pause – the ducks are halfway down the lake by now – and then her last shot rips into the side of the *boat* – our fucking goddamned cedar strip! – *crack* above my head. I was picking shot out of the hull with tweezers half the night.'

'I guess you should've taken the swim, Doris, and let Jack handle the shooting.' Mom smiled as she said this, and the two women exchanged a look I couldn't read. That look was like the passage in a book I'd been told to study but hadn't bothered to, hadn't thought I'd need it. Couldn't believe they'd question me on *that*.

'Annie Oakley.' McAllister was shaking his head.

Everybody was laughing, laughing or at least smiling. Teeth were visible all around the room. You know how old teeth go all yellow, tawny-beige. You can't hide it, it doesn't matter how much you brush. And I looked at them and I looked back at McAllister, who was smiling only a little, smiling and watching them, and I thought: What? With his Annie Oakley comment he'd almost handed it to them, and they still didn't get it.

❧

The driver is craning over his wheel, peering ahead, and Cate knows they're about to stop. She has to close her eyes just to get away from him for a bit. She doesn't believe he's heard anything, no tangent has grazed him, though she's unsure how much of it she said out loud, and anyway it doesn't matter. The bean surge is nasty with eyes shut, the mind out ahead, galloping unencumbered in total blackness, no local sight to lasso and brake it a little.

Finally the air brakes hiss and she feels a gentle gravity settle her into the seat, which smells, she only now realizes, a little like a lot of things, but mostly like wet raincoats.

Eyes shut, she tells herself, a high-speed mantra – *ishutishutishut-ishutishutishut*. Especially when he touches you. Though when it happens, a gentle poke of her arm, the needle peak of a pyramid of expectation, her heart jumps into her throat and it's everything she can do to stay in the dark. But when his fingers close on her forearm and gently tug, she thinks – she has to think – a little groggy blinking is permitted even the safely doped, she can't quite go blind where she's taking her.

And sees, in lash-strobed blur, not uncomfortable sights. A little sleeping compartment like a roomette in a train, only smaller, bed like a gym mat on a shelf, blankets jumbled at one end. He's behind, directing her by hands on her shoulders. When they get to the bed she flops with rag doll finality, closing her eyes as she falls. Then feels, then hears, him moving away, back into the cab where he makes fussing sounds, clicks and bumps and rustlings. What a relief to open her eyes again. Even bland, low-lit objects – the faintly luminous pearl moulded plastic of the cubicle walls, a little humless box fridge an arm's length away, TV on a shelf above it – billow and snag in her speed, parachutes braking the space shuttle. Raising herself slightly, she peeks out a porthole-like window and sees a vast area of whitish pavement, beyond it a cluster of shining buildings behind symbols for eating, sleeping, gas … an international shorthand that makes her feel entirely displaced and comfortable. *In the suburbs of my affection*, she thinks, not knowing where she got it, some pale flotsam from an English essay bobbing up in her wake.

The indecipherability of the sounds he is making in the cab is unnerving, but then she hears a muted gargling and is reassured. She's heard it before, the mouthwash prep behind the door, then rolling down the window to discreetly spit. Gary Numan's 'In Cars' comes on the tape deck, twiddled down to funky bleats. *His makeout music*, she thinks, and has to stifle her laughter in a pillow that smells strongly of laundry soap. A shy boy, she decides. A virgin, maybe. Call it a working hypothesis. Just don't mistake it for self-defence.

Now why are you doing this? she asks herself a moment later. There's bean bravado, of course, the disdain of pure energy, and under that, supporting it (though it needs no support) a kind of hypothesis. But what was the hypothesis? Now she can't remember it. Something about her invulnerability, she recalls, with a jittery recognition that signals the bean speed fading, splintering into differently paced shards.

Through minutely parted eyelids she sees, serrated by furry bars, a creature of looming beige that she knows could never harm her.

She keeps her eyes shut tight as he removes her clothes, wincing slightly in the effort not to look. She wants to see what he will do when he can, and is not much afraid. Danger still flits into view, but it is like a rare moth species, notable but weightless.

She has to see without eyes, by touch only, like a blind person. When he tugs on one of her braids she imagines his other arm thrown up over his head, the plaited hair in his fist like the reins of a bronco he is riding … except, really, that doesn't fit. It's all so slow and gentle, tentative and slithery, without a ghost of rodeo roughness. Even him inside, in big wondering strokes, like a piston underwater or a cervical probe under kindly local. So different from what she's used to, what she likes and needs, that she has to drop character and get on top. Horse Mounts Rider.

When she opens her eyes, the expression on his face is one she wants to freeze on a Polaroid and tack up on every fridge she'll ever own: the necrophile surprised when his slab doll blinks. She's going to have to keep him occupied enough that he won't miss his corpse.

*

There is a light over the bed, a little shelf with books, Dutch titles, the squat little fridge – it's like any suburban kitchen in miniature, only better, this cosy no-place tucked in between the unnamed freight and the diesel engine. *Strangers on a Train.* An old movie.

Languid and sprawled, he's so grateful she doesn't need to pretend to be. Though she is a bit, she realizes, faintly grateful and faintly sleepy. She brings him a Heineken, deftly crumbling two of the pink capsules into the neck, swirling them down. Sandwoman.

'Is there a story to this?' He touches the scar at her temple. Yeah, that's where my crazy coot grandpa stabbed me, she could blurt out, but he seems too sleepy to shock. 'No, just another accident,' she says, which is also true.

As she swigs her beer beside him on the bunk, she feels it bring the bean buzz down another notch, lowering her back to earth while he must be sinking under it, though he doesn't know it yet, his cells compacting and closing like buds at night ... they are passing each other like people on chemical escalators going in different directions, one up one down.

And I never got to tell him my last tangent, she thinks, honestly a little regretful now that he is breathing deeply. It was the summer of McAllister's decoys story, but it had the pattern of another summer lying over it, a summer two? – no, one year earlier, the two visits lying over one another like designs on plastic overlays, together making one picture.

My summer of blood. Not sure if she called it that at the time or only made it up later. 1975, she thinks. Only twelve years ago, but history's already going slippery-hazy. Up at McAllister's, the annual visit, she favours as getaways the outhouse or the opposite end of the cottage from the adult chitchat, burrowing in a stack of *Life* magazines commemorating catastrophe. Kennedy, King, Kennedy. She fixates on the Manson murders from 1969, realizing it was the same year she was nicked by her grandfather, in circumstances so bizarre they confer an out-there pride. X's carved in foreheads ... Charlie's girls. She feels herself coming awake, a relentless tug. Bowie's 'Rebel Rebel' will morph within three years to *Low*, her ideal album. For the first time she'd bridled a bit, kicked up a little dust, about going up north. She'd rather stay and train for cross-country (nowhere to run in real country, *especially* the Canadian Shield). She's started menstruating, what a powerful bore. She studies her grandpa's scrapbook, tucked in her dad's bookshelves ... sphinxes are cool. By dieting and running hard – she's heard of girls doing this – she slows the flow down to a weak, sporadic trickle. Now, in summer, it's House of Blood all over again. 'You're so gothic,' her mom says – at odd, seemingly unprovoked moments – which she takes as a compliment. Anything Mom finds odd or disagreeable strengthens her. If she could only horrify her she'd be fine. Her mom plays *tennis*, an improving backhand in a white pleated skirt. Reading the Manson murder accounts, she focuses on Sharon Tate, specifically the knife entering her pregnant belly – the rest of the story is distracting, a woolly nest to hide this bright red egg in – getting supper, she plunges a knife into a tomato, grapefruit – watermelon! – to trap the right feel. There is the idea in her every action of a vein of truth hidden by a mass of detail, so naturally knives define her ... cutting away, trimming the fat, exposing. People get misled. She hardly reads, skims magazines, but following an obsession that springs up with sphinxes and satyrs, centaurs, gorgons, she devours Bullfinch's mythology. Her homeroom teacher glows. The glow cooling to ash during her oral, when, with declamatory boldness and plagiarized subtlety, she proclaims her belief in the reality of occult forces, phenomena like psychic doubling, vampirism, voodoo, as (at least) obvious restatements – perhaps with imaginative elaborations – of the unknowability of life, its iceberg-likeness, the tip visible, the vast sunken bulk (her parents are skimmers, skiers on water and snow). 'The Egyptian concept of the Ba or Ka – the soul's double – is now a proven scientific fact.' *Thank you, Cate! Well....* Horror movies amuse her endlessly. Mistaking the truth for entertainment they commit unintended ironies that unscroll from every scene. She regards with tolerant credulity any account of idols, sacrifice, propitiation.

And one firefly-sprinkled July evening, Bratwurst on the barbie, McAllister telling the story of teaching his wife to shoot, oh this was years ago, when she 'realized the only way to keep an eye on him was to go with him.' The condescending lesson with the surprise ending: Doris 'doing an Annie Oakley, making the soup cans dance.' Her parents guffawing back from McAllister's double martinis; her brothers, sunbronzed from dock work, sprawled over the rug below the host's chair, chuckling reverently. McAllister pop-eyed with recollected shock; Doris modestly shrugging, but with a cocked eyebrow ... *I'm full of surprises.* And that's – *that's* – what McAllister was challenging them to remember a year later. To arrange, to order, to shuffle things in the light of. Doris the hysterical nincompoop missing ducks to blast decoys and a polished cedar boat and damn near McAllister ... *Annie Oakley.* And when no one twigs, when all the faces laugh and bob oblivious, that's when he turns – actually swivels his hips womanishly in his seat – to face her. He was daring her, the prick, to remember the earlier story, daring her to cut through his bullshit and expose the truth – daring her to be a surgeon. His eyes were taking her in, sparkling black and lunging at her, daring her to know what she knew, and she saw all this in a moment and saw how mild contempt could be a workable basis for a long friendship, had been and would be, and then her teenage mind cut across all this with a tense, cross question: What's wrong with these people? Some of them are over sixty, but they act like they were born yesterday.

⚜

She looks down at the sleeping driver. His mouth is open. He looks like a little boy. She seems to see him from a great height. 'What's your name?' she thinks, and then, because that still doesn't matter, 'What's your excuse?' looking down on him without a trace of rancour.

Virtual

They move with slow deliberation through the galleries of the Royal Ontario Museum, examining the works of people who have been dead for nearly five thousand years. He, sometimes straying ahead of her and then returning or waiting with his hands on his hips, is wearing olive green trousers and a cream linen shirt under a tan jacket. She is wearing a linen sheath of a pale wheat colour; if you glanced at her you would think 'off-white', but as she approached, your eye would pick out flecks of grey, brown, gold. They both have thick, lustrous black hair, his frosted with white at the temples, but her face is pale, perhaps a little anaemic, while his is a varnished brown. He is, in fact, of Egyptian descent. They make a striking enough couple that people pause in their contemplation of the dead to watch them pass.

Beginning in the spring of 1999, 'Egyptian Art in the Age of the Pyramids' has been shown in Paris and New York. Toronto, from February to May 2000, will be its last stop.

Like everyone else, they stand longest at the sculptures of King Menkaure and a queen, 'his principal wife, probably Khamerer-nebti ii'. One of the consort's arms is slipped behind the pharaoh's back, the small hand reappearing to hold his waist. The other arm is folded across her middle to rest on his near bicep. The pose is eternal: you could find it in any mall, in a cluster of teenagers on this Saturday, or at the door to a successful dinner party tonight. He slips an arm around her waist now as they wait for the viewers to inch them into the centre, but a glance at his rapt face makes her shrug free and stand alone. The placement of the joined statues exacts a kind of involuntary homage. Life-size or slightly larger, the figures stand on a base of stone, which stands in turn on a raised museum platform. You must look up to view them. You join a restless throng at one side or the other, then shuffle in from the periphery by inches, amid murmurings of awe and annoyance, until at last you hold the spot in dead centre, facing the couple, for as long as you can stand the jostling to displace you.

* * *

In time they drift apart, following their own interests, caught up in eddies of the crowd. She stops at a dress in beaded netting, *found in an intact tomb on the mummy of a female contemporary of the great King Khufu.* This, she thinks, has lasted as long and as well as the great pyramid, and all in all seems as impressive. 'Women and fashion,' mutters Raouf, drifting near. She rolls her eyes: he spends more time and money on clothes than she does. The beads are arranged into diamond shapes, seven thousand cylindrical and ring-shaped faience beads, pale and dark blue. *It is not clear whether, in everyday life, the bead-net dress was sewn onto or simply pulled over its underlying garment. The present example had no fabric underneath it apart from the bandages.* 'Very pretty,' says a melodious high voice, and Cate looks up into a pair of elderly blue eyes seeking her own. The woman's white hair and lined, pallid skin float beside the humidity register on the other side of the plastic display case, like a hologram in a modern art piece. Cate's linen sheath has not been ironed recently and is very wrinkled. It becomes her, gives her a sleepy, dishevelled appearance that contrasts with her alert, sand-coloured eyes. It makes her feel sexy. She nods, and moves away slowly.

When visiting a museum or gallery, she likes to alternate moments of close inspection with spells of dreamy wandering. She roams in large, loose spirals between the display cases, skirting crowds, leaning in occasionally to read a label card. It is not immersion in a culture, nothing so entire; it is more like being enveloped by a mist of ancient Egypt, a fine intermittent rain that flecks her thoughts, bringing soft, pungent scents. Sights are more apt to be revelatory, and the odd can remain merely odd, when not courted too diligently. Like the Fecundity Figures she leans in to view, the men obese, with pendulous breasts and aprons of flab; the women slender, except for the pregnant *Liquid (a feminine word in ancient Egyptian) as she gives all life and dominion.* Whatever, Cate thinks contentedly.

There is a room she thinks of as the Animal Room and a room she calls the People Room. In fact there are plenty of animals and people in each room, but it is a question of her own shifting focus. In the Animal Room she sees two birds from a Nile marsh painted on limestone. Traces of green paint fleck the papyrus stalks; the birds' beaks are interlocked, the talons of one bird stretching toward the other. *Booty animals* include bears captured in the mountains of Syria. A porcupine, its *only known representation in pharaonic art.* A leopard, a wild jackal. The dog already collared. Donkeys walking ankle-deep in stalks of grain on a threshing floor ... what transfixes her is the attention to detail, to difference, no two muzzles exactly alike. In the depiction of a desert hunt she notes the nub of penis on the calf, the pointy teat on the antelope; the arrow that twists the head to an odd, new angle. Late Summer in the Nile Valley is a cornucopia of observation: ibises, terns, a pair of ducks; mullet, beehives; copulating goats and sheep, the ram blindly staring above the ewe with lowered head; one goat sniffing another's arse, nose thrust under tail.

In the People Room there is a bowl with turned-in sections of rim, its walls so astonishingly thin, the rim folds so fluid, that it defies you to believe it is made of stone. Claymation-like figures of the necessary menials: the rib-thin, squatting butcher; dwarf musician; stooped, emaciated potter; woman with sieve; cook with his eternal pot and stirstick. Fishermen haul in a net wriggling with several species of Nile fish. Herdsmen and cattle cross a branch of the Nile: *The man holding the calf uses the maternal instincts of the mother cow as a lure: where the calf goes the mother will follow* – reading this, Cate feels a dry throb under her breastbone, a pump of tender shame. The mother's head strains to touch tongues with the back-leaning calf. Amid his detailed foliage, the sinewy Woodcutter pauses to rest.

They had bodies. It is a strangely simple detail – the lines on the braided rope of a ship under sail – that evokes this summary phrase. *They had bodies.* It is easy to forget this about the ancient Egyptians, just as it would be easy to forget that a sun-worshipping cult knew the simple warmth of spring sun on the back of the neck, the pale disc of December.

After a while Raouf, impatient with their separate tours, comes and crooks his arm into hers. For the space of half a gallery they move in concert, stopping at each display together; though usually only one of them is leaning in to examine, while the other is looking ahead for something of greater interest, tugging slightly at the leash of arms. Raouf is interested in the bound slaves, the kneeling Nubian with elbows pinioned behind his back, the Libyan heads – but Cate finds these routinely brutal. They seem an obvious corollary to the colossal attempts to perpetuate oneself in eternity. She is more interested in the tiny, exquisite frog – this evidence of creature curiosity tracing a nebulous line in her mind to reach her earlier thought: *They had bodies.*

'What impressed you most about the anatomy of those figures?'

'Oh, tons of things. They were amazing. Little details, first. Nipples, cuticles. The soft fleshy earlobes and lower lips. In *stone.*'

'The articulation of his knees. And quadriceps.'

'God, yes. And her knees. The outline of them *through* her sheath dress.'

'Her hands weren't so good.'

'True, but I'm beginning to suspect the Egyptians were good at whatever they wanted to be good at. You couldn't get the tendons of his striding leg so right and miss on her thumb, unless you didn't care so much about a thumb.'

'Selective anatomy?'

'Of course.' Raising and lowering her coffee cup: 'They never missed on eyelids.'

'I couldn't believe the stonecutter could chisel the difference between the male waist and the female. The slight convexity below her navel, with a suggestion of interior space, a faint rounding. How do you make a womb appear through stone?'

'I'm sure you didn't miss the *mons Veneris* dropping into that dark triangle beneath her dress.'

'They were *hot.*' Raouf shakes his head slowly.

'They were.'

When they touch fingers across the Druxy table in the ROM cafeteria, their flesh actually burns. On fire with a five-thousand-year-old heat.

'Ramses Extra,' Raouf smiles. 'With that guy they'd better be.' And peering slyly at her, he contrasts the efficacy of a dash of spermicidal lubricant with the epochal ninety-six-year-old warmaker with his fifty-two known sons. Cate bought the condoms, made sure they were Ramses. She likes symmetry. People sometimes confuse this with a sense of humour, of which she has almost none. It's a fact she regrets, a character flaw, though it's one of the things that turns Raouf on. He's always smiling. A smile like a crease that begs to be closed, sewn sternly shut.

'Old Kingdom,' Raouf says. 'Menkaure and friend. About 2500 BC. Or as far before your grandfather's Amenhotep as Amenhotep is before Jesus Christ. And Jesus Christ is halfway, roughly, from them to us.'

Did she tell him about her grandpa's scrapbook? She must have, but she can't remember. Their evenings have been so sybaritic, so soaked in pure pleasure, that a disclosure could have been served as casually as an oyster or a glass of ice wine.

Lying on his burgundy percale sheets, Cate squints as if she could see Raouf's time markers, obelisks arranged in diminishing perspective on some aggressively vast plain.

'We're talking ancient.' Raouf stretches his slim brown arms up and locks them behind his head. The black curls in his armpits remind her of moss moored in rock clefts.

'Or yesterday, if you think of the Canadian Shield.'

'The stars.' He curls his toes and yawns.

With the bifocal lens that she seems to have been born with, factory issue for her eyes, she admires Raouf's lithe, love-languid limbs and knows that she is happy, and sees also that she is almost at the end of where suavity can take her. The first throb of departure announces itself as an itch she can't scratch, can't even locate exactly. By now she doesn't try so hard to find it.

In her own North York condo there is a postcard from her parents on the fridge. It shows table-flat white sand with a cactus in pink bloom. 'Once every 19 years!' her mom has written on the back. After affairs on both sides, one suicide attempt Cate is sure of, alcoholism and drug dependency, betrayals, lies, and good times, sure, Cate and her three brothers – after all this, her parents have found their way to a desert room with a pool, hot dry air for arthritic joints. An oasis. This is the other side of divorce, the survivors' story, its dogged, triumphant facts. This not uncommon fact, which lately, locked by a fish magnet to her fridge, strikes her as a miracle, of continuance. Her mind flies back to Menkaure and his principal wife. Not their *personal* continuance, she thinks – and for a culturally relative moment denies their naïveté in thinking so – but the continuance of the moment they inhabited, embodied. One step forward, together, forever. You could look at it that way. Didn't you have to in the end? And for a wilfully obtuse moment allows herself to forget the simple greed of the powerful.

Late one Wednesday night, one of the first times they make their thorough, thrilling love, Cate is lying in the tangled sheets afterwards, and Raouf, dressed in a chocolate dressing gown with silver piping, brings in two Scotches from the bar of his Yorkville condo.

'This is amazing. What is it?' she asks after a sip. The Scotch has a complex smoky smell that translates into a long lingering aftertaste, like a weave of flavours unravelling on her tongue.

'Lagavulin. Eighteen-year-old. From the isle of Islay.' His Scots accent is terrible.

'It smells amazingly like a campfire. Or more settled, ingrained. I know – campfire *clothes*. Your clothes when you're camping. As if you could bottle and drink that smell.'

The corners of his mouth turn up uncertainly. He's never camped. 'It's peat. Peat aging.' The two vertical lines between his black eyes deepen. 'But I guess in either case you're talking about complex carbons breaking down. In a way, you could say a peat bog is a very slow fire.'

'My mom loves Scotch. She *liked* Scotch, a little too much. Now she's strictly pop and juice, as far as we know. With Dad it's always a new cocktail: martini, old-fashioned, daiquiri. Switching around. And fanatical about blends and precision. Don't *bruise* the gin. You know?'

'The anaesthetist,' Raouf says. 'Tinkering with dosages.'

They exchange a smile. A while ago a joke went round the hospital. A photocopied page, thumbtacked to bulletin boards: 'The Bartender's Guide to Doctors' Drinks'. How the bartender could guess the specialty by the order. Obstetrician: Bloody Mary. (Chief Obstetrician: Bloody Caesar). Gynecologist: Screwdriver (or Two Fingers Over Ice). Urologist: Banana Daiquiri. Proctologist: Two Fingers on the Rocks. Psychiatrist: Surprise Me. G.P.: Whatever's on Tap. Etc. It had been a big hit in the staff locker rooms.

Someone had scrawled a snippet of dialogue, medical graffiti, at the bottom. *Internist: Complex, full-bodied wines, with enigmatic bouquets and long lingering finishes. Must be imported, expensive, and frequently unavailable.* (Not quite fair in Raouf's case, his other favourite drinks being Dubonnet on the rocks and Campari and soda.)

Surgeon: Let's kill that bottle and open a new one.

'Was your father a doctor?' she asks. 'I can't believe I've never asked you.'

'My parents immigrated to Canada in 1957. Right after the Suez crisis. They operated a restaurant on Gerrard Street.' This sounds to Cate like the first clipped sentences of an autobiography; Raouf looks stern and sad, saying them. 'They aimed me at success like an arrow. I was always going to be a doctor.'

'Or else?'

'Or else nothing. A doctor.'

'They must be proud then. Happy.'

'Proud, definitely. But the first time my mother visited here she burst into tears.'

'Over this?' She raises her hands at walls that have a waiting list from *People.*

Raouf smiles thinly. 'That's what I told her. The maintenance fees here are more than the mortgage on the house. But you see, I'd lost Tamara and the kids. It's all a package to her. To my dad too. For them being a doctor is much more than a career. It's more like a family business – wife, children, home, community niche – with everybody working together in their roles. It makes no sense alone.'

'A mistress?'

'A mistress is no problem. There are always openings for mistresses.'

Another time she believes she catches the scent of a woman in Raouf's bathroom. A trace, cloyingly sweet and floral. Young. Something duller and more shameful than jealousy prods her. As she uses his toilet she thinks, a bit ruefully, some garbage she must put out soon as it is beginning to smell, that she has been too comfortable with the seducer type. With his overmastering need to feel he is leading, which dovetails so neatly with her not-always-attentive mime of following. She has become lazy, she thinks. It grew with ambition, with something that claimed her core energies for itself.

'I'm guessing your grandfather was a successful man,' Raouf says.

'No, actually. Far from it. But why do you say that?'

He wriggles his long brown fingers above the bed. A complex series of small gestures, rhythmic movements that look almost like language.

'Your father settled for anaesthesia. He didn't feel like he had to get to the toppermost of the poppermost.'

'Dad's a bit lazy.' She smiles. 'Smart and lazy. I think he wanted the maximum of medicine for the minimum of work. He figured it out like a dosage. He was good too.'

'I've heard. The Sandman.' He puts his hand on her thigh; his fingers give off heat. 'So what's that make you – less smart or less lazy?'

'Restless maybe. David kept saying to me, "We're two GPs working our buns off. We can retire at forty-five if we want. Fifty, tops." I don't think he had any idea how that thought chilled me. Freedom fifty-five, right. But I *know* how my starting surgery scared him. Like signing up for a suicide mission, I think he saw it. Remember Martin Sheen in *Apocalypse Now*, shaking his head over Kurtz joining Special Forces? "Humping it over those hills at forty, and it almost wasted me at nineteen." Something like that. That was David, I think.'

'Maybe kids would've kept you together.'

She shakes her head. 'I think we would've split sooner with them. There's something in me that just has to keep going, I think.' She hears a little pop in her ears as she says this, as if she's just changed altitude in an elevator or plane.

Raouf's fingers are at the bump on her left temple. 'And your grandfather did this, you told me. Right?' It's odd how she can hear the frown in his voice while she's staring at his terra cotta ceiling.

'Yup. Five years old. Me, I mean. He was almost eighty.'

'Crazy? Senile?'

'Who knows.'

'Alzheimer's?'

'I doubt if they used that word then. Not automatically, like we do now. But I think that was the consensus. He'd gone to World War I as a doctor, and when he came back he worked as a janitor in the steel company.'

'Shellshock?' These words, like boxes on a diagnostic check sheet, are driving her a bit nuts. She turns to face him.

'People said that. People always say things. But I don't think so. I remember a quiet, peaceful old guy. An odd duck, I guess, but not to me. Not then. He seemed content, not troubled in any obvious way. It was his wife who was the hoot owl.'

'I can see why. She marries a doctor and gets a janitor.'

'Caveat emptor,' Cate says, staring into his eyes until Raouf raises his eyebrows, shrugs.

They don't talk for a while after that.

'Sometimes I think *he* was the surgeon in the family. One flick at a girl's temple and he solves so many problems. His. His wife's. My dad's. He was their only child. "Dad in the Home? Dad in the Home yet?" It had been a dithering question, a hanging sword, for years. He cut to the chase.'

'He cut a little girl.'

Cate just stares at him. Thinking: *Duh, a surgeon.*

'Are we seeing each other tomorrow?'

She is dressing with her back to him, something she knows he likes.

'It's Sunday. I've got the kids.' She catches the wince in his voice; can see, without turning, the lemony downturn of his mouth. He needs her to dislike children, it's easier for him than her neutrality. In truth she has no particular – or, no, no *general* – feelings about children; she finds them not essentially different from adults; smaller usually, but with the usual mix of types and temperaments. What would really rattle Raouf is the not-small number of children she is genuinely fond of. Without for a moment wanting to be their mother.

'I'm on call tomorrow night anyway. I better do some power-napping if I can.'

'We wore each other out,' he says.

'We did.'

There is something epicurean, or perhaps just gluttonous, about their sex together. It is almost exclusively oral. They pleasure each other with their lips and tongues, artfully and intensively. Crudity and sophistication mingle without jarring. Details matter intensely; details *are* what they savour together, which is as removed from mere necessity as the orgasm can be. Lack of the brute – that's what will do us in, Cate thinks, cabbing it home one night when Raouf has to work early – and grins so at her own melodrama that the driver stops ogling her. *Sheer* delight – delight like a cliff dropping into water – was what she knew the first time he went down on her. The circling, nibbling, laughing frenzy of his tongue – her pleasure radiating out from it in twitching shimmery starfish limbs. But she knew she surprised him – never mind the towels and creams laid out thoughtfully on the bedside tables, the fastidious dual shower he suggested and oversaw – when she rotated him by a pressure on his hip and attended to him with the same care. Rolling his balls one at a time in her mouth like wrinkly-skinned, warm plums, licking flat like a mother cat the black hairs of his thighs, between his cheeks, flicking the hairy crinkled rim of his ass, his damp buttocks tensing to grip her tongue, then lapping outright while he twisted and moaned in a high voice. For all his urbanity, she wasn't sure he'd ever had good sex before.

My wife didn't like to use her mouth, he said after.

Something moral … religious…? she suggested reluctantly. Catching unwelcome glimpses of the mother of his children, a lipglossed dark beauty in alimony clothes.

She said I didn't taste right, he said sheepishly, twisting on the pillow to get her first reaction.

You taste fine. In truth there was very little taste for her when it was this good. After the first few licks the taste buds were overwhelmed, small sensitive nodules with a buffet pouring past them.

'I just want to give you gifts,' Raouf says, embracing her in his bathrobe before she leaves. There is nothing in his hands.

Oh no, not that, Cate thinks vehemently, recoiling from something she can't even name.

Sitting behind an agreeably silent, turbaned driver, she watches the companionable spray of lights on Avenue Road. Fireworks in slow motion? she wonders, remembering Raouf's *slow fire* image. She likes him. (Is that the trouble? barks a pesky voice, a mutt in a dark alley). The first time she'd left his place late, they'd had a brief but acrid argument when she said she would be taking the subway home. She likes the long steps down below the street, the lights glowing then blazing in the dark tunnel, even the strange furtive stares, heels echoing on the tiles. But for Raouf the point was non-negotiable. *This* is your taxi money, he said with a comical solemnity, willing her attention to the bills fanned in his fingers. He's sly and naïve … slyly naïve, naïvely sly … she toys with the difference as she rides behind the driver's tightly wrapped head.

In the lobby of her building the concierge hands her a thick brown envelope, unstamped and unaddressed, just her name printed in block capitals in one corner. On duty now is the slender, doe-eyed Chinese woman who calls herself 'Joyce' and who amazes Cate with her ability to look daintily chic inside the drab hanging blue of Skypoint's security uniform. As the elevator doors begin to close, Cate hears brisk clicking steps on the marble floor, and a man slips sideways inside. She glimpses the Jell-O colours she still thinks of as 'golf clothes', though increasingly they are accepted as general leisure wear. He stands behind her, in the opposite corner of the box which now smoothly lifts. She feels a hot spot of scrutiny, like a lamp, on her buttocks. Other times she would handle it differently, but tonight she turns and says brightly, 'Hello.' He glares at the featureless steel doors, she examines her featureless envelope.

Raouf loves surprises too much to be expert at them; he telegraphs his delight in advance. 'Imagine seeing the real thing,' he'd murmured ardently in the museum, but at that moment, feeling a bit tired, she was unable to imagine Egypt other than as a larger – much, much larger – museum, with relics no more real but far more numerous. She is sick of travel, she decides (even though the last of her many trips abroad was several years ago). She had that bug for a long time, bad, like a lingering flu, but she got over it. What do I have now? she wonders idly, toying with Raouf's envelope before opening it in her kitchen. History? (*He* thinks.) No, definitely not. The future maybe – that's going around.

When her parents were cleaning out their townhouse to move to Arizona, Cate went over for last-night takeout amid the boxes. 'We'll rent when we're up here. Oh, that must sound awful, dear,' her mom said. 'Not really,' she answered, though she was uncertain. It might sound awful. They gave her her grandpa's scrapbooks, the top items in a box labelled *?Precious*. Meaning (Cate wondered): Are they precious? Or – outside chance – precious, but in what way?

Inside the envelope she finds Raouf's travel arrangements for a ROM-sponsored trip to Egypt, a fourteen-day Nile cruise hosted by the married Doctors Davis-Cadeaux (pictured smiling – high-powered but casual – beside a partially excavated tomb), the glossy brochure giving a detailed itinerary and an insert of 'get-prepped' Web sites.

The liquid crystal display of her laptop glows a dark blue. She imagines she is looking at the Nile itself, effulgent under a cloud-veiled moon. She takes a sip from her glass of Chardonnay.

She never used the computer much when it was a stack of boxed cir-
cuitry on her desk. But the laptop has changed her relationship to the
machine. It rests comfortably on her thighs, a slim black rectangle of
reassuring weight whose top flips up, with small sensitive keys. A
brushed grey mouse pad – like a mouse *skin* actually, stretched and cut
to an elegant oval – on which a brush of her fingernail produces a
command. Only the electronic death rattle as she connects to the server
– that hapless string of choked squeals, groans, squawks and hisses –
reminds her that she is not quite one with the electron, that
www.communion costs.

But then she is at a coloured billboard with a white slot for *Search*.
The Egyptians would have loved this, she thinks. The edifice of power
grids and nerdy research cubicles, all to reach this weightless darting, the
soul's flitting passage beyond the gates, through and about the world's
ethers. Pure Old Kingdom.

Landing on the Virtual Tour of Egypt, she follows the links to the
Colossi of Memnon, wondering if, among all the high-res graphics flipping past, she will ever find the faded snaps her grandpa used to show
her – but she is amazed to recognize them right away. Again the particu-
larizing power of the Egyptian artisans strikes her forcefully. Her eyes
hop down a bit of prefatory text – *the Colossi of Memnon – originally
some 65 feet tall, two quartzite statues of Amenhotep III – virtually the only
remains of the king's funerary temple on the west bank of the Nile in Thebes*
– and then she clicks on an icon and finds them.

Two massive figures seated on stone thrones, spines erect, arms bent
at the waist and laid straight along the thigh – crumbling in the legs, the
torso, the head and face. The thrones themselves are the most solidly
preserved, sheltered by the huge bodies they support. They summon
immediately her grandparents sitting in their straight-backed chairs
(though their bodies were slumped by this time) in adjacent rooms in
AltaVista. Though they saw each other in the dining room, they did not
eat at the same table, nor (Cate was told later by her mom) did they visit
each other or even ask for news about their next-door neighbour. When
he died, a few months before her, the nurses eased her door shut so that
the stretcher carrying him could be wheeled past discreetly. She was
playing solitaire in her chair and did not look up. 'Totally senile,' her dad

concluded, with a wan smile to show that they were safely skirting tragedy. Her mom wasn't so sure – whispering to Cate about it, as she did now and then after it had evolved into an illicit topic, she would say, 'Him maybe. I can't be sure. But her, no way. She plays her solitaire like a hawk, snapping cards onto the piles. You notice the nurses don't call it senile. They know better. Doctors can afford these terms, they come in and go out. Nurses have to live there.'

(Cate, who had no idea yet whether she wanted to be a doctor, promised herself then, at age eight, that she would never be a nurse.)

'The head nurse apologized to me that they couldn't arrange for rooms on different floors,' her mom said with an expressively blank stare.

Scrolling down the text beside the pictures, Cate is mildly shocked to discover that the two statues are not of the pharaoh and his consort, but of himself. Pharaoh and pharoah. Clones. *Oh himself,* she thinks, rolling a slug of wine around in her mouth, wondering if her grandpa could possibly have known that he was showing her only double-ness, not a union. He was a sly old bird. Wouldn't the pharaohs have gone nuts over the human genome project? Sterilize everyone and start pumping out replicas of yourself, every lab working 24-7. *Ass,* she thinks suddenly. And laughing, pours more wine.

Somewhere in the pre-dawn before she goes offline she has a studious interlude in which she ignores the candy graphics and reads text intently. Twenty years of schooling to become an MD, and now this residency: learning is a hard habit to break. It's one of those wine-bleary times when she will focus with desperate sincerity and remember nothing afterwards – each fact agreeably urgent and disposable. The reign of Amenhotep III represented the height of the New Kingdom empire, which disintegrated after his death into factional squabbling between rival groups of priests and the pharaoh. The sun-worshipping religion established by his son, Akhenaten, said to be the world's first monotheist, may have been an attempt to bring back unity to a hopelessly divided kingdom. His reign, though glorious and revolutionary, was short-lived, however; after his death, his tombs and palaces and monuments were destroyed, defaced, raided, and obliterated.

Memnon – variously the son of Eos (dawn) and a Trojan warrior slain by Achilles – is identified with two seated statues commemorating Pharaoh Amenhotep III. Partially broken by an earthquake in 26 BC, they then became famous for the musical note, like a breaking lyre string, which they gave out at sunrise. A popular Roman tourist attraction, the 'stone singing' ceased abruptly when Emperor Septimius Severus tried to repair it in AD 199, presumably blocking air passages which had been affected by the temperature change at dawn.

Yawning, she puts Raouf's envelope in a drawer. Somewhere far off, but approaching, she can see their affair ending, the last scenes coming into focus like riders on the horizon. She doesn't want to go to Egypt. Virtual travel is all she needs right now. All she can see herself needing for as far as she can see ahead. This surgery in the day – or night – her fist squeezing the pulp of a man's lost heart, and by night this featherless winging about the cosmos, adrift in space and time. Annihilating, not crossing, distance. She wonders in a spasm of doubt if she can handle a world that severe and paradoxical. Sun and shadow purely, her thin goal the sundial's arm that divides and joins them. Herself a simple, simple and savage, clock? Decides that for now she would have to try, will try, to be just that. Could. Could be.

Scribe

Cate was having a dream she was glad to be wakened from. It involved a thing like an auger twisting down into the ground, or where the ground should be, except that instead of soil the substance was whitish and flaky and soft, like punky wood. The drill-thing turned and bored, no sign of who or what was turning it. And after boring one hole it started another; she never saw it move, just its progress in a new spot in the punky white. And the last hole filled in right away, its sides caving and rising, somehow both. *Stand back,* she told herself, *You're too close* –

'Doctor?'

She opened her eyes, and the nurse who had touched her shoulder stepped back a pace. She sat up on the staff lounge couch, felt the chill of recirculated air as she left the burrow of warmth her body had made. ER blood, adrenalized waves of it, was already pumping in her chest, a warm tingling in her arms and legs, but not enough reaching her head yet. Cobwebs there.

'My pager,' she said. Local problems and corrections sometimes a useful startup gambit. A few mental pushups and crunches to speed the pumping. 1:58 a.m. by the clock over the nurse's shoulder.

'We tried several times.' Cate had the black thing out of the pocket of her greens and was pushing its small soft buttons: On/Off, Vibrating Mode Test, Message Display. No light, nothing. She threw it in the garbage can beside the couch.

'New batteries this morning,' she explained, but the nurse was backing toward the elevators, one of which had its doors keyed open, a softly glowing box. Should've noticed that, Cate thought, grogginess disappearing with a last sullen lurch. Or this nurse's eyes: flat calm, calculating, an ER veteran. When they reached the ground floor, the nurse started swiftly down the long corridor, striding stiffly like someone who wanted to run. Cate sprinted ahead of her.

There was already a small crowd around the stretcher in Room 1. The casualty officer, an intern, two nurses: the triage nurse must have put out a general call. The paramedics could be seen beyond the glass doors, packing up equipment in the glow of red and white blinking lights. *End of the party*, Cate thought, images rising out of the phrase with the frivolity of champagne bubbles. She'd learned to tolerate their hallucinatory clear contours, and their sudden pops, part of the process of a line emptying itself so it could receive new contents under pressure. Part of *all business*, she'd learned, was a little two-beat intro of *all play*.

Dr Chandler, the casualty officer, was busy with a nurse at the patient's middle, so she went to the patient's head, the intern withdrawing a step to let her in. *Always check the face first*: a wise tidbit she'd picked up on her first six-month rotation. *The wound's not going anywhere, and the face can tell you a lot.* This face was massively pale, its whiteness heightened by a sheen of sweat – getting on to bleached paper, polished rice whiteness ... the eyes were wide and staring (their colour didn't register on her), expressing both lucidity and confusion, some darting apprehension of approaching catastrophe. Lips parted just enough to emit the rapid shallow breaths. No grimace or frown of pain: nothing inconsistent with a state of advanced shock. Veering again, Cate thought of a dedicated student confronted with an unexpected and totally perplexing exam question. It was the face, she noted last, of a twenty-five-to-thirty-year-old white male.

A rasping sound. Chandler's arm sawing back and forth behind the patient's back, a blue-suited maintenance man backing wide-eyed out the door. The nurses were holding the patient on his side, the intern pressing towels around something protruding from the abdomen.

She went round to the other side of the stretcher. A thin stream of sawdust was trickling onto the floor from between Chandler's steadying left hand and the patient's back. The bar the blade was cutting through cued a scene in Cate's mind, which matched with eerie precision the story she later heard. A young man driving home behind a truck loaded with lumber; a metal strap not quite tight enough; a two-by-four slides off, through his windshield, impaling him. (Through the seat too; the paramedics sawed at the scene to get him out.) From the exit angle she thought it might have missed his spine. There was only a little rim of blood around the wood coming out his lower back, and the towels under the intern's hands had been dry. *Process that.*

'Easy now,' Chandler said as the end he'd sawn off fell to the floor.

'Gently onto his back. We've got to get him lying flat for some pictures,' he added to Cate, who hadn't done a thing yet except steady the man's shoulder as they rotated him. For these first few moments – just a few moments more – she knew that Chandler needed her most as a witness to his own procedures, actions he did not doubt but had to have processed and certified by another.

The iv nurse had already got a large-bore needle inserted in one arm; another nurse was disappearing with a tray of blood samples, and the iv nurse was hanging a bag of normal saline. As soon as he was on his back, in semi-cruciform position, his arms just out from his sides, she started another line. 'Pressure?' Chandler said to the nurse cuffing the patient's upper arm. To Cate: 'We're cross-matching for ten units could you start the catheter before you scrub?'

Chandler put his stethoscope to the patient's chest. Bent over the man's groin, a nurse handing her the opened catheter package, Cate pressed two fingers into the thick muscle of the inner thigh. Deep in the cool, slightly clammy flesh she located a faint pulse. He didn't need his legs now, and the core of him knew that. Nor his arms or feet or hands; nor most of his organs even, except for his heart, lungs and some parts of his brain.

A bright backwash of red spurted down the catheter when she inserted it. Chandler glanced down and met her eyes. The blood gathering in the bag was bright and barely thinned by urine. 'I ordered the pilogram anyway,' he murmured – though the evidence of a punctured bladder and zero urine output was pooling in the bag – 'along with chest and abdomen shots.'

Cate nodded, and stood up to go.

She stayed by his side on the trip to X-ray, walking by the head of the stretcher, patting his shoulder, saying the comforting and reassuring things that no longer really registered on her as she was uttering them, but were crucial nonetheless. She helped shift him into position – not a wince, even as they did that – and she helped the nurse starting the arteriogram to find the femoral artery, like feeling the flutter of a moth's wings through a mattress. 3:05, she noted by the clock over the elevator on their way up to the OR. Over an hour, even with everyone hustling and no wasted movements or words. Too long for a TV hospital show, and we haven't even got him on the table yet. And yet – a deeper mystery – she knew he wasn't in any imminent danger. He was young, healthy, and, she guessed, the wood that had impaled him was acting as a kind of internal compress, a huge hard tampon – *until we remove it*. Vasoconstriction caused by shock – that faint femoral flickering – was helping to minimize blood loss. She looked down at him; she had to remind herself to do that. The eyes were still wide and staring, but something had changed in them. Some slight blurring or glassiness, a loss of focus. He was trying to keep his gaze fixed on a rock, but an undertow was sucking him away from it by degrees. He seemed slightly smaller too, as if he'd crept back from the borders of his large frame and was stationed tensely there, a few millimetres inside his own skin. He hadn't said anything, not a word, since he'd arrived. Now Cate placed her face close to his and said, 'We're going to take you upstairs, put you to sleep, and get that thing out of you.' Three simple steps. He blinked slowly. 'Doctor,' he said. Uninflected, the word seemed to hang in space, a marker at the beginning or end of a longer speech that had been ripped from its context. The elevator doors rubbered open.

A team of five was waiting in the operating room: Dr Meade, the surgeon, and Russ Ashley, a junior resident two years behind Cate; Dr Shiraz, an elderly anaesthetist who had worked with her dad; Lena, the scrub nurse; and Andy, the circulating nurse. All except Andy were gowned and gloved. At the entrance of the stretcher they stepped back a pace with gloved hands raised, like people surprised at something illicit. Cate and the nurses from downstairs got the patient onto the table, then retreated again, the nurses to return to ER and X-ray, and Cate to scrub.

At every point in her training, scrubbing had been impressed upon Cate as her first and crucial responsibility as a surgeon. *You'll kill more people dirty than you will drunk*, said an early instructor, with only a little pedagogical hyperbole. But she couldn't help wondering what chance, or scientific honing of the available facts, had made this bacteriological imperative such a welcome break too. A good scrub couldn't be hurried, and required light but steady concentration. At a time when she was most likely to rehearse what was about to happen – when she was tempted to operate in advance, so to speak – the vividly blooming mental scenarios kept dissolving in the face of the concrete facts of hands, soap, water, stainless steel, and counting.

One thousand, two thousand, three thousand ... ten seconds on the back, front, left side, right side of her thumb; then on to the index finger: *one thousand, two....*

A nurse put on her gloves, gown and mask, and she bumped seat-first through the doors of Operating Room 4. The gut-roiling tension she still felt here was tempered, given focus, by a growing confidence in her abilities. More often now she caught herself thinking of the OR as *home.*

The man she'd spent the last hour with had mostly disappeared. In his place was a great green linen sheet that rose from his upper chest in a tent or wing-like shape over the metal halo behind which the anaesthetist sat with his machines and tubes, communing with the head and monitors while, on this side of the curtain, the surgeons worked on the body. Blood bags hung from poles on either side. The square of torso framed by green might have been a piece of modern sculpture: the base of flesh painted amber with proviodine; the end of two-by-four (stamped, she saw now, with the sawmill's red inventory code) jutting up at an ineffably blunt and graceful angle. The body was under already: an inertly massive quality that came right through the layers of linen. *Gone:* the thought rushed her down a mental alley, and she kicked it aside. She hadn't learned the man's name, much less used it. Several of her teachers had stressed the importance of names, especially in the most critical cases; paradoxically, they became more important the less time and use there was for them; but it was a lesson she had trouble remembering.

She joined Dr Meade at the light board, where the X-rays were pinned up. Dark clouds, wisping at their edges, floated in the peritoneal cavity. 'You see where the dyes ended up?' Meade said.

She nodded. *Everywhere.*

'Let's try to control some of the vessels before we tackle that stick.'

And so the struggle around the table began in earnest. Meade made a modest midline incision above the wood, and with Russ suctioning up what he could with both hands, Cate found the lower end of the aorta and tied it off with a strip of cotton. The scrub nurse handed her a clamp, and she slipped it over the tied end and fastened it. Loosening the tie and clamp would return some flow to the lower extremities when they required it. She followed the same procedure for the inferior vena cava, Russ suctioning generally and Meade more precisely, with a light touch, where she was working. The pool of blood rose less eagerly to the sucker ends.

As soon as the second clamp was on, Meade said to her, 'Now pull out the wood, straight as you can on the entry angle, and get back as fast as you can. I'll go for the iliac first.'

It felt like pulling a stake out of firm moist ground. Following the end of the wood came a vile-smelling ooze, a lava of blood and urine and stool. Cate backed away. On her way out she dropped the gore-tipped stick in the garbage hamper.

Mindful of Meade's warning, she made her second scrub as quick as she could. Thorough enough to take her from the class of 'dirty' back over into 'clean', though not what a punctilious examiner would have considered 'completely sterile'. Andy, the circulating nurse, ducked out to glove and gown her.

At the table Meade was straightening with a wince. His temper flared more readily when his back was acting up. 'Suction, Russ, c'mon. Suction, suction. If we can't stop that shit let's at least get it the hell out of there.' Russ continued doing what he had been doing. Cate met the scrub nurse's eyes over their masks. Meade was a good surgeon, precise and painstaking, if a bit slow – no one of his earned adjectives exactly suited to this case. 'More saline,' he snapped. The nurse handed him a huge syringe, holding two more in her hands; one by one, he pumped them into the abdomen, like someone sloshing out a muddy vat with a series of small pails. Russ suctioned the diluted mess away. To Cate, Meade muttered, 'The iliac *was* ruptured. Sigmoid colon, the bladder. The spine's about all it didn't hit ... the lucky bugger.'

'How are we?' he said, his voice strangely lowered and undirected.

'Low, but holding,' came a high, soft voice from behind the raised curtain.

Meade looked at Cate. 'Help me clean him out some more, and then let's try some stitching.'

It could've gone like that. It was the course, with minor variations, Cate had foreseen in glimpses while she was scrubbing. But events forked another way. As Cate and Meade turned from examining the X-rays, Shiraz said, 'I'm losing him.' Meade shot him a surprised, almost an affronted look, but the sheet of green hid the source of the voice.

'Dropping?' Meade said.

'Almost gone ... flickering. We're losing him.'

Meade frowned deeply. He hated the repeated phrase, hated the collusive 'we'; for a moment, he even hated the body being lost, whose condition had been a lie. So did Cate; she felt these things too. You had to – it was only for a few moments, though it felt interminable; better to let disaster possess you purely for a time, paralyse you frontally, than have its venom sink deeper into your system, warping and slowing your movements. As they both frowned down at the table, the rectangle of brown-yellow sculpture began to change alarmingly, as if the artist had rigged it with tiny motors, compressors and dyes that would kick in during the installation, surprising the viewer with some revelation of static and dynamic processes.

Around the interface of wood and skin, which had been dry enough that its rim of blood had crusted over, new blood began to well, oozing out of the crack between foreign object and the body. At the same time, evidence of the same pressure, the abdomen began to swell visibly, the flat brown plain the stake had been driven into ballooning slowly out, as if by a mischievous breeze; as if Shiraz, insane behind his curtain, had stopped his drugs, taken out his oxygen tube, and the reviving patient were drawing in a long, deep, diaphragmatic breath.

'Tamponade?' Russ said. The two-by-four might have been acting to compress a ruptured blood vessel, which now, with a slight shift in the wood – getting him on the table, perhaps – had begun to bleed freely into the abdomen. The difference between a first and third-year resident lay in the fact that these realities skipped through Cate's mind too fast for words to follow them. Meade already had a scalpel in his hand.

He made a long slash from the xiphoid sternum down to the pubis, opening the man. Pinkish, glistening intestine fumbled out at them, like the tentacles of a creature trying to escape. Russ held the wound open, a nurse mopped at the bleeding sides of it – no time to tie off the vessels according to normal procedure. Eight hands worked in a small space, creating, with the slipping coils of bowel, the impression of one many-limbed creature, struggling confusedly. There was not a shocking amount of blood; most of it would be pooling in the deep well of the pelvis. 'Get control of the aorta,' Meade said. 'I'll occlude it, then go after that artery.' He meant get the stick out, too – *that thing* was an unspoken impediment – but for now the wood had become strangely irrelevant, a prologue and possible future, but of no present significance.

Someone handed Cate a thick dressing. Her gaze had narrowed to the small square of glistening intestines, the size of a tray of shrink-wrapped sausages, directly below which the aorta pulsed. She could see it in her mind, throbbing like a bright red garden hose, and she pushed the dressing down through spongy loops toward the picture. She felt the hard knobs of the spine first, then next to it, the lunging blood. Using the spinal cord as a backstop, she pressed down as hard as she could. The vessel surged in her hand. She pushed her other hand through and laid it on top of the first. Pressing as hard as she could, the ache running up both arms and across her shoulders, she felt the flow lessen … down to half, down perhaps to a quarter of what it had been. It was like trying to stop the flow in a high-pressure hose without the simple option of dou-bling it back against itself.

'Still dropping,' came the unseen, strangely flat voice.

'Too young,' Meade said, as if it were a curse. That sense of affront again – not *too young to die*, but something less Hollywood and more surgical. *He should have more reserves, vasoconstriction should have bought more time.* A surgeon was inured to surprises, had to be, but could still be offended by flagrant violations of the rules. Something had cheated.

'His heart's stopped,' Shiraz said. A moment before, Cate felt the pulse in the hose flicker out, her shoulders relaxing in treasonous grati-tude.

'Christ!' Meade said. He flung aside the cotton tape he'd been start-ing to tie. 'Hold on,' he said to Cate. He reached through her straining arms, their arms criss-crossing, to get to the diaphragm. The tendons in his forearm jumped as he found the bottom cone of the heart and started squeezing. 'Hold tight,' he murmured, his face an inch from hers. She pushed hard where there was no resistance, saving a bank of pressure against future loss. 'Open him up,' Meade said to Russ, 'Fifth interspace.' Cate was glad she couldn't see Russ's eyes.

The acrid smell of their sweat was strong enough now to vie with the odours of urine, stool and blood. Glancing to her right Cate saw a scalpel drawn between the ribs, through the intercostal muscle with a *ssstht* sound. She reached out her right hand, keeping her left on the slack aorta, and tugged the lower rib hard towards her. Russ pulled the upper rib outwards and pushed the retractor blades in between them. A few hard cranks and the ribs cracked with a sound like sticks broken over the knee. Russ made a flick through the pericardium. He reached for scissors and slipped them into the narrow oval space. Then he was massaging the stopped heart, his forearm tensing and relaxing like the arm of a man in a gym. Cate saw and felt what he was seeing and feeling. The muscle steak-red but tinged with blue already, starving for air; a limp mass that could bulge and go hard instantly, like a weightlifter's sleeping bicep.

'Ripples,' Russ said.

'Anything?' Meade said to Shiraz, as if the green sheet were an actual boundary requiring relays, translations.

'Not really, no.'

'There,' Russ said, 'a strong contraction.' Cate felt it under her hands and clamped down harder than ever. He couldn't afford even a few drops. 'Choppy beats, now.' Cate knew the picture that went with the excitement in Russ's voice; she felt it inside her own chest. The amazing compression down to half its size, the rhythmic convulsions like an irrepressible bursting. The only sight she could compare it to was the crowning of a baby's skull, or a lover's tremors during orgasm.

'What's the score? What's the score?'

'No real rhythm. Give it a second,' Shiraz said, with a calm that might have been intended to provoke. Anaesthetists and surgeons developed complex relationships, like any two people doing complementary but dissimilar jobs. Who knew what had transpired between these two in a hundred cases of crisis?

There was a pause around the table, a hush Cate could hear. She knew the silence was its own distinct sound because she could hear the beep of the electrocardiogram *alongside* it, a lesser sound. The flabby hiss of the respirator. Russ was poised, his arm halfway inside a man. No one moved. She had a few seconds to wonder what wisdom or economy was keeping Meade on the other side of the table. A lost cause: let the junior resident cut his teeth on it? Saving himself for a final assault, the strongest leg of a relay? She'd been on rotation with him five months, and respected him as a surgeon, but knew him only fitfully. His moments of transparency surprised more than his usual opacity.

'No,' Shiraz said.

'You're running sodium bicarb?' Meade said as he rounded the table to take Russ's place. Cate's arms were jelly from leaning on the aorta, but perhaps she wouldn't've been strong enough anyway. For heart massage, yes, she'd done it often; but not for a desperate *show* of strength.

'Since he dropped off,' Shiraz said. 'I don't think he's overly acidotic.'

Meade groaned, and rolled his eyes at the ceiling. 'Spell off Cate, Russ.' Cate shook her head. 'Suckers, then. Keep clearing the fluid.'

Meade plunged his hand into the man and seized his heart, tightened his whole arm, let go. Each time he leaned in with his whole body, a lunging motion that lent his hand the strength of his legs and back. Cate wasn't sure if the technique, much more forceful than Russ's had been despite the twenty-year difference in their ages, was more correct or just more brutal. It seemed odd not to know even at this late stage of her training. She could feel the surges of blood caused by Meade's squeezings, like waves hitting the breakwater of her hand.

Meade paused a few times – tremulous flutters under her fingers, wavelets only – and then resumed. No comment came from behind the sheet, and Meade didn't ask any questions.

'Fuck.' Meade lowered his head. 'Fuck, fuck, fuck, fuck, fuck, fuck....'

He said it many times, perhaps a dozen times in quick succession, until the word was drained of force and meaning. Reliving the night later, Cate would consider this the pronouncement of death; though immediately after saying it, Meade asked for the paddles and applied them at intervals, interrupted by more heart massage and adrenaline injections, for the next thirty minutes. 'PR ... for the family,' Meade had said, in an ebullient moment early in their rotation together, about this long post-mortem struggle to resuscitate. 'You know after five minutes.' That was after they'd lost a twenty-year-old woman, another car crash, and they'd been sitting in the surgeons' lounge drinking contraindicated coffees, jittery and talkative and, in Cate's case, guiltily elated. Adrenaline was a great deceiver, always wearing the same eager mask to each event. There was no way of predicting how a case would affect you.

The one that had undone her the worst, left her sobbing in a locked linen room, had been a shrunken eighty-five-year-old, riddled with cancer, stoically agreeable to yet another useless surgery. After a long helpless cry, she'd actually laughed through her tears, telling herself that she was mourning a dandelion puff, its last filaments detached by a breeze. And nothing in Meade's work now, even to her eyes, seemed perfunctory; his actions to restore life, all their actions, were vigorous and incessant; just like the ardent flurry around the 'Clear!' moment in the TV drama, except that this went on far longer and more doggedly, and was leached of the hope that would have permeated the film version.

Finally Meade stepped back from the table, a small step but so sudden it seemed he had been pushed. 'That's all,' he said. 'We're not getting this guy back.'

The hush that had prevailed throughout the crisis deepened a notch, a human silence that surmounted the fans, beeps and clicks of machines. Every head shifted and looked somewhere else, a necessary realignment, no pair of eyes meeting another. Not yet. Cate looked at the clock: 4:03. A nameless time. Not quite the end of night, not quite the beginning of day ... pre-dawn, she'd heard it called. There was a click from behind the canted curtain as the ventilator was turned off. As if at a prompt, everyone started moving in different directions, spacing themselves like identically charged electrons about the room.

Shiraz was still invisible. Meade pulled off his gloves and tossed them at a garbage hamper, one of them falling to the floor. He sat down on a stool near the door, his head lowered, squeezing his forehead between his thumb and fingers. He wouldn't wait long before going to find the family. The scrub nurse and Andy were gathering up instruments. Another circulating nurse, whom Andy must have pulled in as the crisis deepened, was sitting on a stool in the corner, writing quickly, finishing up the case notes. Russ took two strides away from the table, then stopped; there was nowhere to go in the small room without purpose. He stood in the centre of the room, his face flushed with competing emotions.

There was a very soft, almost hallucinatorily subtle, sound of sobbing, but when she looked around the room there was no one the sound could have come from.

* * *

Cate stepped back from the table. She sighed and took a deep breath, her first real respiration after the shallow and stopped breaths of crisis. She stared for a few seconds at the carnage on the table, willing it to cease being a man in her mind, then turned her back on it. She pulled off her gloves, then her mask and sweat-soaked bonnet, and dumped them in the garbage by the wall. In one fluid movement she untied her bloody gown, shrugged out of it and tossed it in the linen hamper. She crossed the room to the nurse who was writing in the corner. She grabbed his free arm; he followed unresistingly. She took him a few steps down the hall to a linen supply room. Cate had often been accused, by her mom and by the occasional female friend, of choosing men for mere convenience. There'd been a joking acronym: NAM: Nearest Available Man. But this was the only time that it was literally true. She wouldn't remember what he had looked like later, couldn't have picked him positively out of a police line-up. He was young, but she wouldn't have cared if he was old. Flinging out her arm she swept some linens from a shelf onto the floor, lay down on them. She pulled him down on top of her. Her greens were rust-stained in the front; she could smell her sweat, acrid with adrenochrome. She closed her eyes. Pulled off her green pants and her underpants. She spread her knees wide around him, opened herself as wide as possible. The bulk on top of her moved sluggishly, confusedly perhaps. She gripped his buttocks, clenched under his greens, and moved him back and forth, back and forth, until he was excited enough by friction to take over himself. The brief act they accomplished was mainly a victory over numbness. Cate could feel him moving inside her, but the feeling was faint and faraway, like chewing when the freezing isn't quite worked out. But the feeling intensified slightly, a wake-up call from inside. From *her* body. *I'm* not dead yet. He came with a silent stiffening shudder, collapsed on her. She came while opening her eyes a crack, saw white fluorescence dim to a grateful blur. Closed her eyes, heard the door click behind him. It was a tribute to something – to what Cate wasn't sure, but to something – that the episode didn't immediately become a joke or gossip item. Macabre stories abounded about bodies, living and dead, but her body's sudden frenzy – which hadn't required any input from her mind – didn't immediately become a part of hospital legend. There was a delay, perhaps for tongues to find the right spin, or minds to file it properly. There was a young nurse who gave her timid, hopeful glances for a few days. She had to avoid him pointedly, then reprimand him sharply one night when he handed her a wrong instrument, to put them back on an even, working keel.

When she re-entered Operating Room 4 she experienced a moment of disorientation. During the short time she'd been gone the room had altered slightly, like a stage set in the last act, but the biggest change was in the actors, all of whom had either disappeared or assumed new roles and positions. Shiraz was gone; since the start Cate had never seen him; his voice might almost have been a shared hallucination. So was Meade. And Russ (to somewhere and for reasons never explained; Meade called it 'buggering off' and dressed him down harshly for it, thus distinguishing his absence from Cate's brief errand, which he never mentioned).

Andy and the scrub nurse remained. They stood with a queer stiff dignity on either side of the table. Sentinels, Cate thought, then realized they were waiting for her. They wouldn't leave the body now, not until it was prepped and shown to the family, but they couldn't proceed without her. It was the last of a surgeon's jobs, one Cate had seen performed with slow care, a methodical, perhaps calming, dignity; and also with brutal haste, the remains a rebuke to good intentions.

The man on the table was not the man she had met in ER, and not the painted torso they had laboured over, slicing and draining and squeezing. He was a new man, one she hadn't seen before. For one thing, he was naked. Andy (she guessed), who had the confidence to put humanity ahead of protocol when required, had removed the gory covering sheets. His face might almost have been the face of a restless sleeper, one with damp hair and pale skin, eyelids (bizarrely) requiring tape strips to keep them closed, and parted lips. This face (handsome, she thought, and batted the thought away), the untouched muscular legs with turned-out toes, and the wreckage in the middle: like a magician's assistant, male for once, mangled during the box trick. The man in the cape and top hat mad, or incompetent, or just freakishly unlucky.

The materials she needed now were very simple: needles, black thread, scissors. The same homey stuff her mother had used to close a turkey at Thanksgiving. What the embalmer needed, all he insisted on, was a body that didn't leak from more than the usual places. The hospital needed a patient that wouldn't unnecessarily shock (or spur to litigation) grieving relatives. Cate went a little further than these demands. She felt a need to walk delicately backwards through the mess they'd made (the stick, as garbage, no longer blameworthy), like someone stepping backwards through her tracks in snow.

She sutured the iliac artery, which they'd never had a chance to get to. She sutured shut the sigmoid colon and the bladder, then asked Andy for one of the huge saline hypos. She sluiced it over the last brown-yellow ordure that had leaked out, the image of basting unavoidable. Andy suctioned it away. Then she sewed, in tight rapid rings, the long incision down his middle, gently pushing the bowel back in ahead of her stitching. Images came, unwelcome, hindering: the overstuffed bird, the suitcase pressed shut in advance of the zipper – how much training would it take to achieve the clear blankness of proficiency? As she worked, shimmers passed occasionally under the skin – muscles with shrinking oxygen that didn't yet know the deprivation was permanent. These shimmers, which she caught in the corner of her eye, reminded her (again she fought the ease and sentimentality of the comparison) of the blush-like ripples of breezes over grass. She sewed up the pericardium, though it wasn't strictly necessary. Removed the rib retractor, the broken struts creaking partway shut. Sewed up the incision. With the two main chest holes closed, his torso resembled again that of a man. Waxy, though; already beginning to acquire that heavily inert, glazed look, unmistakable even through the proviodine.

Andy washed the patient's face with a kidney basin of water and a cloth, then removed the tape on his eyelids, pressing his dark fingers lightly down on them for a moment. He moved to the other end of the table and washed his legs, though this too was unnecessary. Cate closed the puncture hole last. It was small and shrunken, ragged lips around a glum 'O', too modest-looking to be the cause of such ruin. Andy poured alcohol onto a cloth and removed the proviodine with brisk, circular sweeps. A second alcohol rub, a third; it had been smeared on. Then he washed him with water. Cate watched in silence. The alcohol and more minutes had heightened the waxiness, giving him a kind of polish: a man transformed into a statue.

The scrub nurse returned with a stretcher. There was a white sheet folded on it, which they unfurled to drape him from neck to feet. Cate had experienced a stab of insight about this sheet, applied at this moment. She'd told a student on rounds that she was still learning something new every day, even now, more than a dozen years after she'd started studying to be a doctor. The student had smiled indulgently, but it was true, it was more than a veteran's veiled boast or recruiting pitch. This sheet was necessary, not only for simple decency, but also as a necessary separation, a thin cotton divider between the dead and the living. She grasped his ankles through the sheet – Andy and the scrub nurse lifted his shoulders – and they transferred him to the stretcher. The scrub nurse went out again. Andy took one of the thick green OR linens and began unrolling it, with a touch of slow ceremony, upward from the toes. This again was not standard. He seemed to be courting another kind of etiquette, inserting – with his own delicate insistence – elements of warmth and creativity into the cold technicality that prevailed, that had to prevail, here. When he reached the neck, he stopped and glanced at Cate.

The man on the table looked tucked into bed, the last roll of green blanket below the hem of white. Within that same twist of fantasy he looked asleep, also both much younger and much older than the thinking, staring adult she'd met downstairs. *Boy and mummy.* She felt little now except a kind of hole, a preparatory scouring somewhere deep inside her. A space some later feeling might fill, or which might remain just empty, a crater. She dwelt a few seconds longer on the harsh miracle of their meeting, waiting until a kind of sombre recognition overspread their time together, and then slowly pulled the sheet up over his face.

Taking her end of the stretcher, she rolled him toward whoever might be waiting for him.

Acknowledgements

Thanks to the following magazines, in which most of these stories, sometimes in slightly altered form, first appeared: *The New Quarterly*, *Prairie Fire*, *Queen Street Quarterly*. Thanks also to the Ontario Arts Council for financial support.

Individual stories have been reprinted in the following anthologies: 'Don and Ron' in *Hard Boiled Love* (Insomniac Press); 'Karaoke Mon Amour' in *The Journey Prize Anthology (13)* and *99: Best Canadian Stories*; 'Cogagwee' in *The Journey Prize Anthology (14)*; 'Scribe' in *03: Best Canadian Stories*. 'Scribe' also won the Silver Medal at the 2003 National Magazine Awards.

Unattributed newspaper quotations in 'Cogagwee' are taken from *The Globe*. Much of the factual material was found in *Tom Longboat*, Bruce Kidd's short, vivid account of the runner's life and career. My father, Dr William H. Barnes, generously shared his memories of his career as a surgeon, which were invaluable in constructing the world of 'Scribe'. Needless to say, any inaccuracies are my own.

For their comradeship, guidance and enthusiastic support of these stories, I would like to thank especially Kathleen Miller, Sue Barnes-MacDonald, and my mother, Mary Barnes. John Metcalf, once again, has been an astute editor and a loyal friend. I esteem him as both.

Tim and Elke Inkster devote untold hours and rare skills to the making of beautiful books. I am honoured that they have made another one of mine.

Kim Jernigan, the remarkable editor of *The New Quarterly*, has given most warm, perceptive and thoughtful support to my fiction almost from the time I started writing it, for which I am deeply grateful.

For nine years, the most fortunate of my life, Heather Rose Simcoe has been my partner in life and art. Her help to me cannot be summarized on this or any page. This book is dedicated to her, with love.

HEATHER R. SIMCOE

Mike Barnes is the author of *Calm Jazz Sea*, shortlisted for the Gerald Lampert Memorial Award, *Aquarium*, winner of the 1999 Danuta Gleed Award, and *The Syllabus*, a novel. He lives in Toronto.